WATTERS · LEYH · ROGERS · LAIHO

LUMBERJANES™

MIND OVER METTLE

Published by

BOOM! BOX™

BOOM! BOX™

LUMBERJANES Volume Sixteen, December 2020. Published by BOOM! Box, a division of Boom Entertainment, Inc. Lumberjanes is ™ & © 2020 Shannon Watters, Grace Ellis, Noelle Stevenson & Brooklyn Allen. Originally published in single magazine form as LUMBERJANES No. 61-64. ™ & © 2019 Shannon Watters, Grace Ellis, Noelle Stevenson & Brooklyn Allen. All rights reserved. BOOM! Box™ and the BOOM! Box logo are trademarks of Boom Entertainment, Inc., registered in various countries and categories. All characters, events, and institutions depicted herein are fictional. Any similarity between any of the names, characters, persons, and/or events, and/or institutions in this publication to actual names, characters, and persons, whether living or dead, events, and/or institutions is unintended and purely coincidental. BOOM! Box does not read or accept unsolicited submissions of ideas, stories, or artwork.

BOOM! Studios, 5670 Wilshire Boulevard, Suite 400, Los Angeles, CA 90036-5679. Printed in USA. First Printing.

ISBN: 978-1-68415-616-0, eISBN: 978-1-64668-028-3

THIS LUMBERJANES FIELD MANUAL BELONGS TO:

NAME:_____

TROOP:_____

DATE INVESTED:_____

FIELD MANUAL TABLE OF CONTENTS

LUMBERJANES
FIELD MANUAL

For the Intermediate Program

Tenth Edition • April 1985

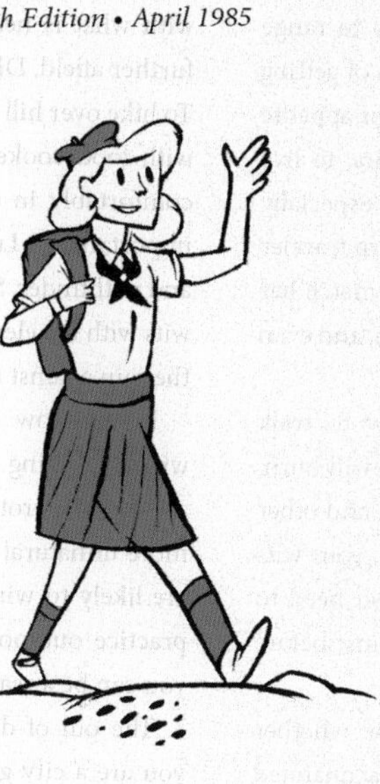

Prepared for the

Miss Qiunzella Thiskwin Penniquiqul Thistle Crumpet's

CAMP FOR [redacted] HARDCORE LADY-TYPES

"Friendship to the Max!"

A MESSAGE FROM THE LUMBERJANES HIGH COUNCIL

miss Quinzella Thiskwin
Penniquiqul Thistle Crumpet's
Camp for
HARDCORE LADY TYPES
FRIENDSHIP to the MAX!

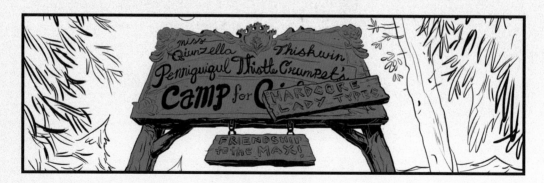

When you are working toward a goal, the image of your success is bright and vivid in your mind. You fall asleep at night imagining where you'll be in just a few months or years, or you fantasize about the future while you wait for the bus, or brush your teeth. It starts to feel almost like reality, like it is just barely out of your reach. Just a half step away from your current life.

But the truth is that nothing is guaranteed. A half a step forward can become a half a step to the left or right, or even a half step back, and suddenly everything that was on the precipice of coming together falls apart. The puzzle pieces that you were assembling are all scrambled, their picture irreconcilable with the one you had in your head.

We of the high council do not say this to upset you young and eager Lumberjanes, who we know all hold your own hopes and dreams dear to your hearts. Rather, we wish to share with you the knowledge that even when it seems like everything is going wrong, and even when it feels like the only options before you are bad and worse, there are ways through and help to be had. You may not always see it from the outset, but just like you could never have predicted how things would break apart, you also cannot know how they will come back together again.

After all, dissonance is only one note away from harmony. But even if you continue to move away from that first, glorious note, the one you thought was perfect, and that you cherished in your mind, you will eventually find another harmonic tone. Perhaps not the original one, or the one that you had hoped for, but one that is just as beautiful, in its own way.

THE LUMBERJANES PLEDGE

I solemnly swear to do my best
Every day, and in all that I do,
To be brave and strong,
To be truthful and compassionate,
To be interesting and interested,
To pay attention and question
The world around me,
To think of others first,
To always help and protect my friends,
[redacted]
And to make the world a better place
For Lumberjane scouts
And for everyone else.

THEN THERE'S A LINE ABOUT GOD, OR WHATEVER

LUMBERJANES™

MIND OVER METTLE

Written by
Shannon Watters
& Kat Leyh

Illustrated by
AnneMarie Rogers

Colors by
Maarta Laiho

Letters by
Aubrey Aiese

Cover by
Kat Leyh

Designer
Marie Krupina

Editor
Sophie Philips-Roberts

Executive Editor
Jeanine Schaefer

*Special thanks to **Kelsey Pate** for giving the Lumberjanes their name.*

Created by
Shannon Watters, Grace Ellis, Noelle Stevenson & Brooklyn Allen

LUMBERJANES FIELD MANUAL

CHAPTER SIXTY-ONE

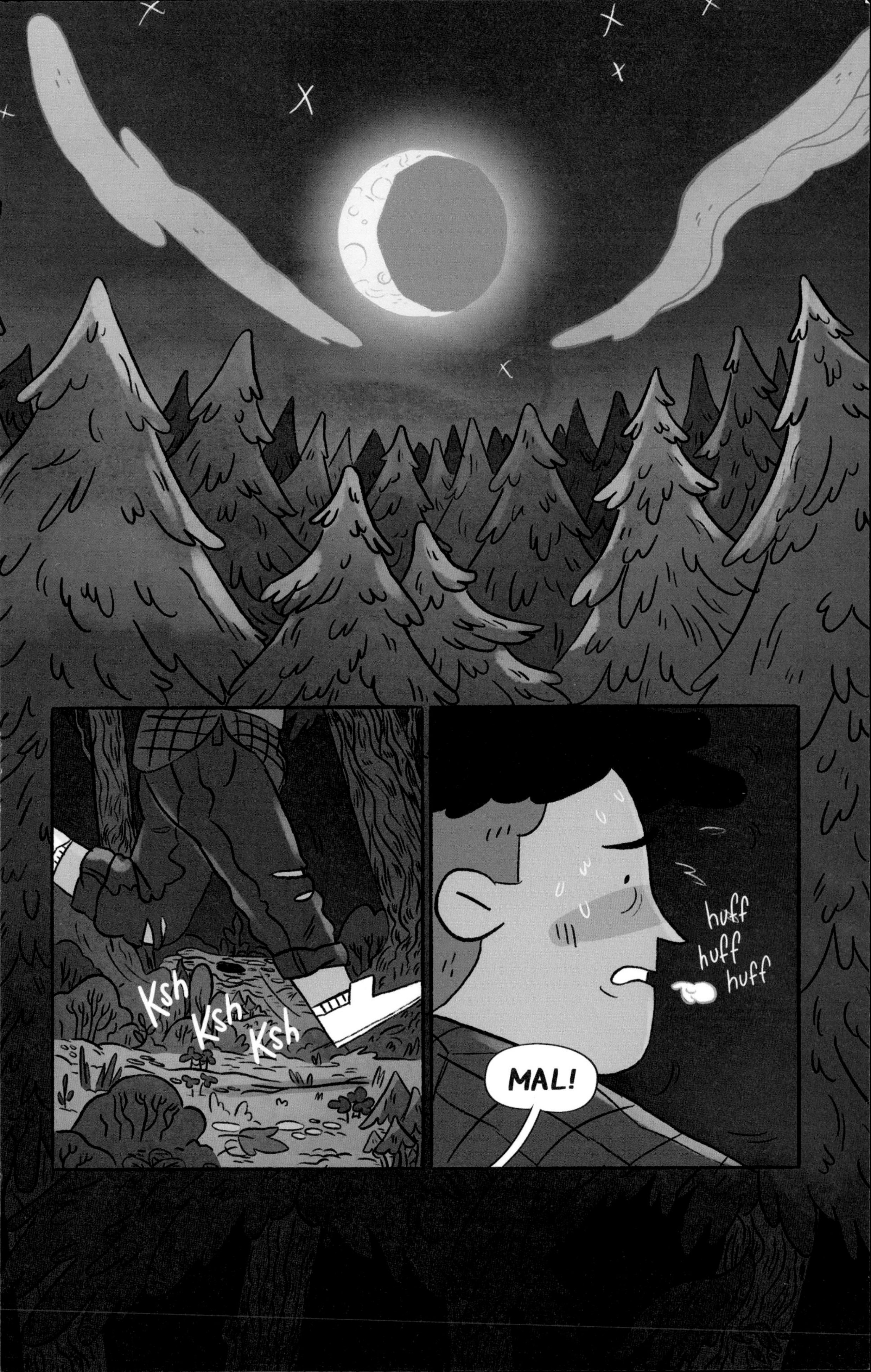
Ksh
Ksh
Ksh
huff
huff
huff
MAL!

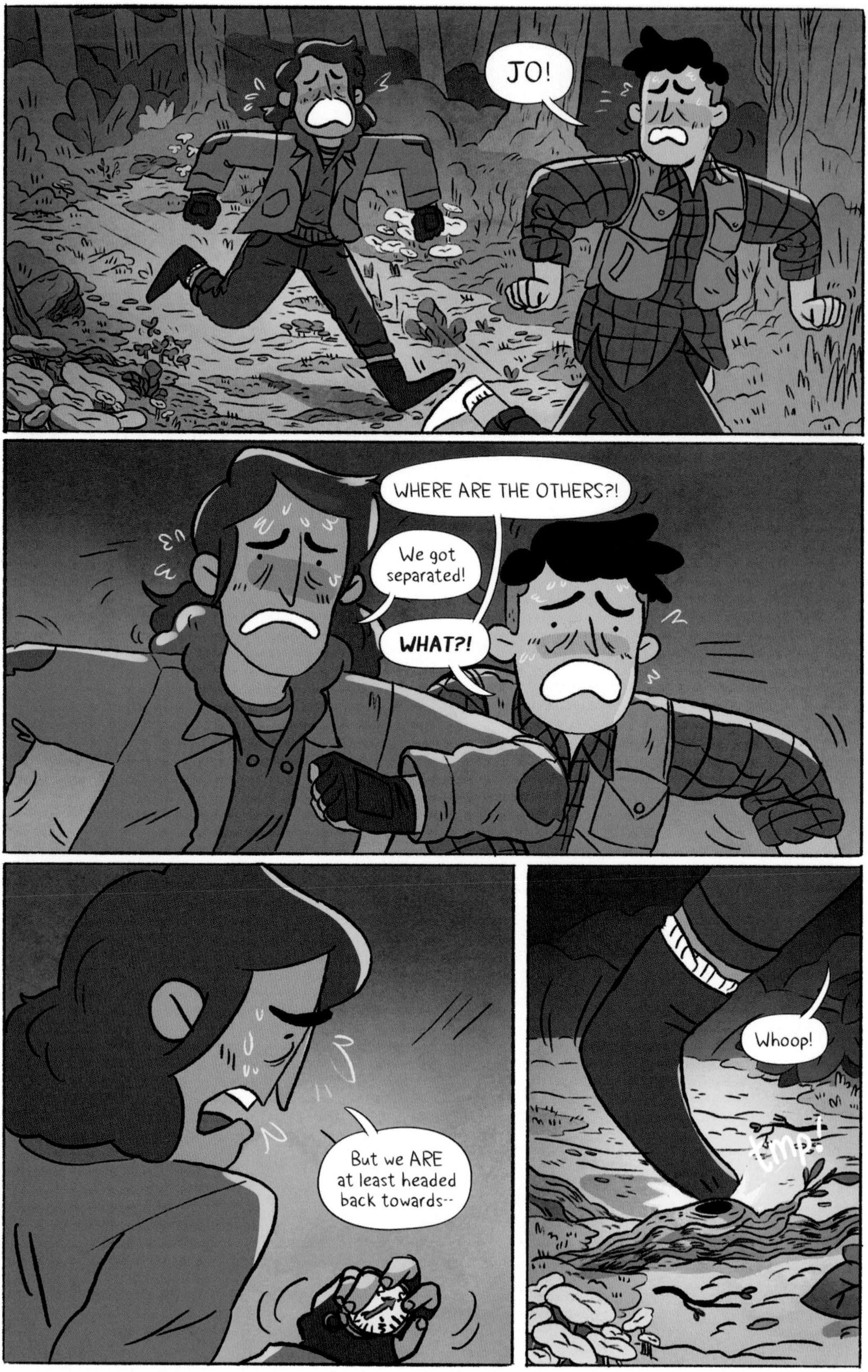
JO!
WHERE ARE THE OTHERS?!
We got separated!
WHAT?!
But we ARE at least headed back towards--
Whoop!
tmp!

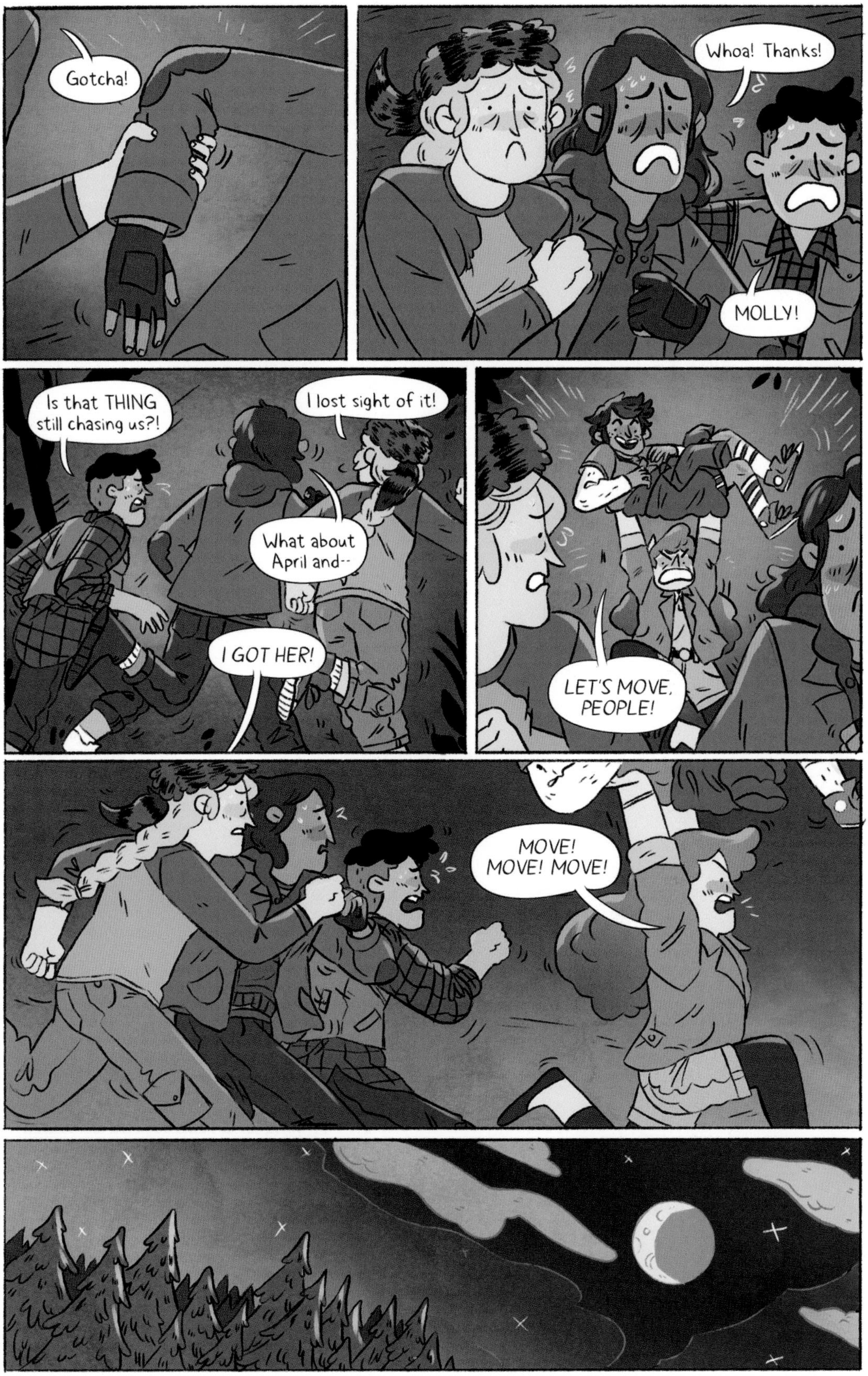
Gotcha!
Whoa! Thanks!
MOLLY!
Is that THING still chasing us?!
I lost sight of it!
What about April and--
I GOT HER!
LET'S MOVE, PEOPLE!
MOVE! MOVE! MOVE!

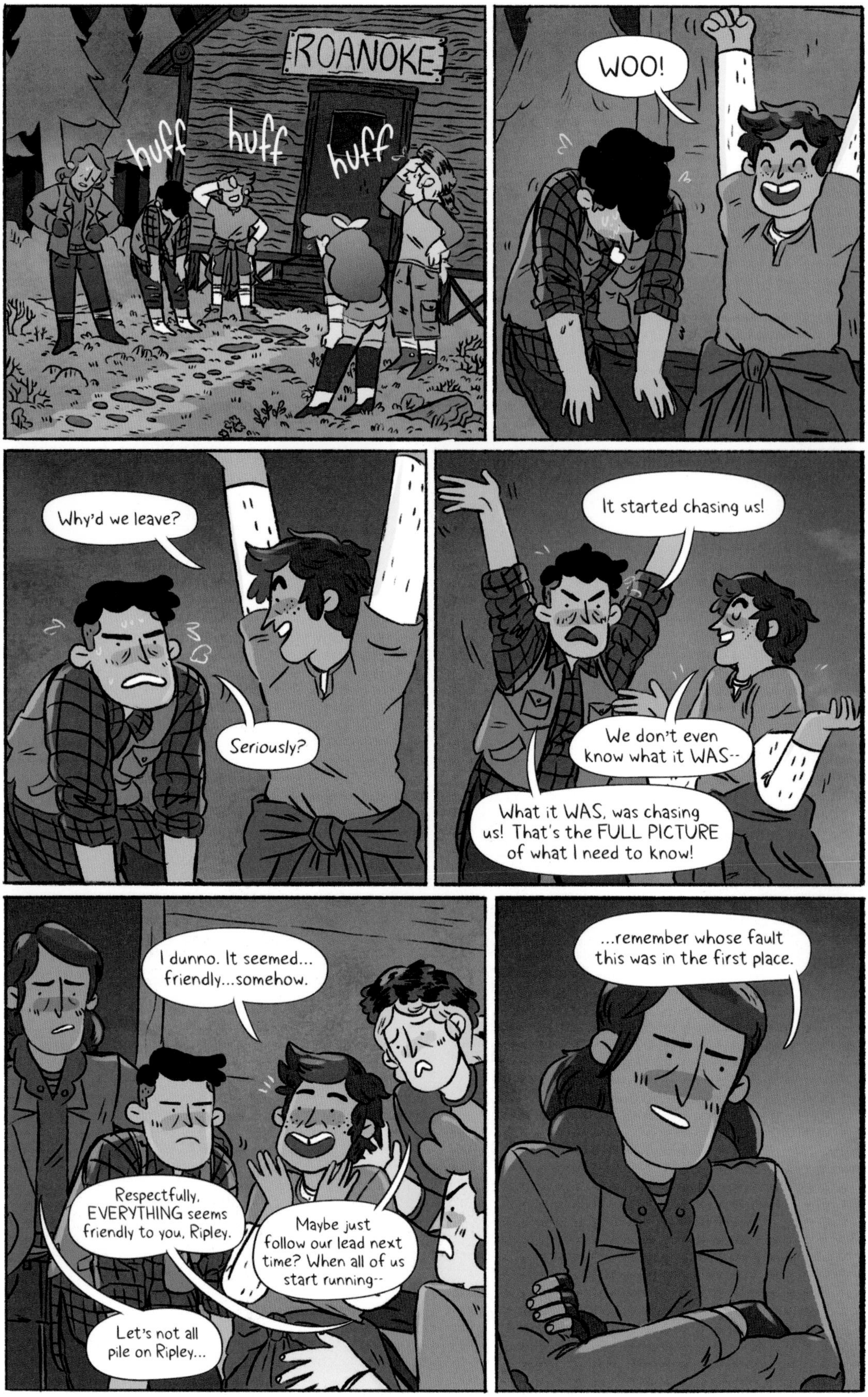
ROANOKE
huff
huff
huff
WOO!
Why'd we leave?
Seriously?
It started chasing us!
We don't even know what it WAS--
What it WAS, was chasing us! That's the FULL PICTURE of what I need to know!
I dunno. It seemed... friendly...somehow.
Respectfully, EVERYTHING seems friendly to you, Ripley.
Maybe just follow our lead next time? When all of us start running--
Let's not all pile on Ripley...
...remember whose fault this was in the first place.

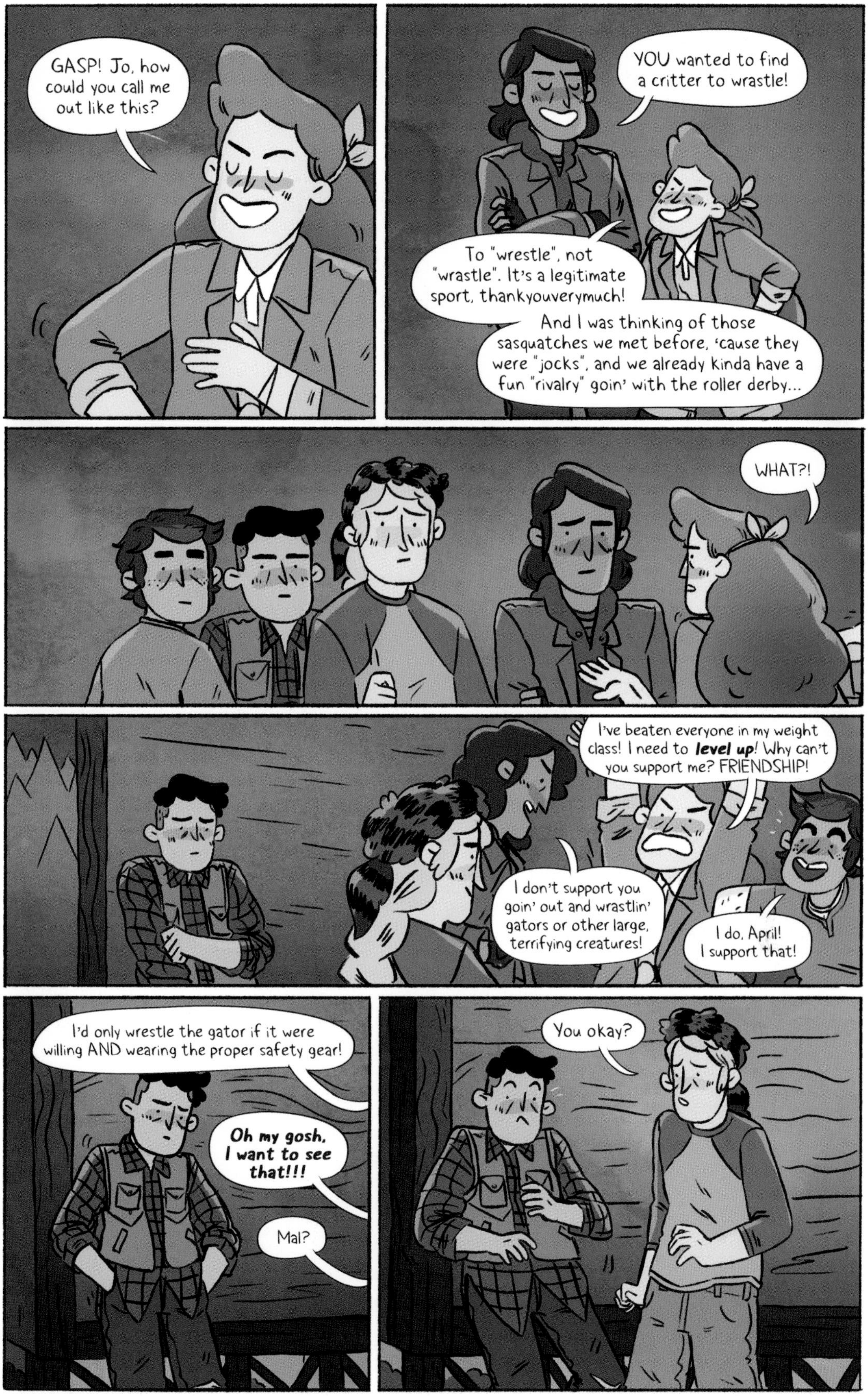
GASP! Jo, how could you call me out like this?
YOU wanted to find a critter to wrastle!
To "wrestle", not "wrastle". It's a legitimate sport, thankyouverymuch!
And I was thinking of those sasquatches we met before, 'cause they were "jocks", and we already kinda have a fun "rivalry" goin' with the roller derby...
WHAT?!
I've beaten everyone in my weight class! I need to **level up**! Why can't you support me? FRIENDSHIP!
I don't support you goin' out and wrastlin' gators or other large, terrifying creatures!
I do, April! I support that!
I'd only wrestle the gator if it were willing AND wearing the proper safety gear!
Oh my gosh, I want to see that!!!
Mal?
You okay?

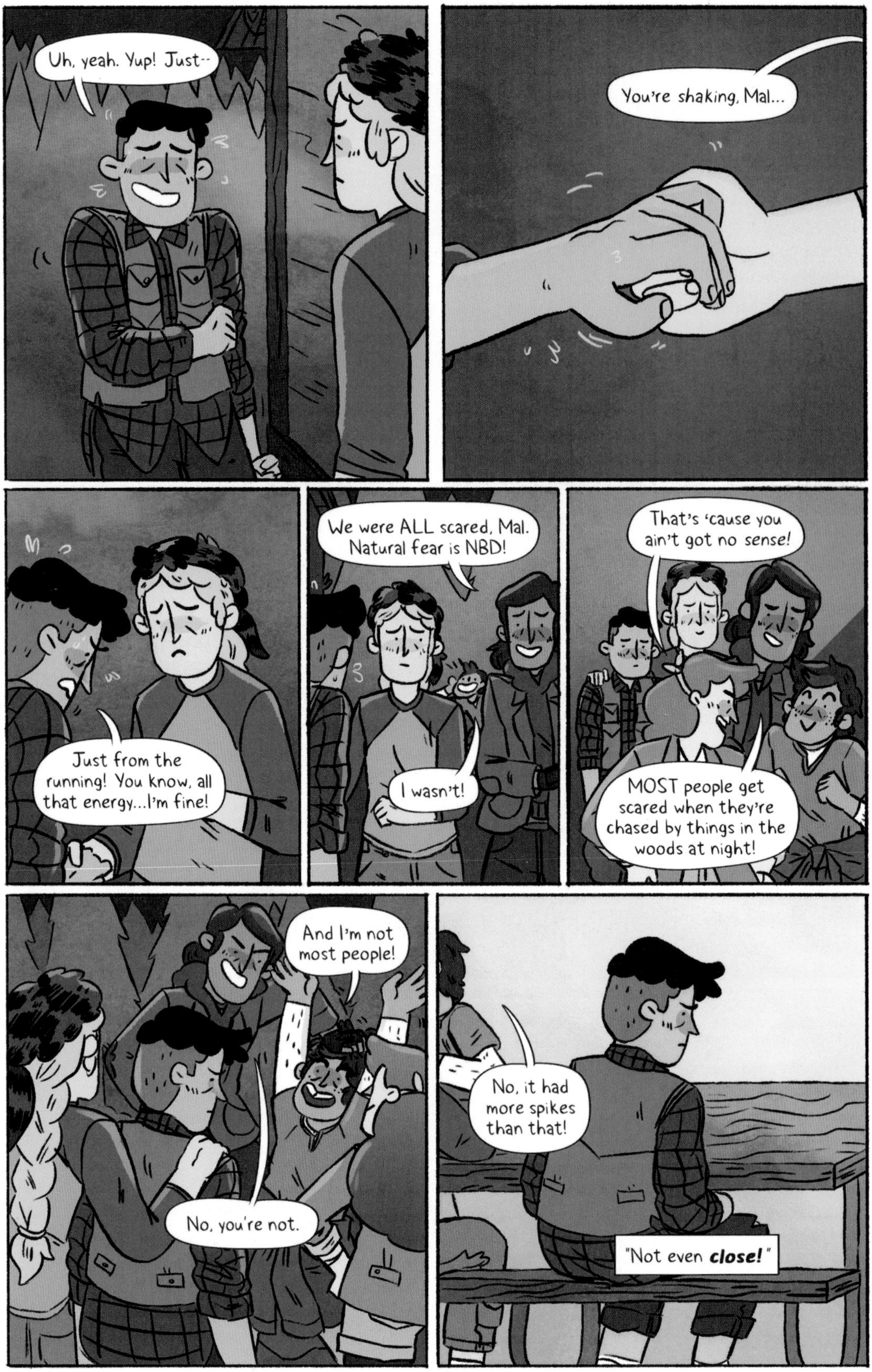
Uh, yeah. Yup! Just--
You're shaking, Mal...
Just from the running! You know, all that energy...I'm fine!
We were ALL scared, Mal. Natural fear is NBD!
I wasn't!
That's 'cause you ain't got no sense!
MOST people get scared when they're chased by things in the woods at night!
And I'm not most people!
No, you're not.
No, it had more spikes than that!
"Not even close!"

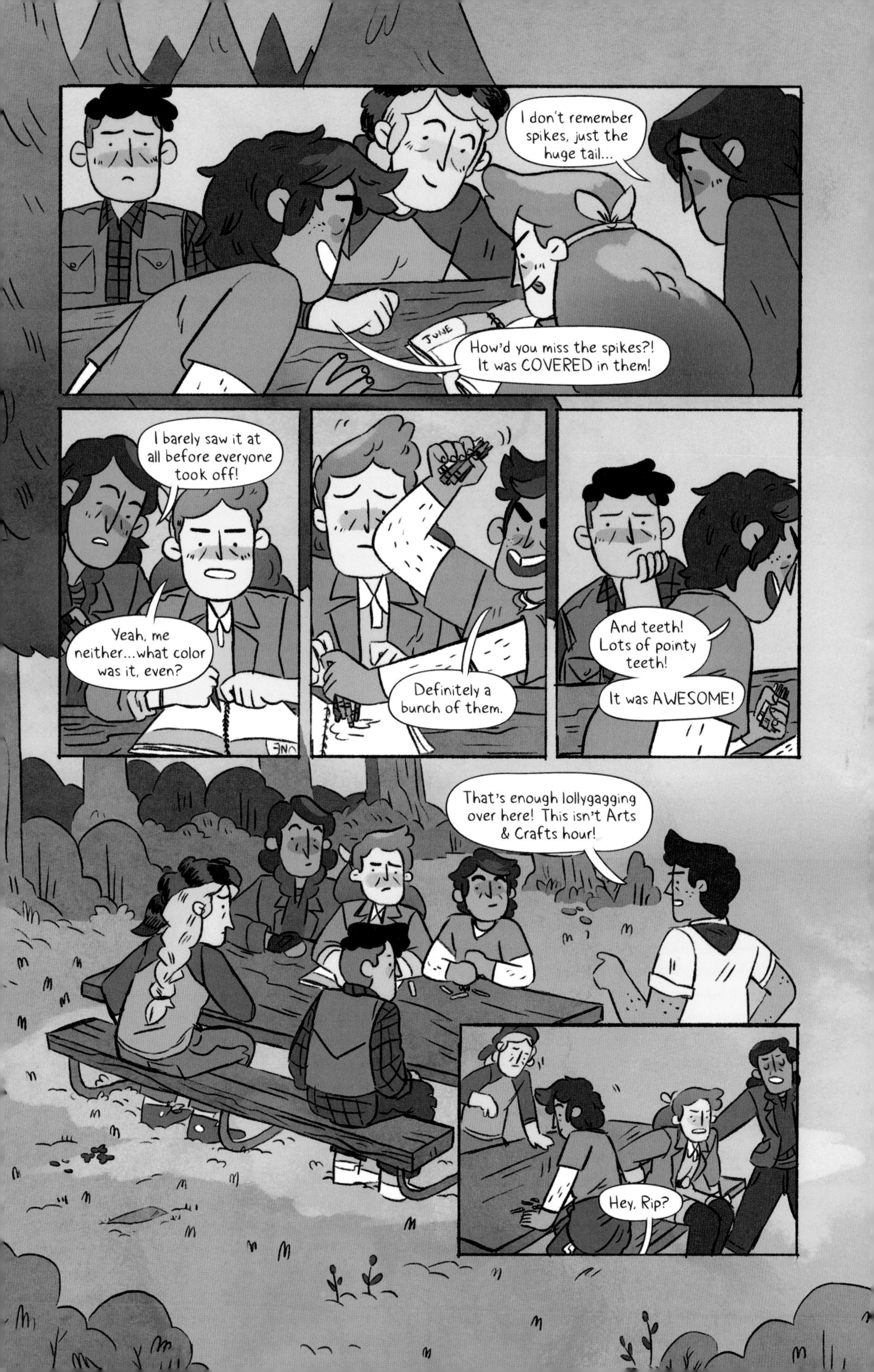
I don't remember spikes, just the huge tail...
JUNE
How'd you miss the spikes?! It was COVERED in them!
I barely saw it at all before everyone took off!
Yeah, me neither...what color was it, even?
Definitely a bunch of them.
And teeth! Lots of pointy teeth!
It was AWESOME!
That's enough lollygagging over here! This isn't Arts & Crafts hour!
Hey, Rip?

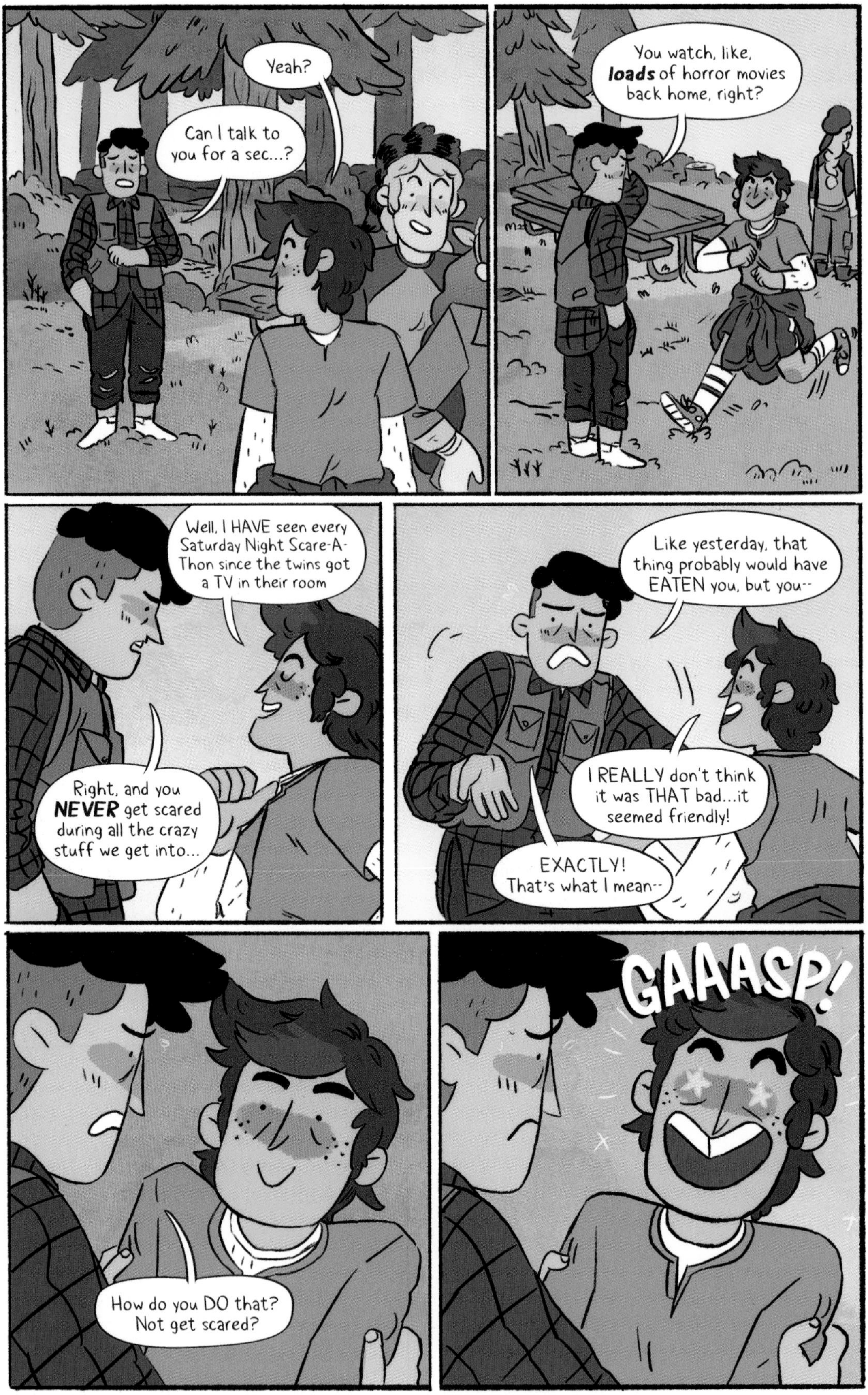

Can I talk to you for a sec...?
Yeah?
You watch, like, **loads** of horror movies back home, right?
Well, I HAVE seen every Saturday Night Scare-A-Thon since the twins got a TV in their room
Right, and you **NEVER** get scared during all the crazy stuff we get into...
Like yesterday, that thing probably would have EATEN you, but you--
I REALLY don't think it was THAT bad...it seemed friendly!
EXACTLY! That's what I mean--
How do you DO that? Not get scared?
GAAASP!

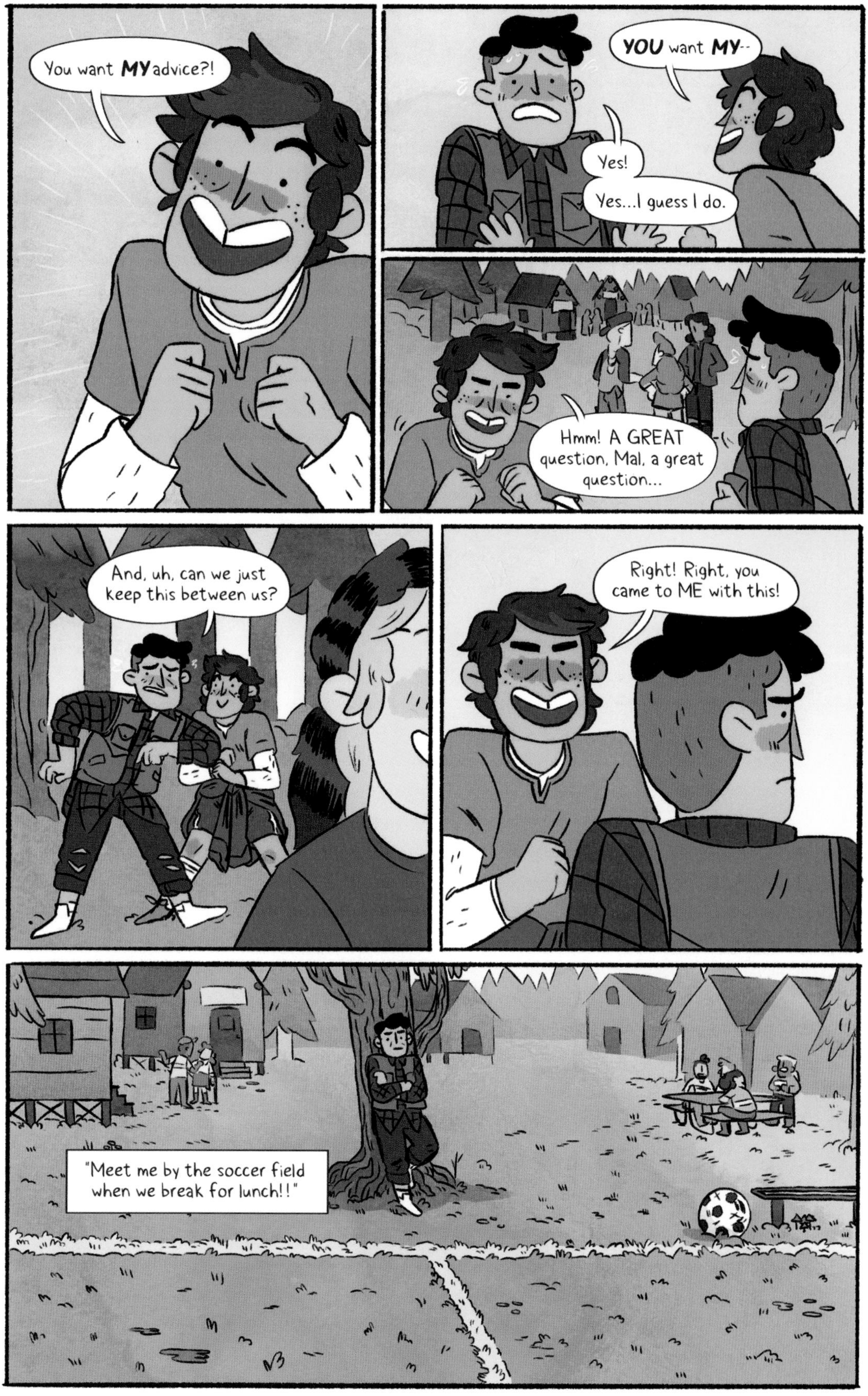
You want MY advice?!
YOU want MY--
Yes!
Yes...I guess I do.
Hmm! A GREAT question, Mal, a great question...
And, uh, can we just keep this between us?
Right! Right, you came to ME with this!
"Meet me by the soccer field when we break for lunch!!"

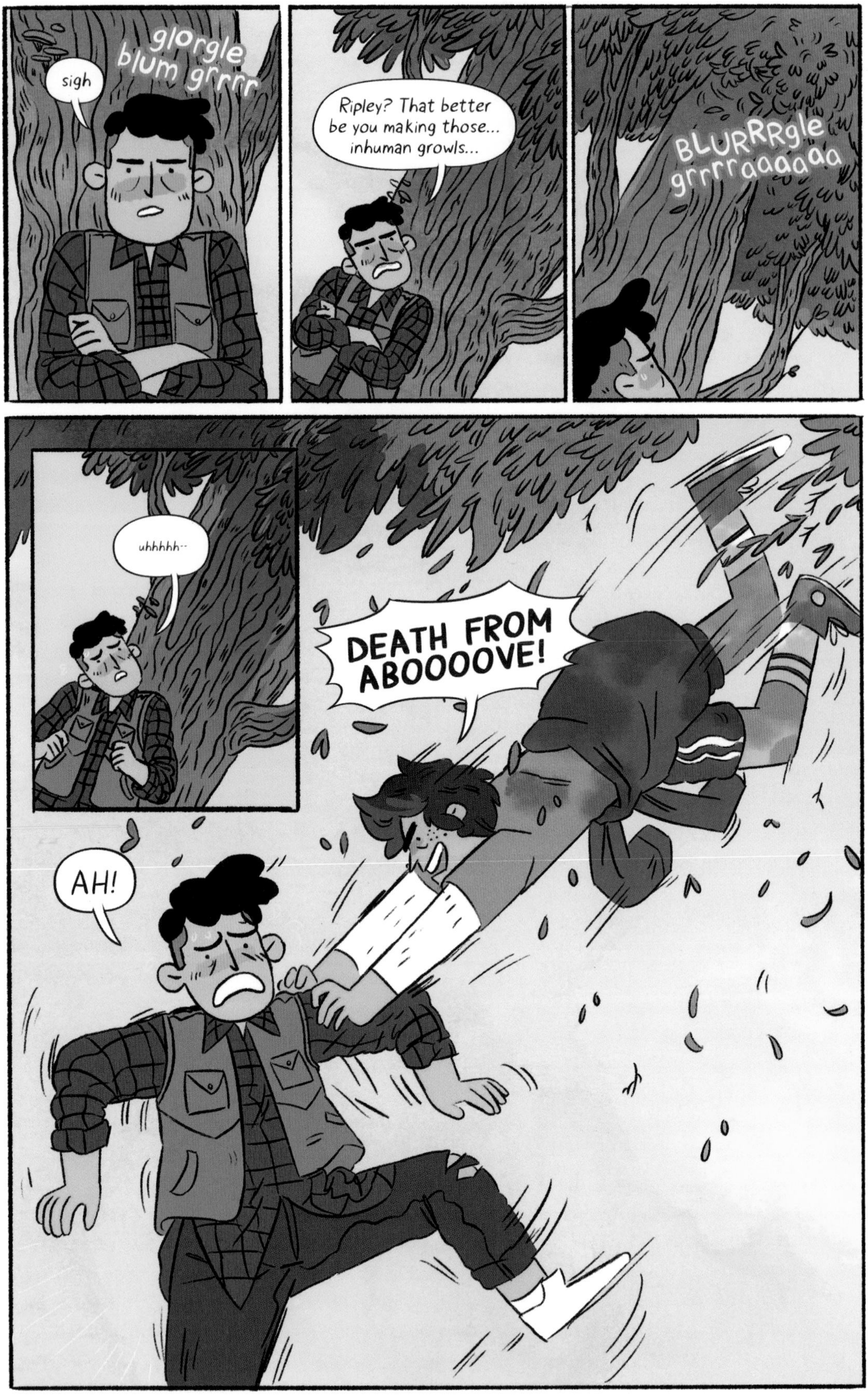
sigh
glorgle blum grrrr
Ripley? That better be you making those... inhuman growls...
BLURRRgle grrrraaaaaa
uhhhhh...
DEATH FROM ABOOOOVE!
AH!

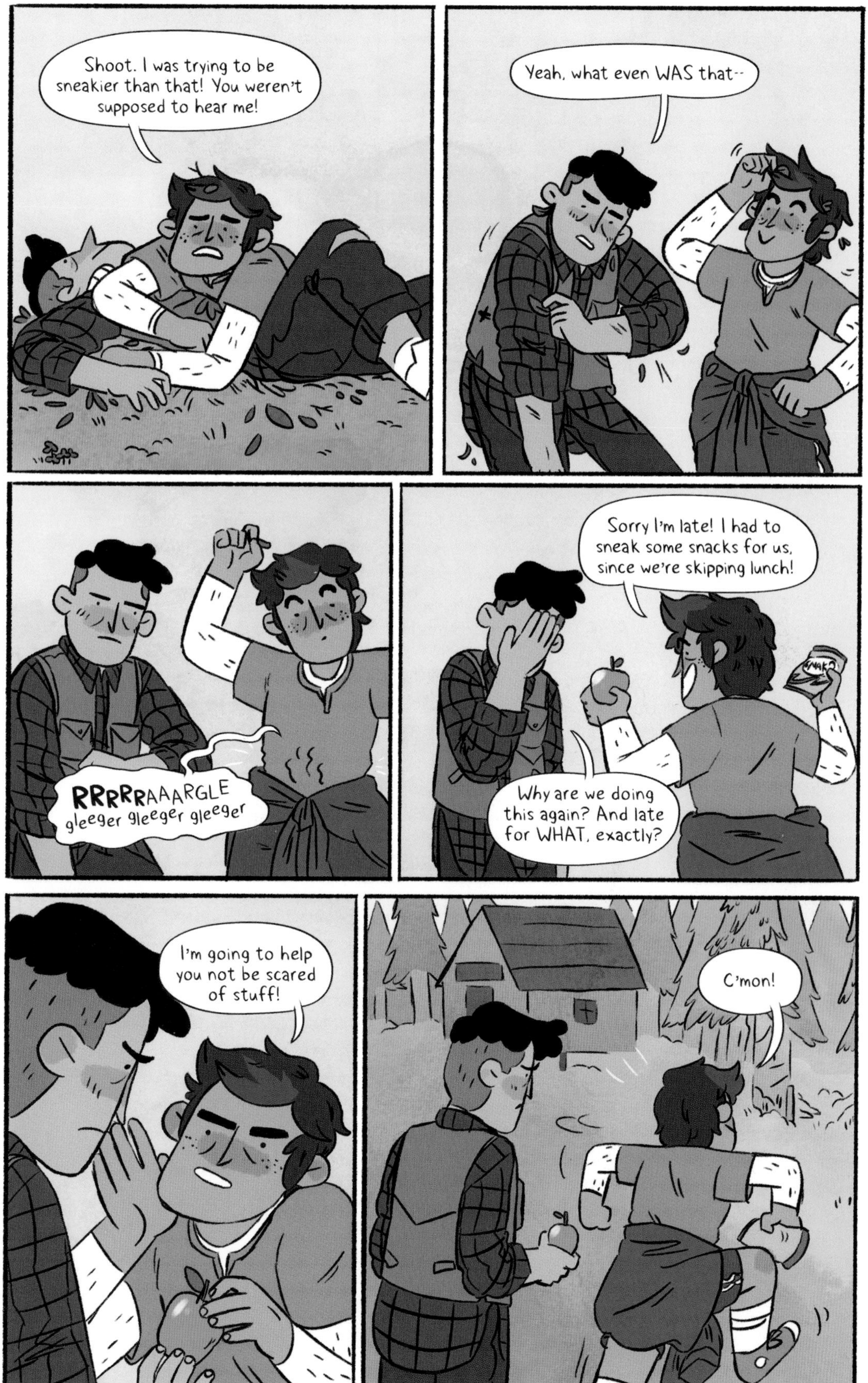
Shoot. I was trying to be sneakier than that! You weren't supposed to hear me!
Yeah, what even WAS that--
RRRRRAAARGLE gleeger gleeger gleeger
Sorry I'm late! I had to sneak some snacks for us, since we're skipping lunch!
Why are we doing this again? And late for WHAT, exactly?
I'm going to help you not be scared of stuff!
C'mon!

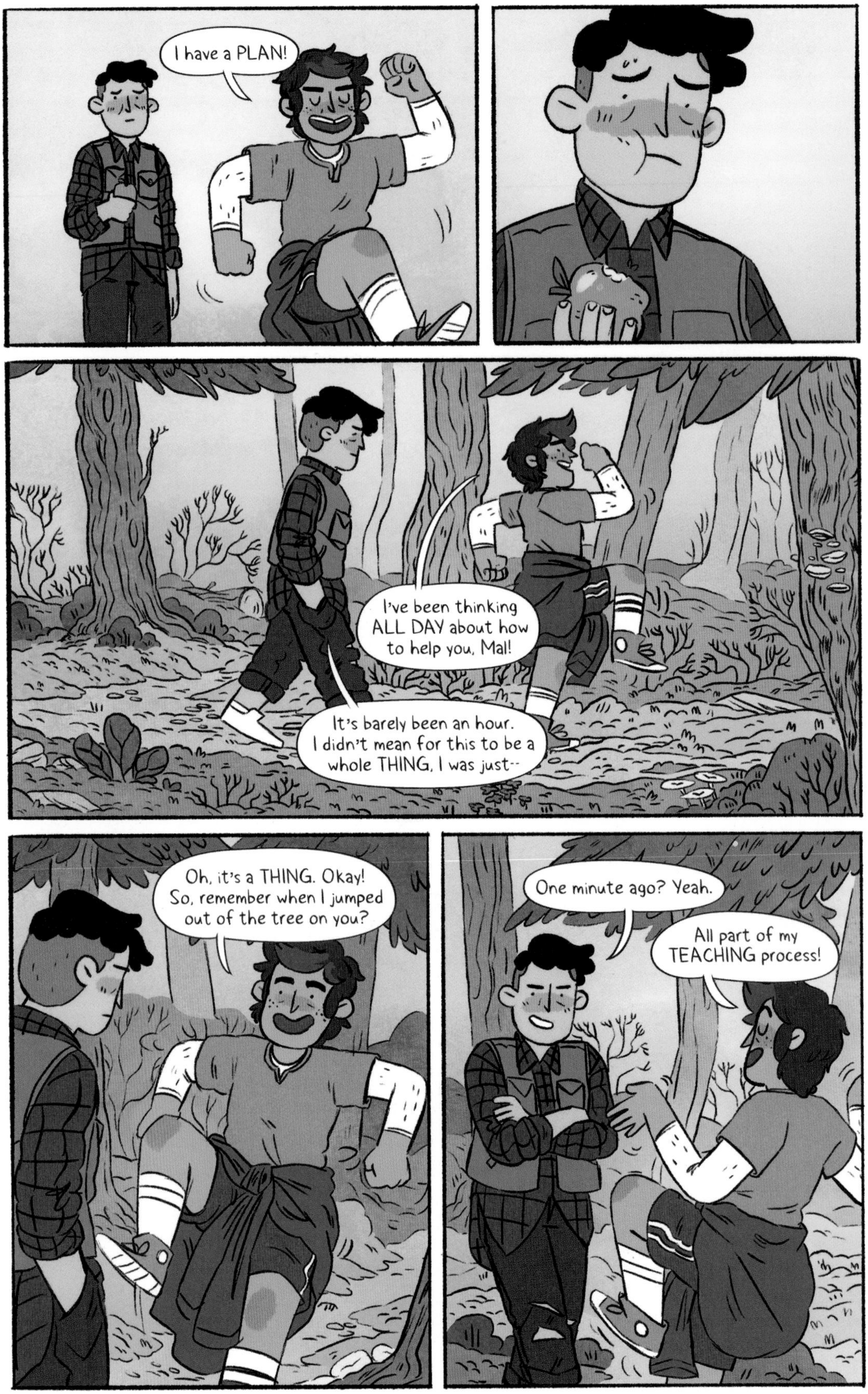
I have a PLAN!
I've been thinking ALL DAY about how to help you, Mal!
It's barely been an hour. I didn't mean for this to be a whole THING, I was just--
Oh, it's a THING. Okay! So, remember when I jumped out of the tree on you?
One minute ago? Yeah.
All part of my TEACHING process!

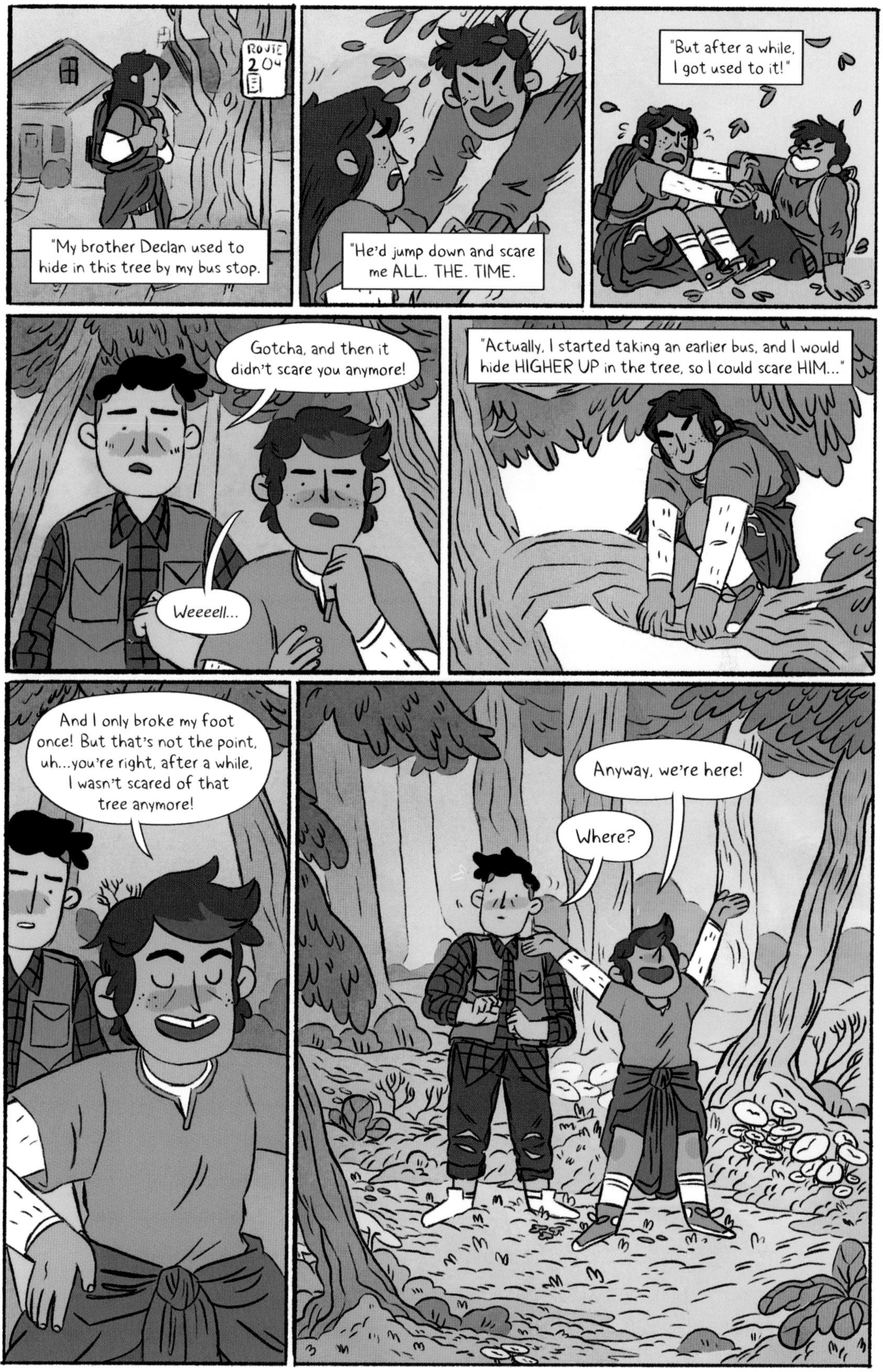
ROUTE 204
"My brother Declan used to hide in this tree by my bus stop.
"He'd jump down and scare me ALL. THE. TIME.
"But after a while, I got used to it!"
Gotcha, and then it didn't scare you anymore!
Weeeell...
"Actually, I started taking an earlier bus, and I would hide HIGHER UP in the tree, so I could scare HIM..."
And I only broke my foot once! But that's not the point, uh...you're right, after a while, I wasn't scared of that tree anymore!
Anyway, we're here!
Where?

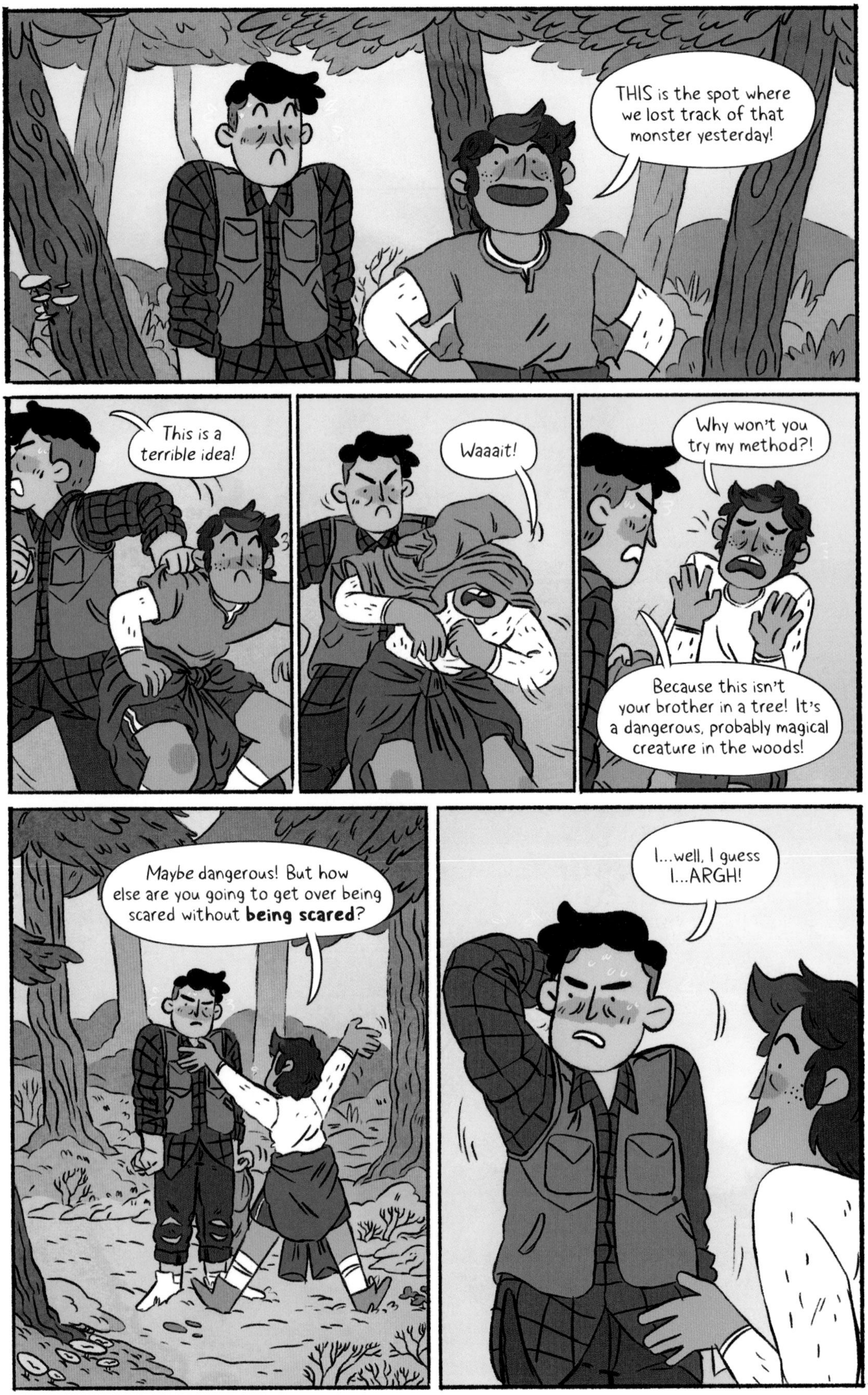
THIS is the spot where we lost track of that monster yesterday!
This is a terrible idea!
Waaait!
Why won't you try my method?!
Because this isn't your brother in a tree! It's a dangerous, probably magical creature in the woods!
Maybe dangerous! But how else are you going to get over being scared without **being scared**?
I...well, I guess I...ARGH!

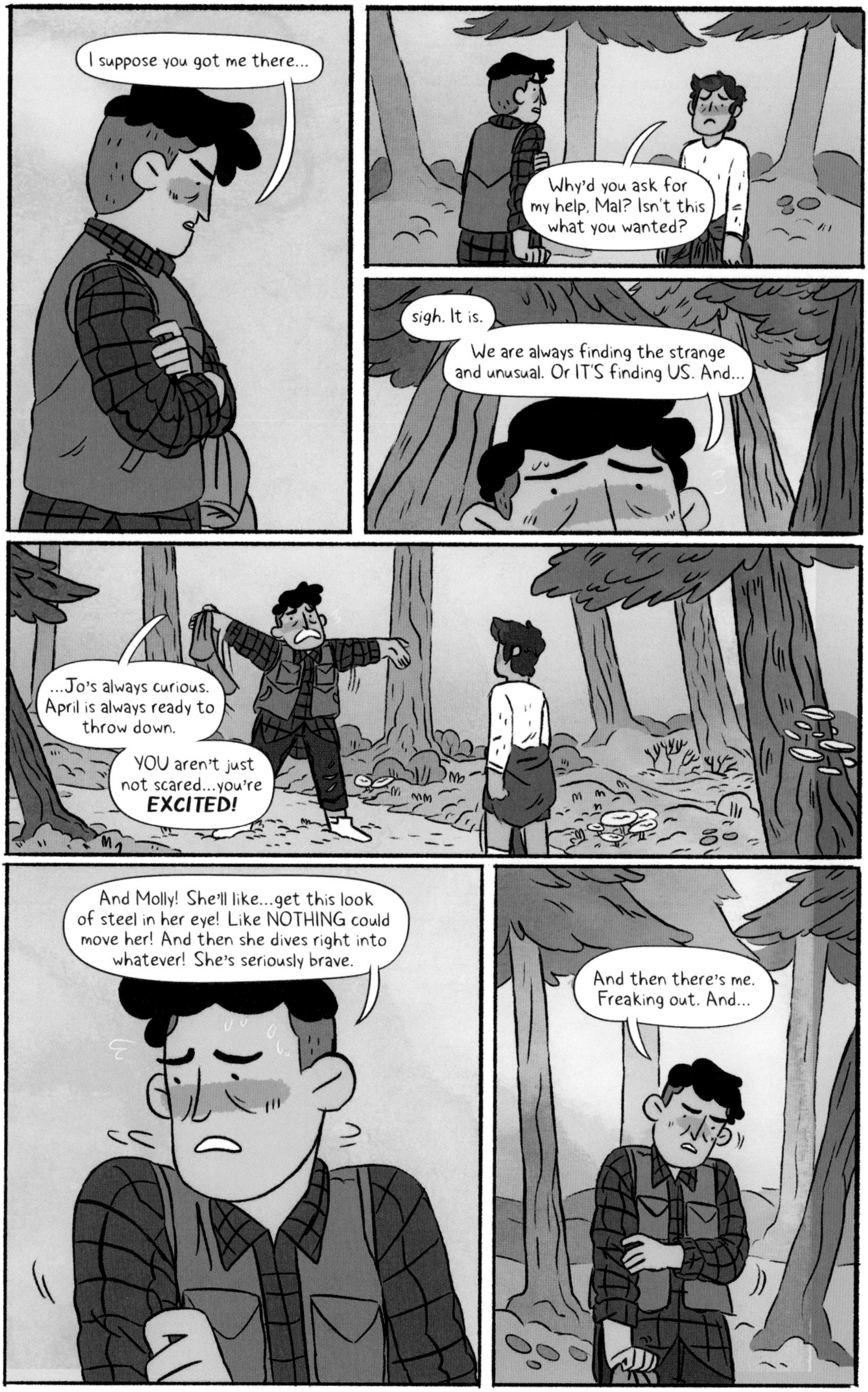
I suppose you got me there...
Why'd you ask for my help, Mal? Isn't this what you wanted?
sigh. It is.
We are always finding the strange and unusual. Or IT'S finding US. And...
...Jo's always curious. April is always ready to throw down.
YOU aren't just not scared...you're **EXCITED!**
And Molly! She'll like...get this look of steel in her eye! Like NOTHING could move her! And then she dives right into whatever! She's seriously brave.
And then there's me. Freaking out. And...

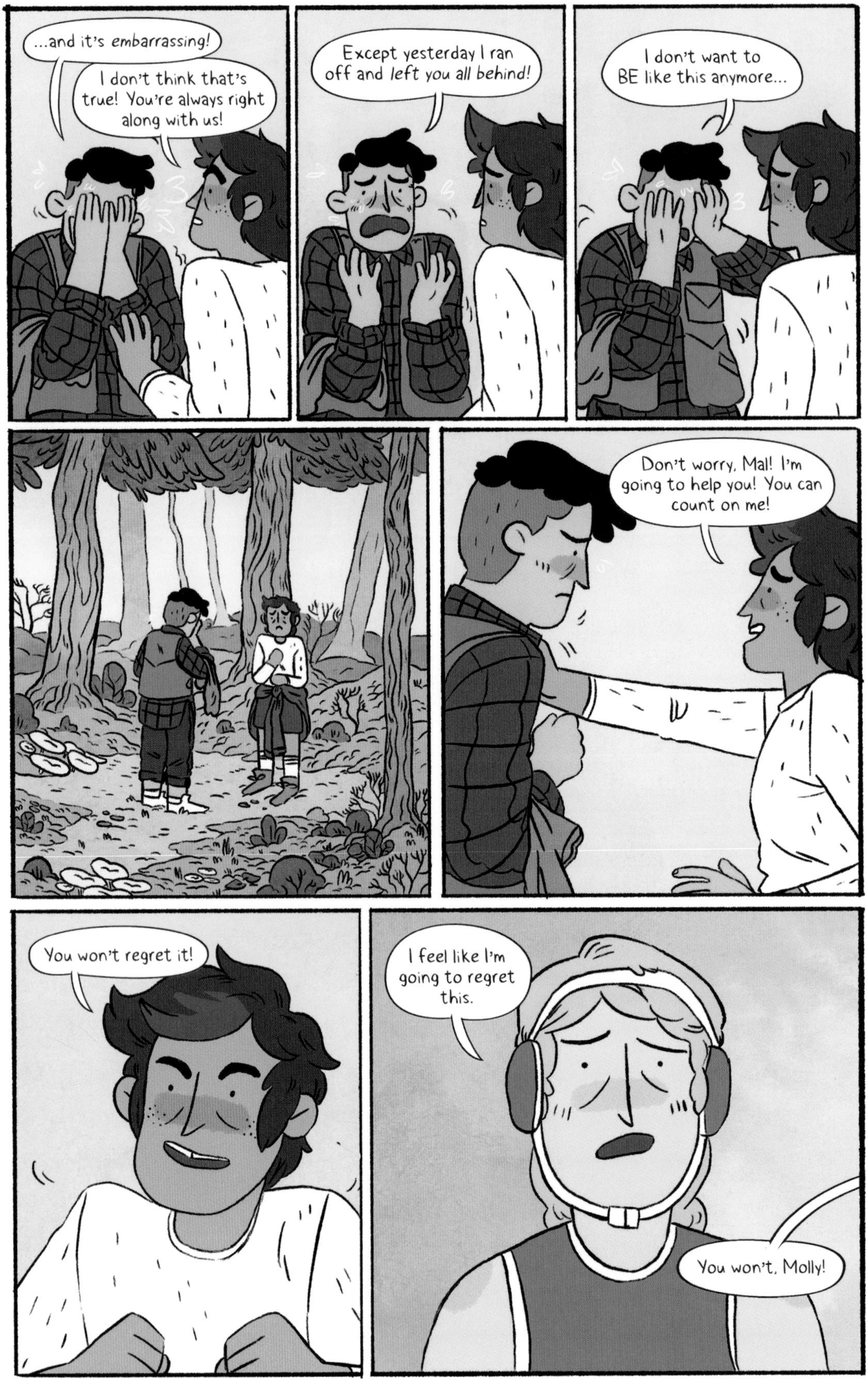
...and it's embarrassing!
I don't think that's true! You're always right along with us!
Except yesterday I ran off and left you all behind!
I don't want to BE like this anymore...
Don't worry, Mal! I'm going to help you! You can count on me!
You won't regret it!
I feel like I'm going to regret this.
You won't, Molly!

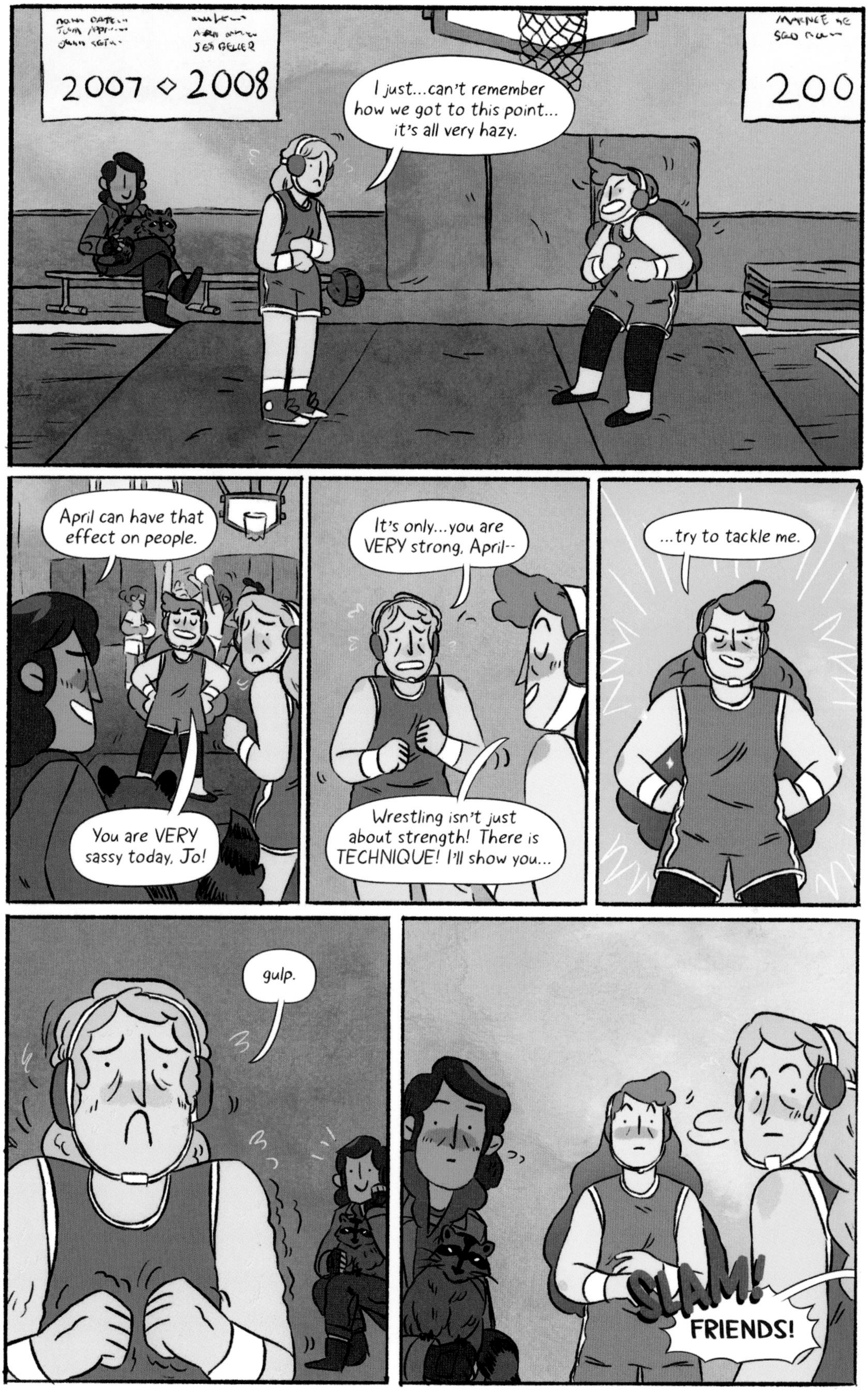

2007 ◇ 2008
200
I just...can't remember how we got to this point... it's all very hazy.
April can have that effect on people.
You are VERY sassy today, Jo!
It's only...you are VERY strong, April--
Wrestling isn't just about strength! There is TECHNIQUE! I'll show you...
...try to tackle me.
gulp.
SLAM!
FRIENDS!

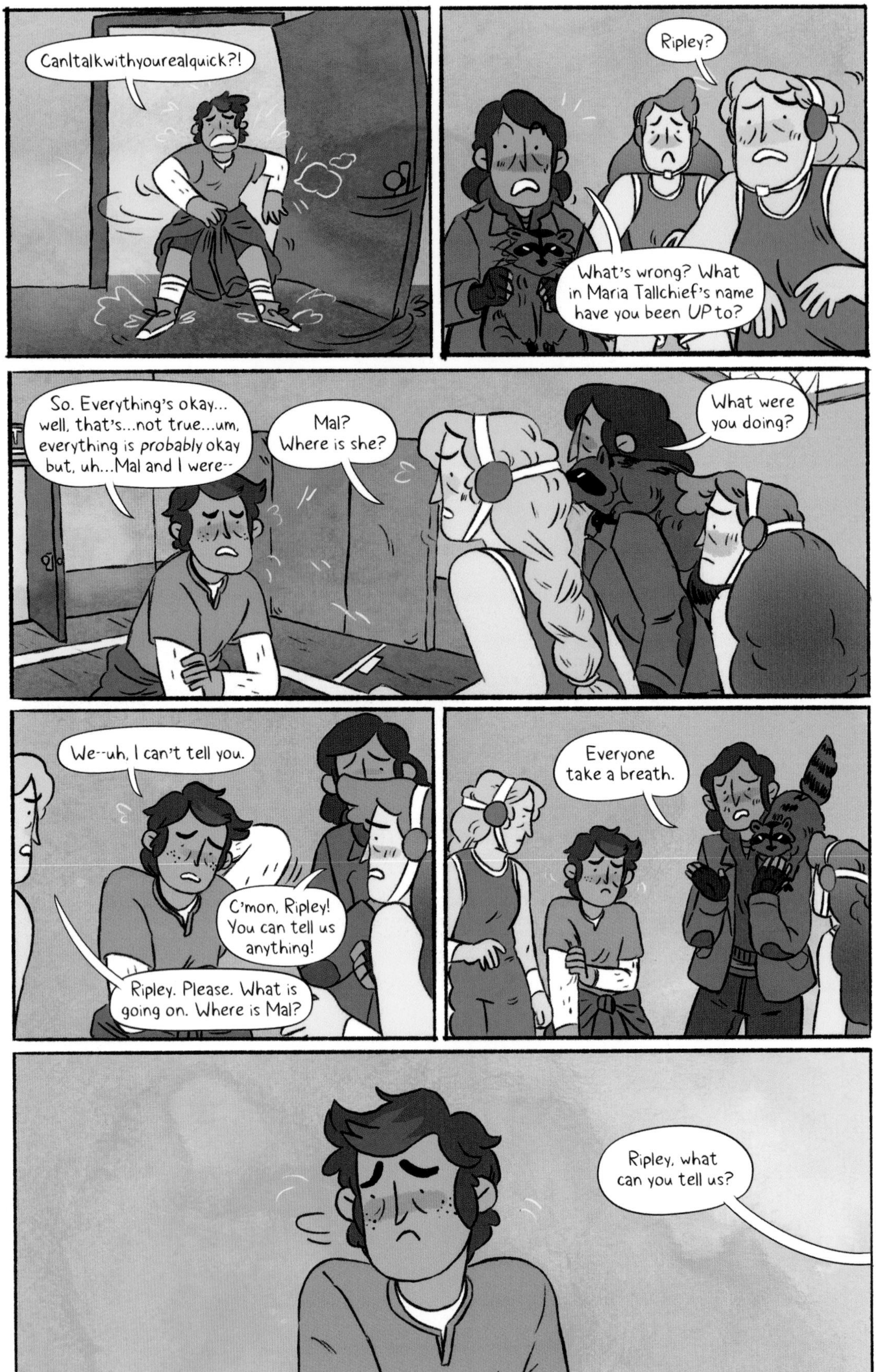
CanItalkwithyourealquick?!
Ripley?
What's wrong? What in Maria Tallchief's name have you been UP to?
So. Everything's okay... well, that's...not true...um, everything is probably okay but, uh...Mal and I were--
Mal? Where is she?
What were you doing?
We--uh, I can't tell you.
C'mon, Ripley! You can tell us anything!
Ripley. Please. What is going on. Where is Mal?
Everyone take a breath.
Ripley, what can you tell us?

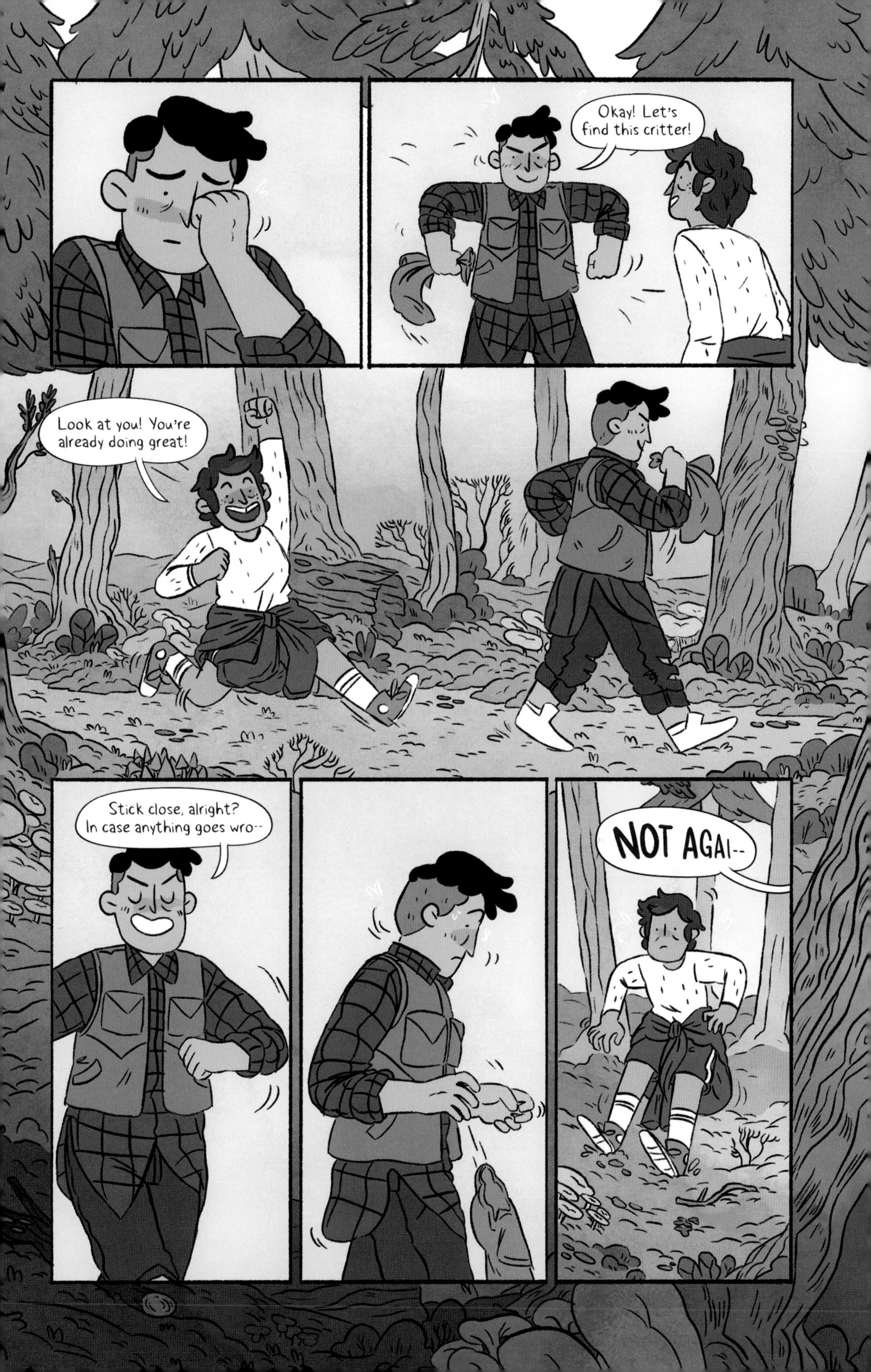

Okay! Let's find this critter!
Look at you! You're already doing great!
Stick close, alright? In case anything goes wro--
NOT AGAI--

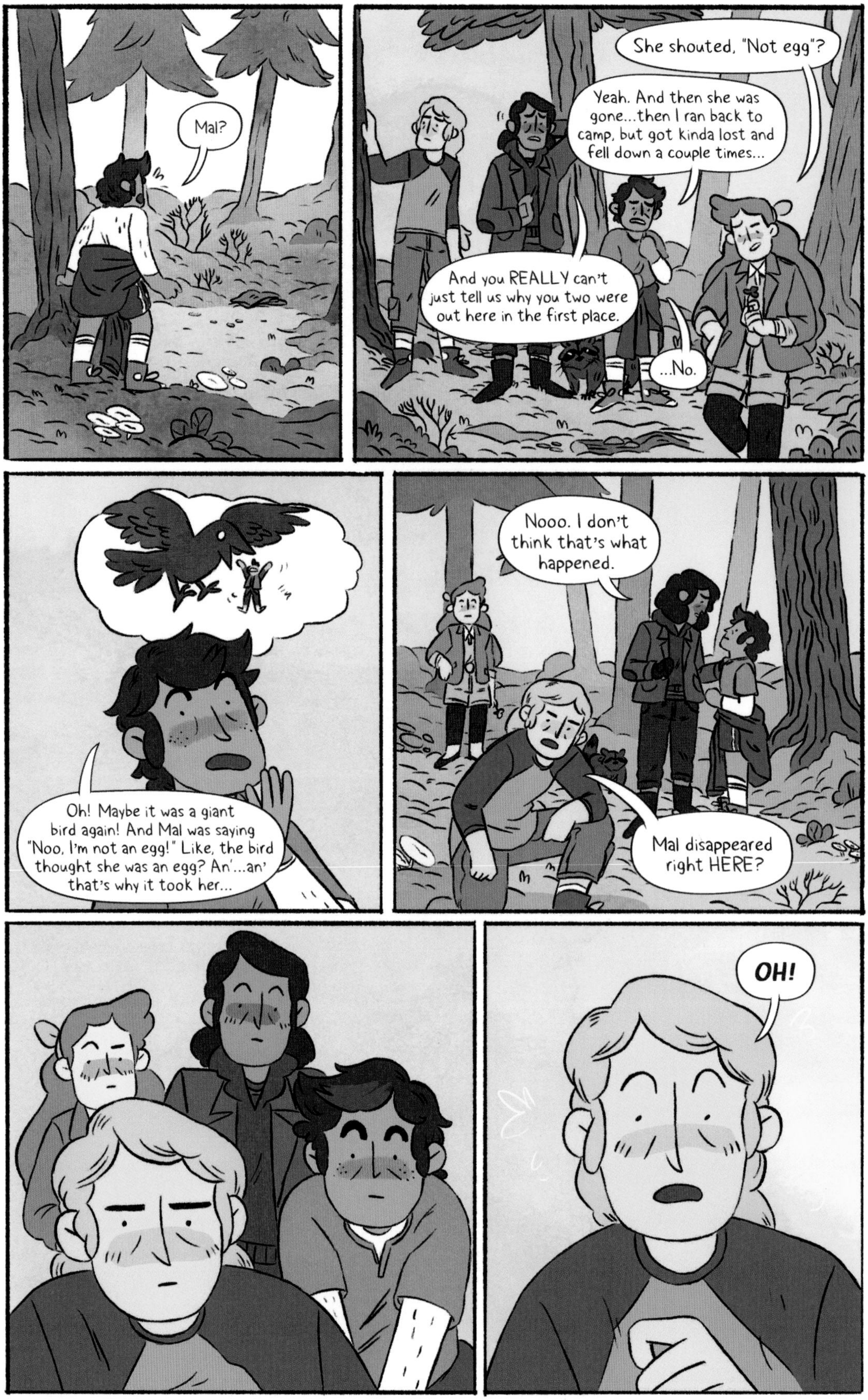
Mal?
She shouted, "Not egg"?
Yeah. And then she was gone...then I ran back to camp, but got kinda lost and fell down a couple times...
And you REALLY can't just tell us why you two were out here in the first place.
...No.
Oh! Maybe it was a giant bird again! And Mal was saying "Noo, I'm not an egg!" Like, the bird thought she was an egg? An'...an' that's why it took her...
Nooo. I don't think that's what happened.
Mal disappeared right HERE?
OH!

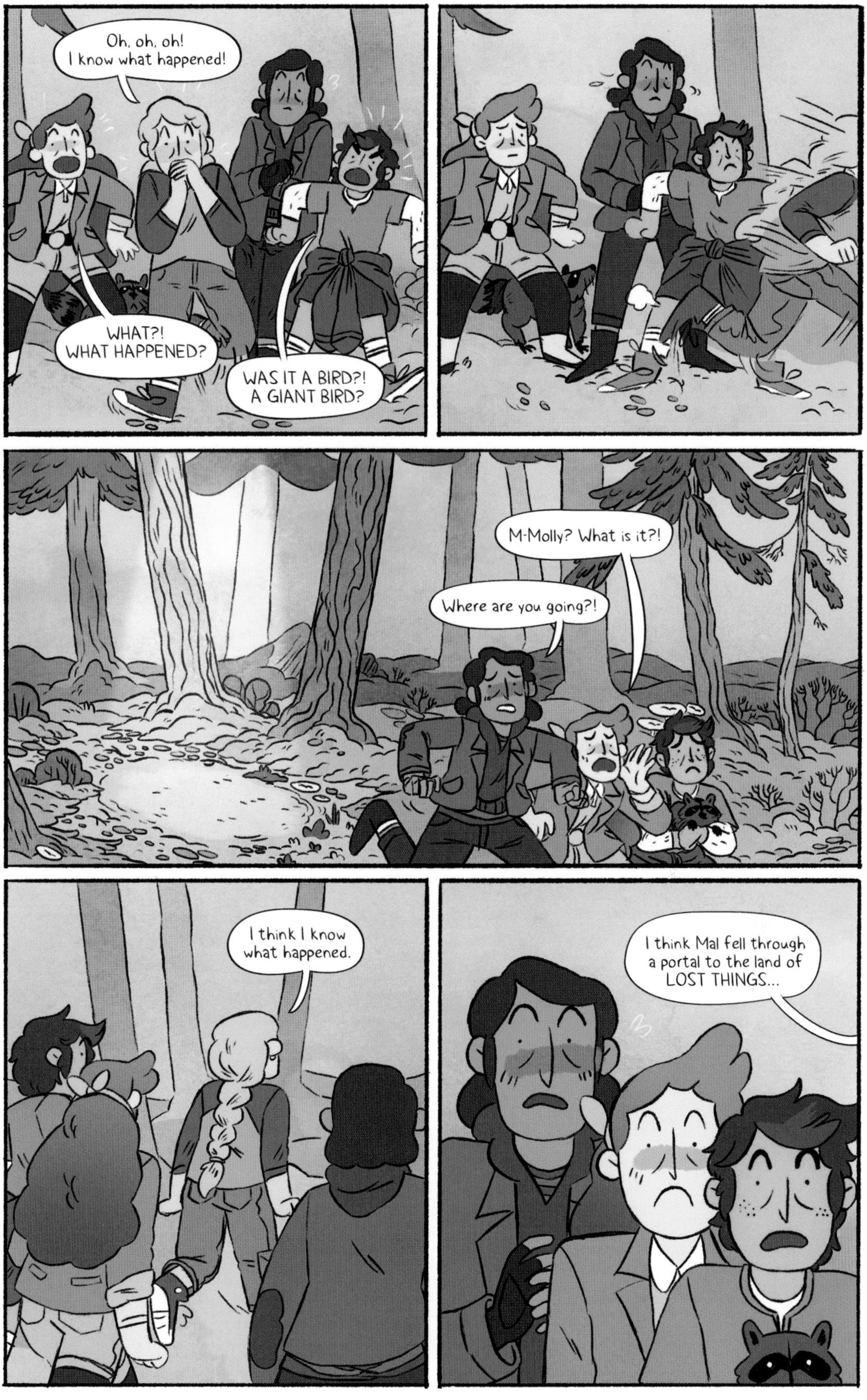
Oh, oh, oh!
I know what happened!
WHAT?!
WHAT HAPPENED?
WAS IT A BIRD?!
A GIANT BIRD?
M-Molly? What is it?!
Where are you going?!
I think I know
what happened.
I think Mal fell through
a portal to the land of
LOST THINGS...

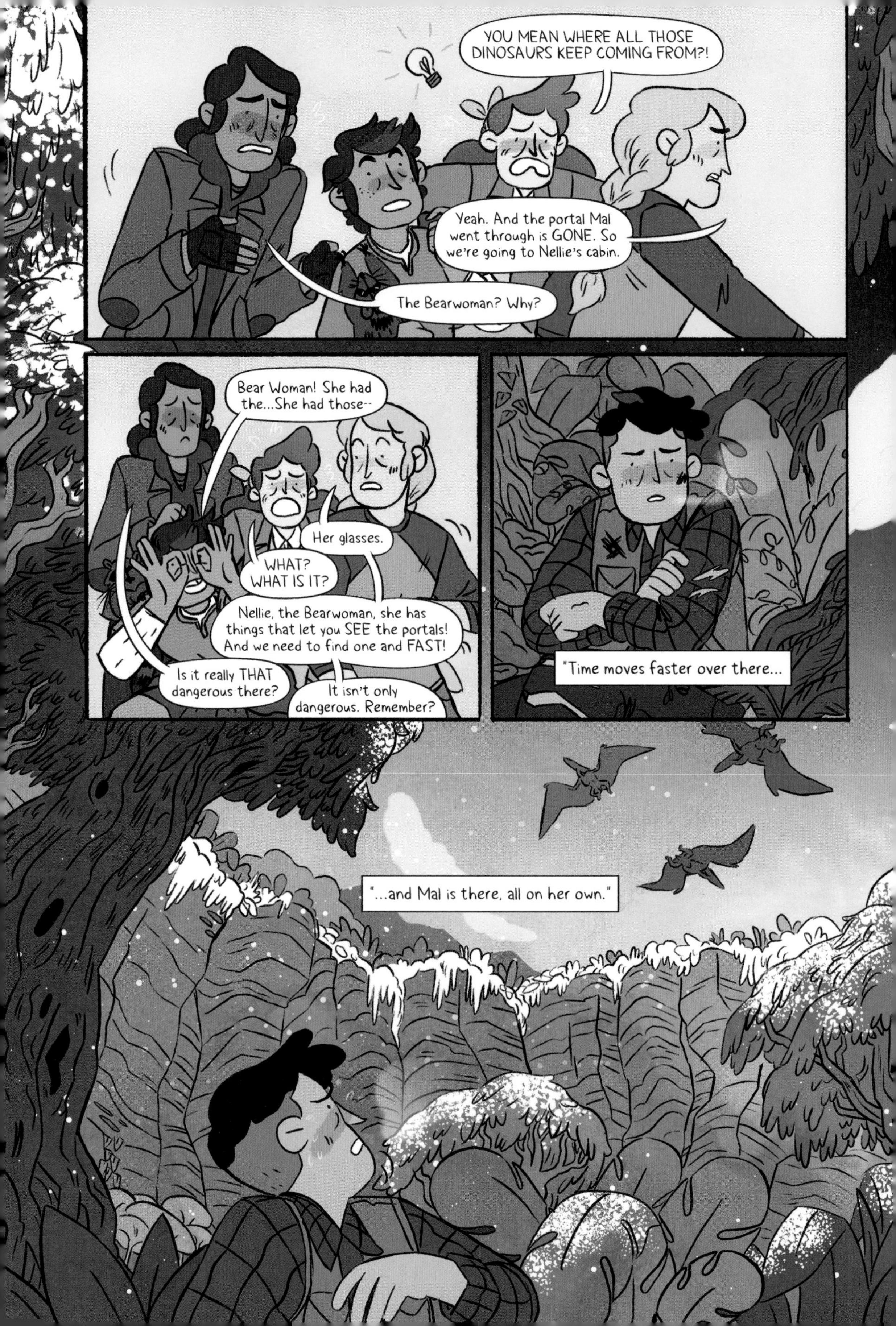
YOU MEAN WHERE ALL THOSE DINOSAURS KEEP COMING FROM?!
Yeah. And the portal Mal went through is GONE. So we're going to Nellie's cabin.
The Bearwoman? Why?
Bear Woman! She had the...She had those--
Her glasses.
WHAT? WHAT IS IT?
Nellie, the Bearwoman, she has things that let you SEE the portals! And we need to find one and FAST!
Is it really THAT dangerous there?
It isn't only dangerous. Remember?
"Time moves faster over there...
"...and Mal is there, all on her own."

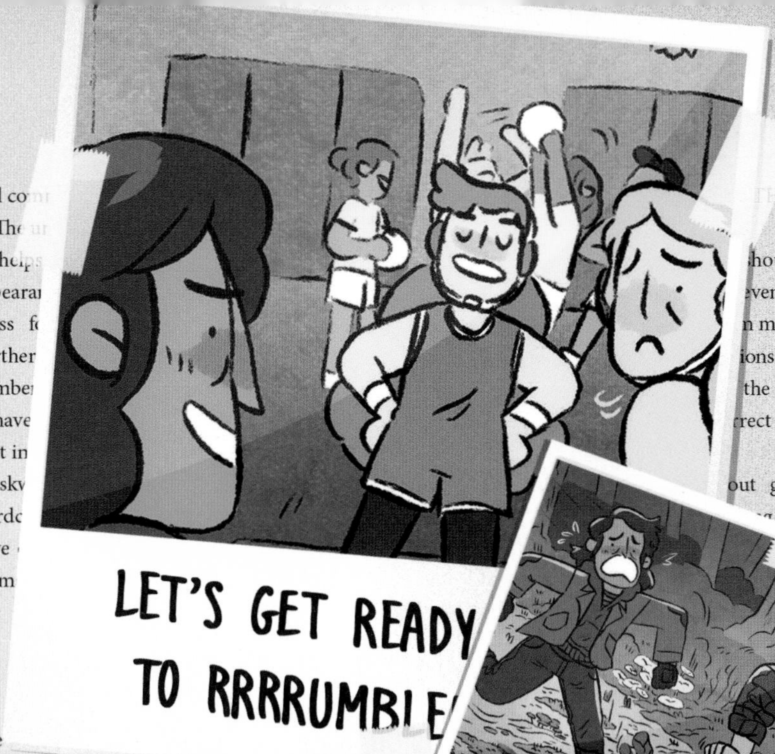
LET'S GET READY TO RRRRUMBLE!

will co…

The u…
It help…
appeara…
dress f…
Further…
Lumbe…
to have…
part in…
Thiskw…
Hardc…
have…
them…

…HE UNIFORM

…should be worn at camp …events when Lumberjanes …n may also be worn at other …ions. It should be worn as a … the uniform dress with …rrect shoes, and stocking or …

… out grows her uniform or … ther Lumberjane. …a she has … her … her

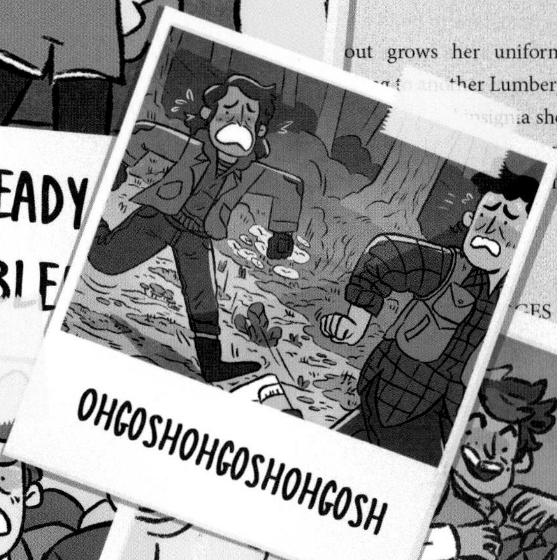
OHGOSHOHGOSHOHGOSH

The …
yellow, short sl…
emb…
the w…
choose…
slacks, …
made o…
out-of-do…
green bere…
the colla…
Shoes ma…
heels, rou… …ings or
socks shou… …with the shoes or wit…
the uniform. Ne…es, bracelets, or other jewelry do…
belong with a Lumberjane uniform.

…GES

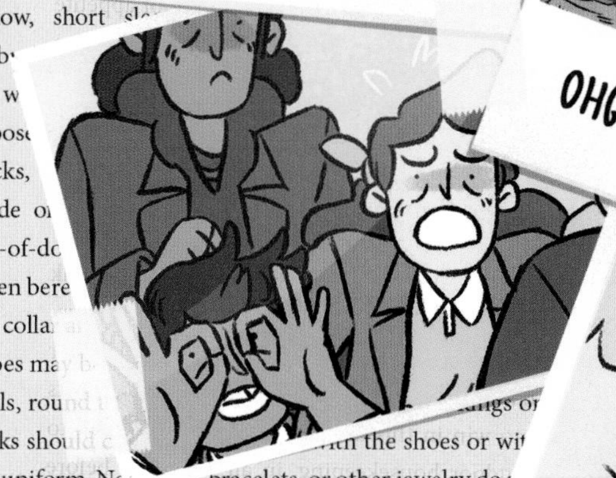

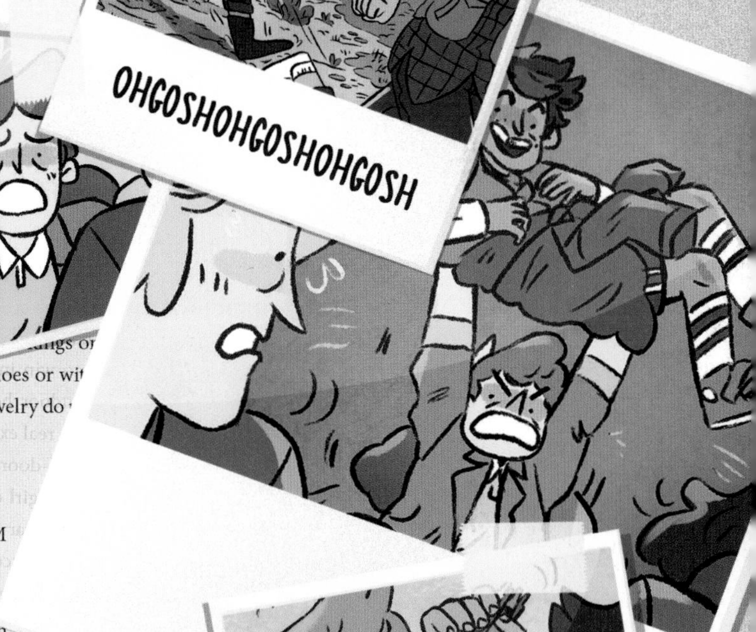

HOW TO WEAR THE UNIFORM

To look well in a uniform demands first of … uniform be kept in good condition—clean … pressed. See that the skirt is the right length for your own height and build, that the belt is adjusted to your waist, that your shoes and stockings are in keeping with the uniform, that you watch your posture and carry yourself with dignity and grace. If the beret is removed indoors, be sure that your hair is neat and kept in place with an inconspicuous clip or ribbon. When you wear a Lumberjane uniform you are identified as a member of this organization and you should be doubly careful to conduct yourself in a way that will show everyone that courtesy and thoughtfulness are part of being a Lumberjane. People are likely to judge a whole nation by the selfishness of a few individuals, to criticize a whole family because of the misconduct of one member, and to feel unkindly toward an organization because of the

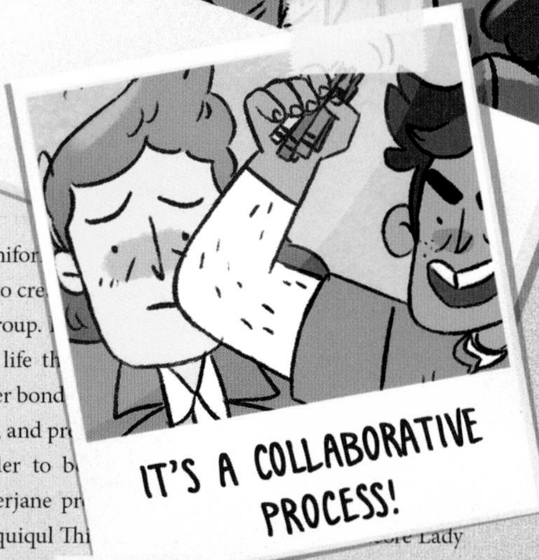
IT'S A COLLABORATIVE PROCESS!

The unifor…
helps to cre…
in a group. …
active life th…
another bond…
future, and pr…
in order to b…
Lumberjane pr…
Penniquiqul Thi… …ore Lady
Types, but m… …es will wish to have one. They can either bu… …uniform, or make it themselves from materials available at the trading post.

LUMBERJANES FIELD MANUAL

CHAPTER SIXTY-TWO

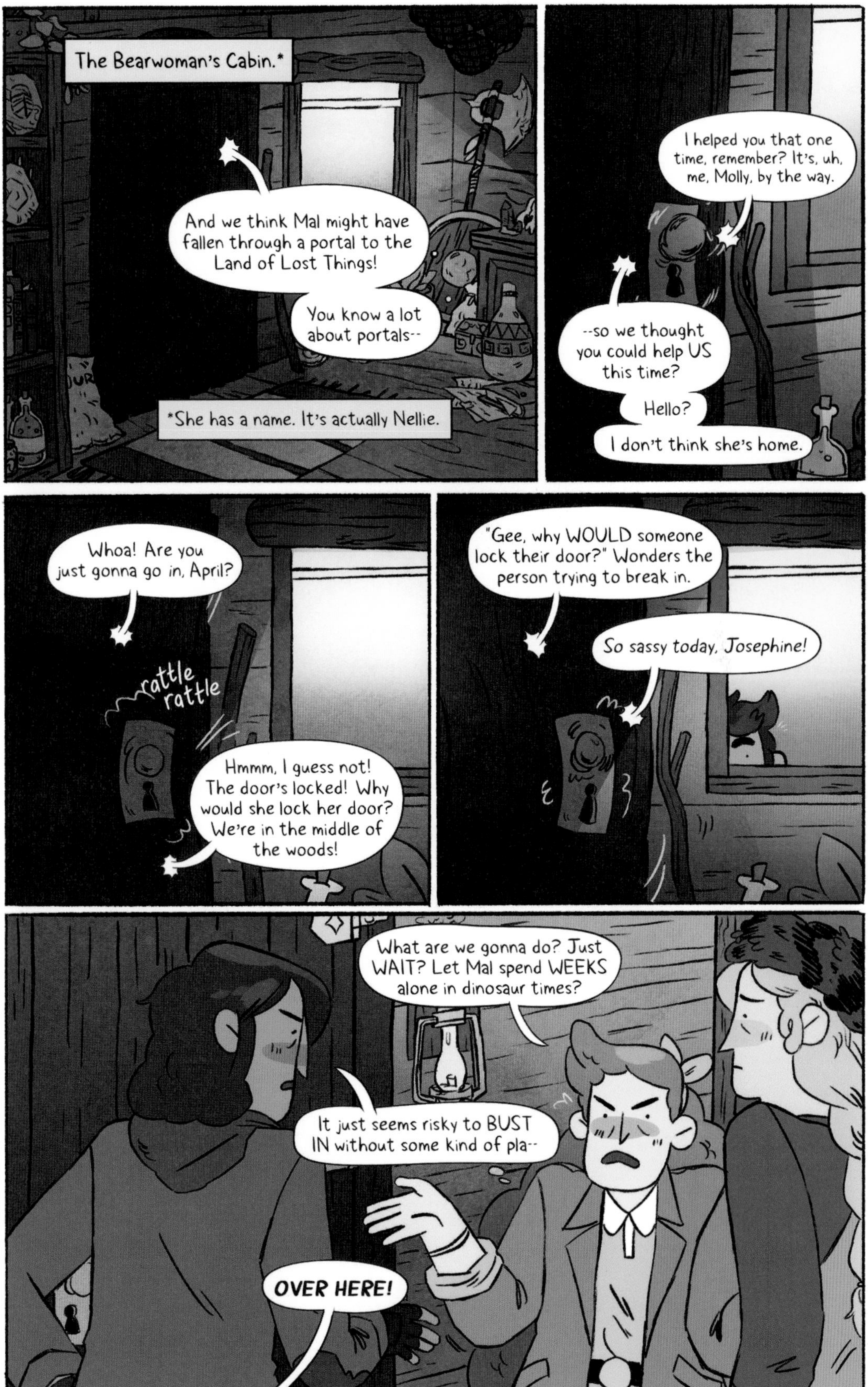
The Bearwoman's Cabin.*
And we think Mal might have fallen through a portal to the Land of Lost Things!
You know a lot about portals--
*She has a name. It's actually Nellie.
I helped you that one time, remember? It's, uh, me, Molly, by the way.
--so we thought you could help US this time?
Hello?
I don't think she's home.
Whoa! Are you just gonna go in, April?
rattle rattle
Hmmm, I guess not! The door's locked! Why would she lock her door? We're in the middle of the woods!
"Gee, why WOULD someone lock their door?" Wonders the person trying to break in.
So sassy today, Josephine!
What are we gonna do? Just WAIT? Let Mal spend WEEKS alone in dinosaur times?
It just seems risky to BUST IN without some kind of pla--
OVER HERE!

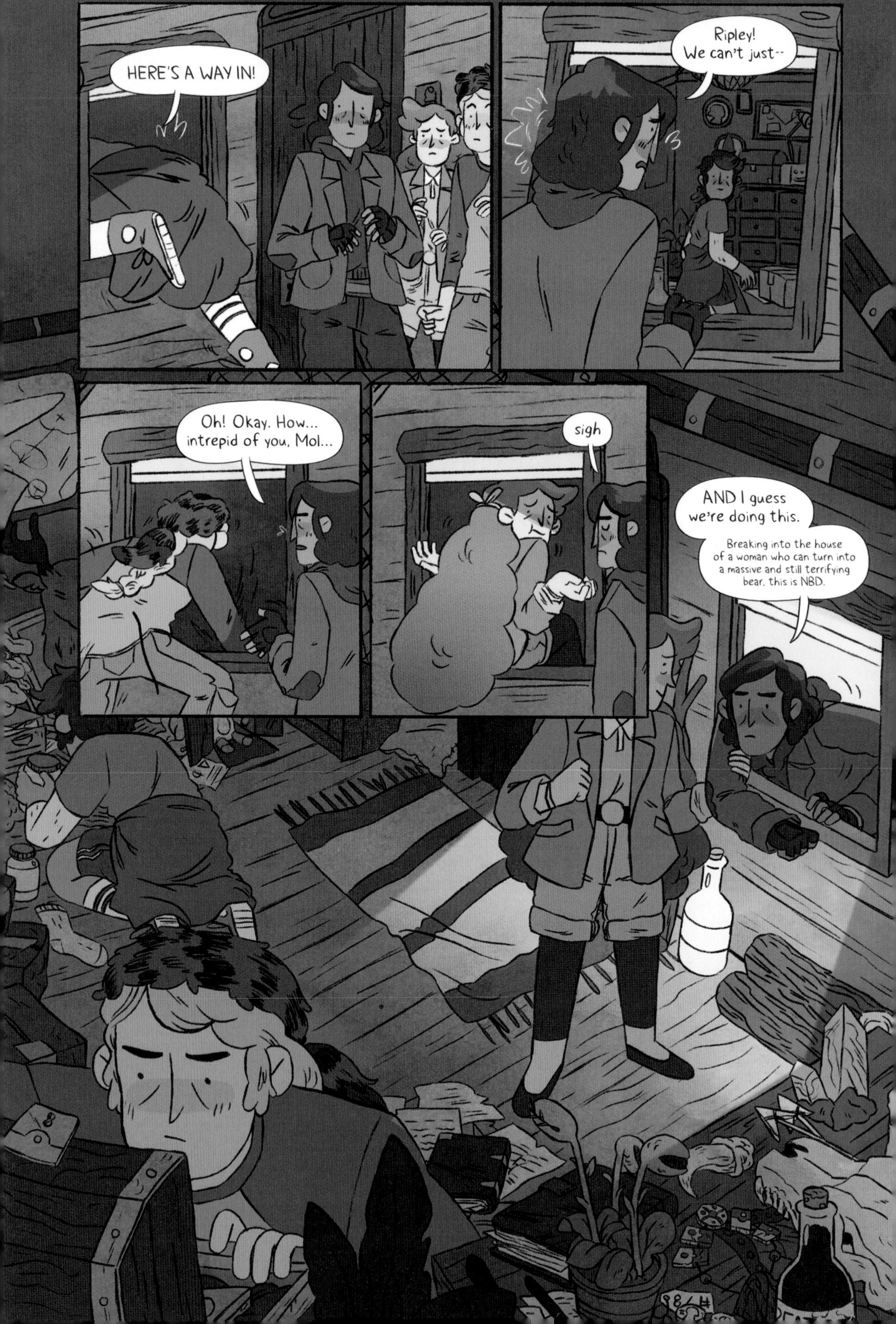
HERE'S A WAY IN!
Ripley! We can't just--
Oh! Okay. How... intrepid of you, Mol...
sigh
AND I guess we're doing this.
Breaking into the house of a woman who can turn into a massive and still terrifying bear, this is NBD.

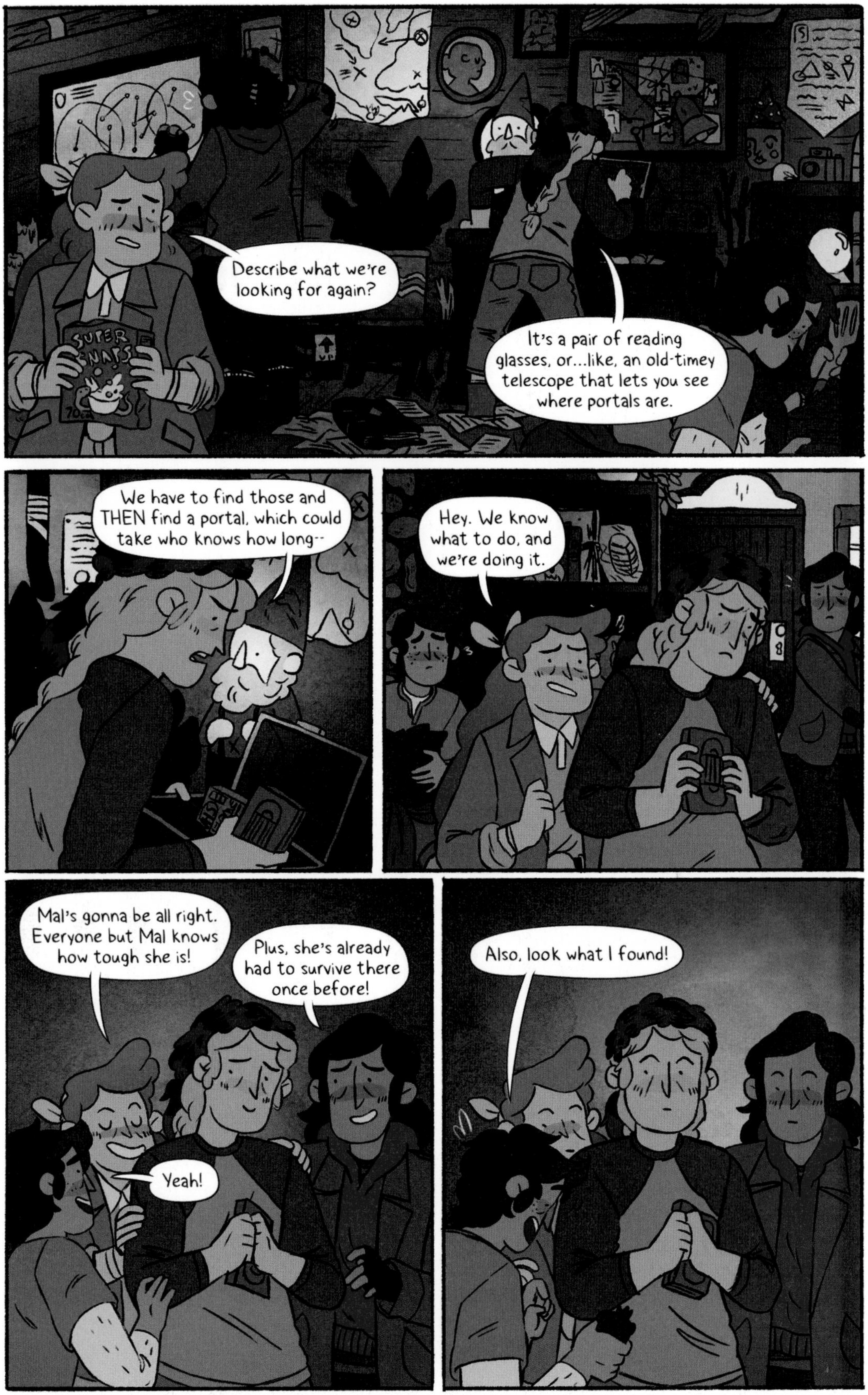
Describe what we're looking for again?
It's a pair of reading glasses, or...like, an old-timey telescope that lets you see where portals are.
SUPER SNAPS
We have to find those and THEN find a portal, which could take who knows how long--
Hey. We know what to do, and we're doing it.
Mal's gonna be all right. Everyone but Mal knows how tough she is!
Plus, she's already had to survive there once before!
Yeah!
Also, look what I found!

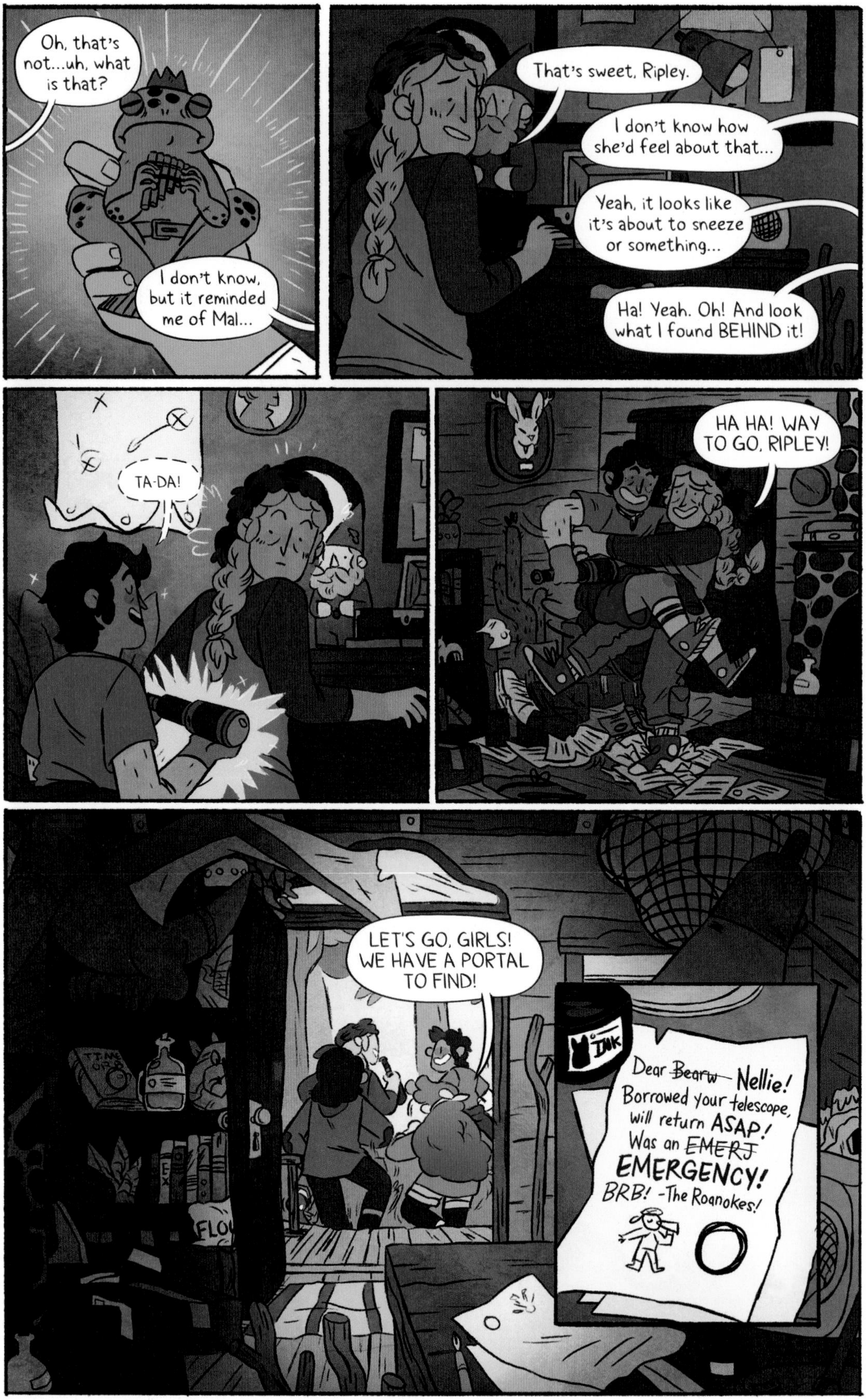
Oh, that's not...uh, what is that?
I don't know, but it reminded me of Mal...
That's sweet, Ripley.
I don't know how she'd feel about that...
Yeah, it looks like it's about to sneeze or something...
Ha! Yeah. Oh! And look what I found BEHIND it!
TA-DA!
HA HA! WAY TO GO, RIPLEY!
LET'S GO, GIRLS! WE HAVE A PORTAL TO FIND!
INK
Dear ~~Bearw~~ Nellie! Borrowed your telescope, will return ASAP! Was an ~~EMERJ~~ EMERGENCY! BRB! -The Roanokes!

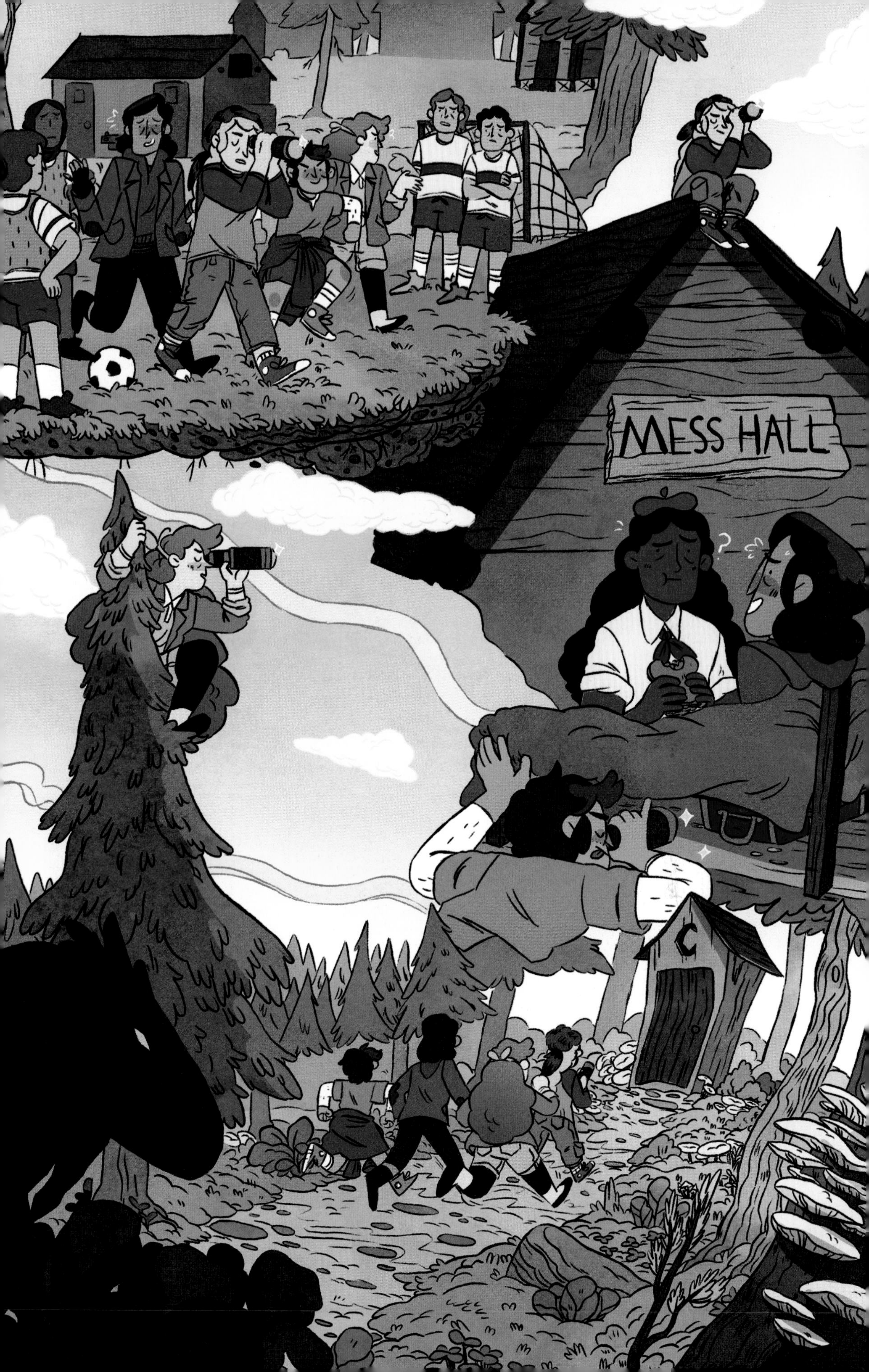
MESS HALL

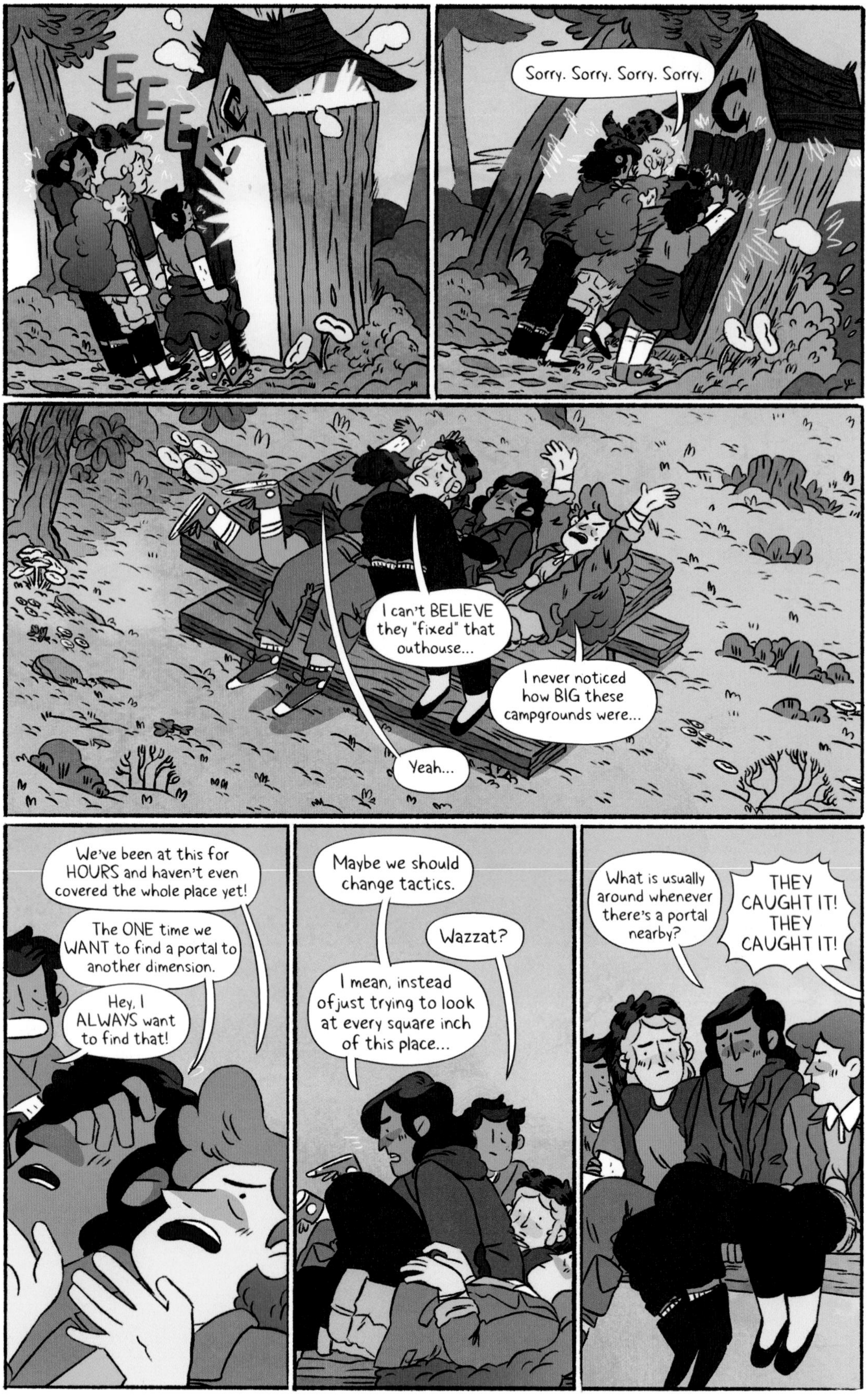
EEEEK!
Sorry. Sorry. Sorry. Sorry.
I can't BELIEVE they "fixed" that outhouse...
I never noticed how BIG these campgrounds were...
Yeah...
We've been at this for HOURS and haven't even covered the whole place yet!
The ONE time we WANT to find a portal to another dimension.
Hey, I ALWAYS want to find that!
Maybe we should change tactics.
Wazzat?
I mean, instead of just trying to look at every square inch of this place...
What is usually around whenever there's a portal nearby?
THEY CAUGHT IT! THEY CAUGHT IT!

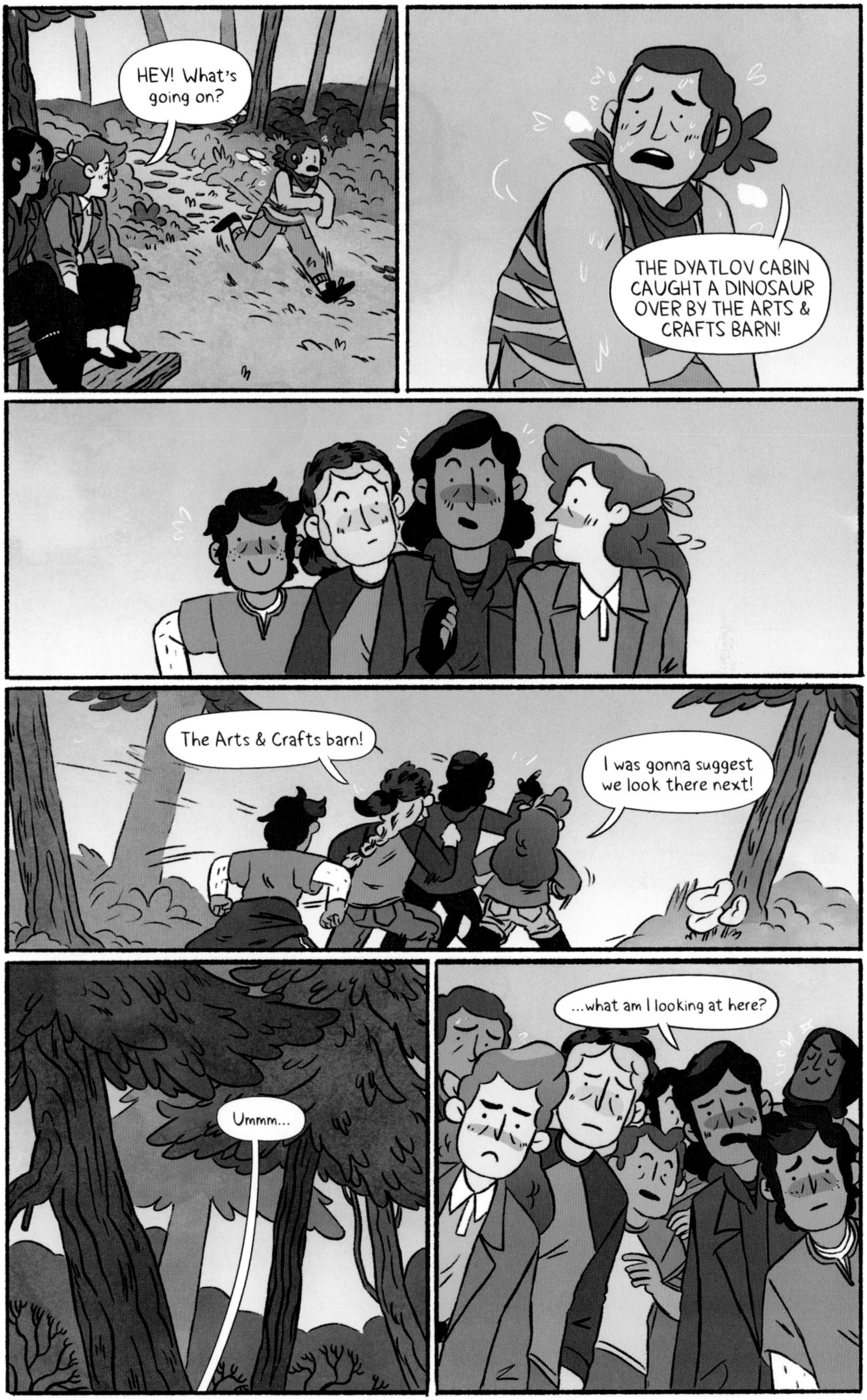
HEY! What's going on?
THE DYATLOV CABIN CAUGHT A DINOSAUR OVER BY THE ARTS & CRAFTS BARN!
The Arts & Crafts barn!
I was gonna suggest we look there next!
Ummm...
...what am I looking at here?

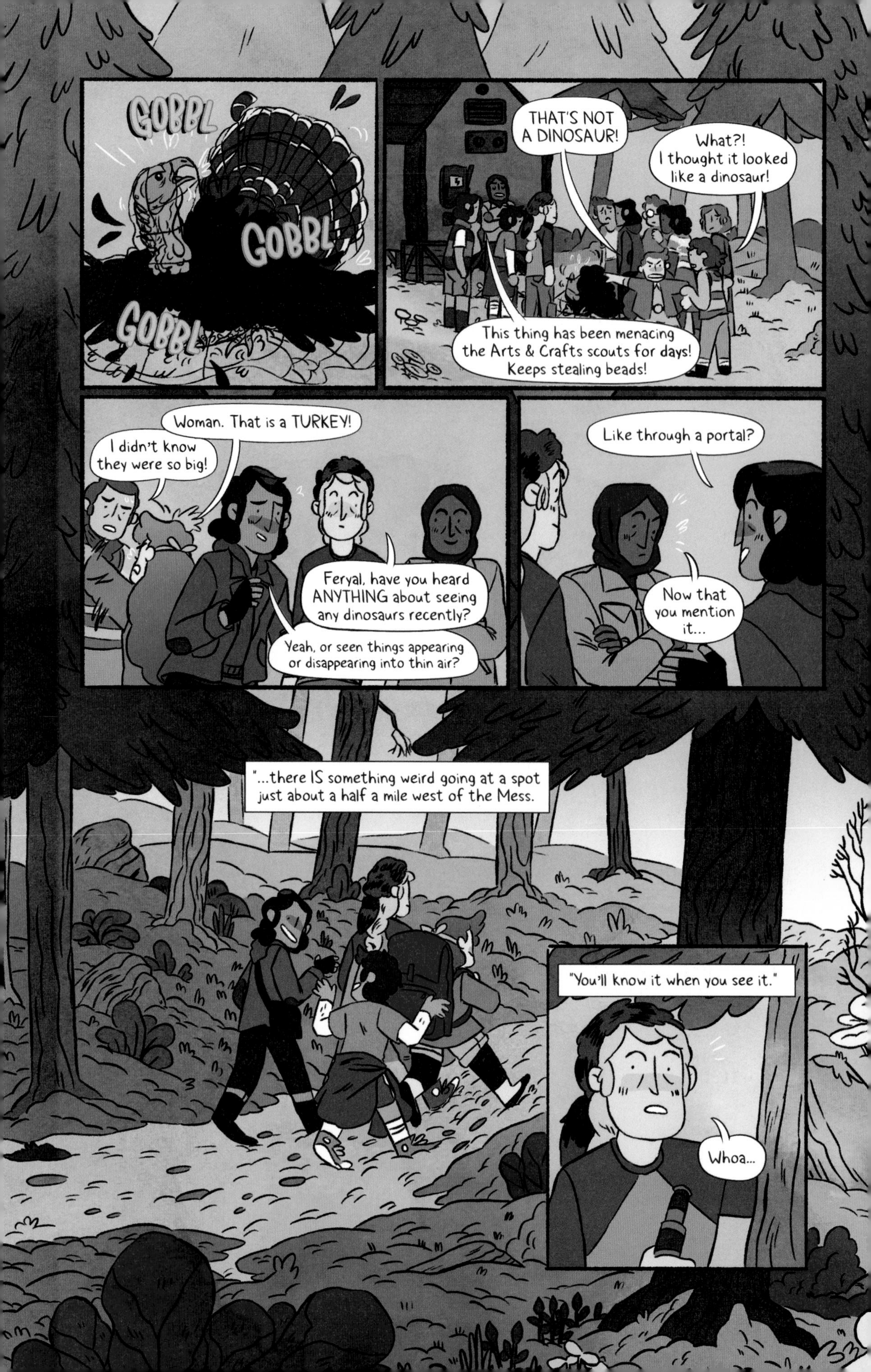
GOBBL
GOBBL
GOBBL
THAT'S NOT A DINOSAUR!
What?! I thought it looked like a dinosaur!
This thing has been menacing the Arts & Crafts scouts for days! Keeps stealing beads!
Woman. That is a TURKEY!
I didn't know they were so big!
Feryal, have you heard ANYTHING about seeing any dinosaurs recently?
Yeah, or seen things appearing or disappearing into thin air?
Like through a portal?
Now that you mention it...
"...there IS something weird going at a spot just about a half a mile west of the Mess.
"You'll know it when you see it."
Whoa...

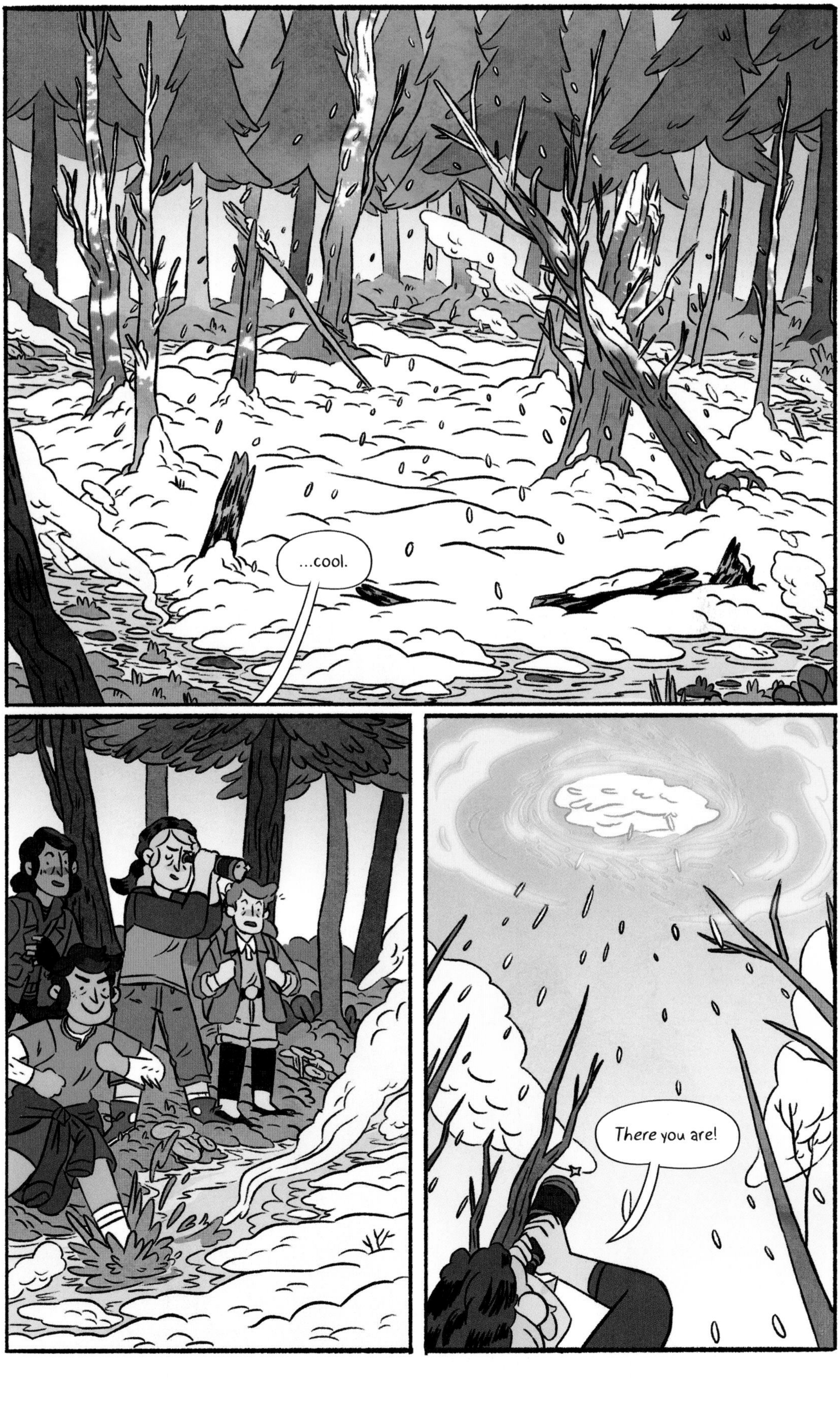
...cool.
There you are!

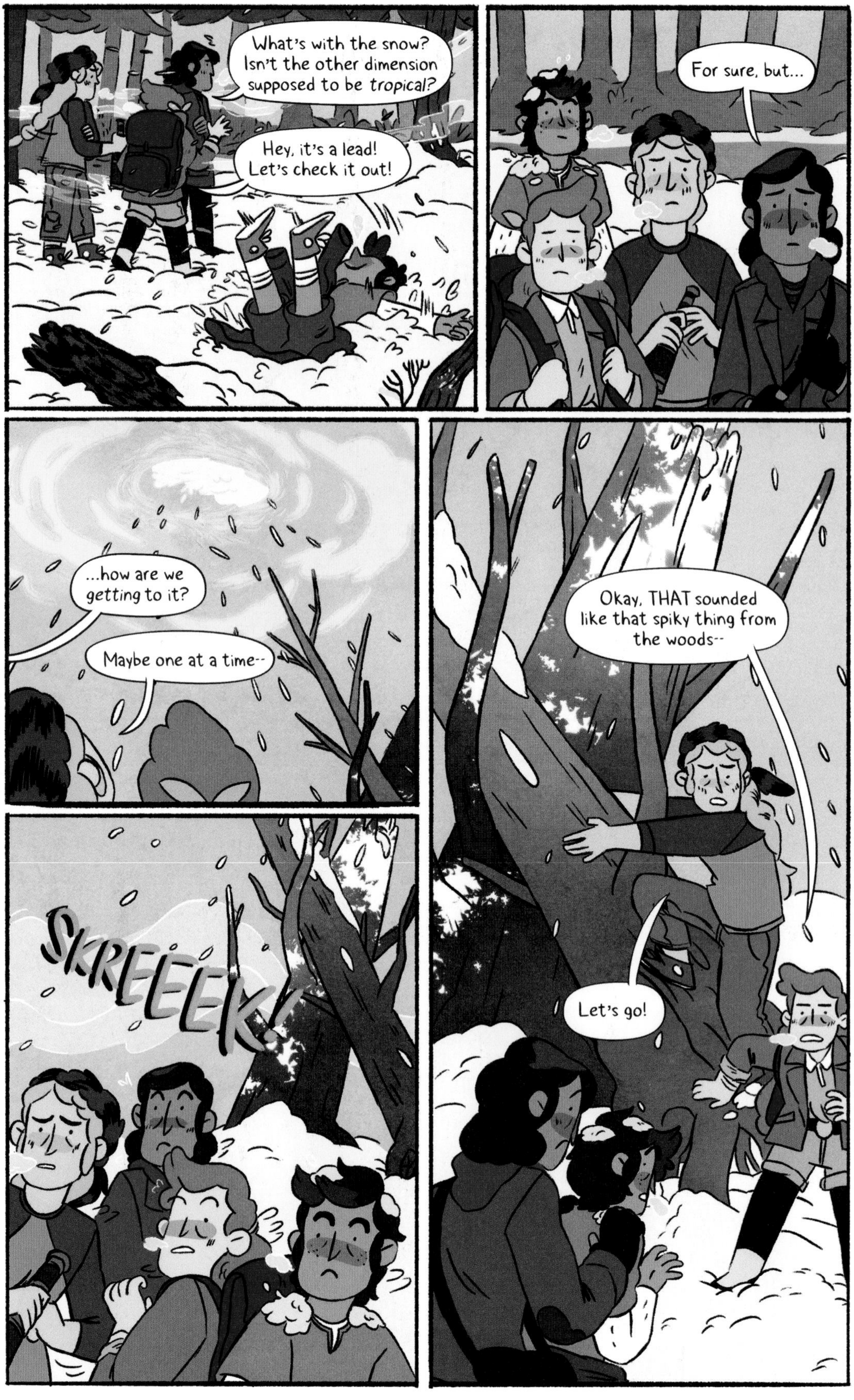
What's with the snow? Isn't the other dimension supposed to be *tropical*?
Hey, it's a lead! Let's check it out!
For sure, but...
...how are we getting to it?
Maybe one at a time--
SKREEEEK!
Okay, THAT sounded like that spiky thing from the woods--
Let's go!

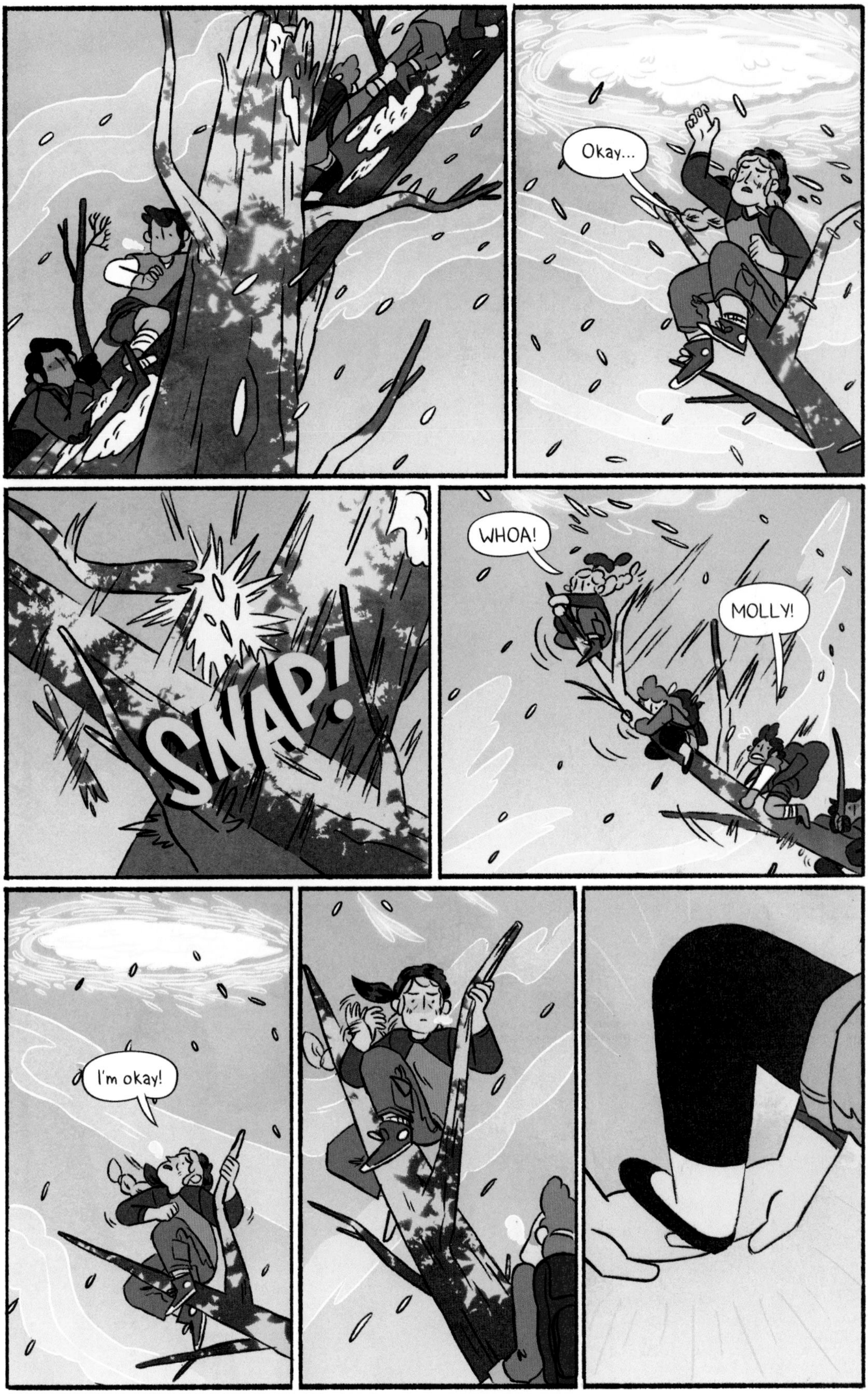
Okay...
SNAP!
WHOA!
MOLLY!
I'm okay!

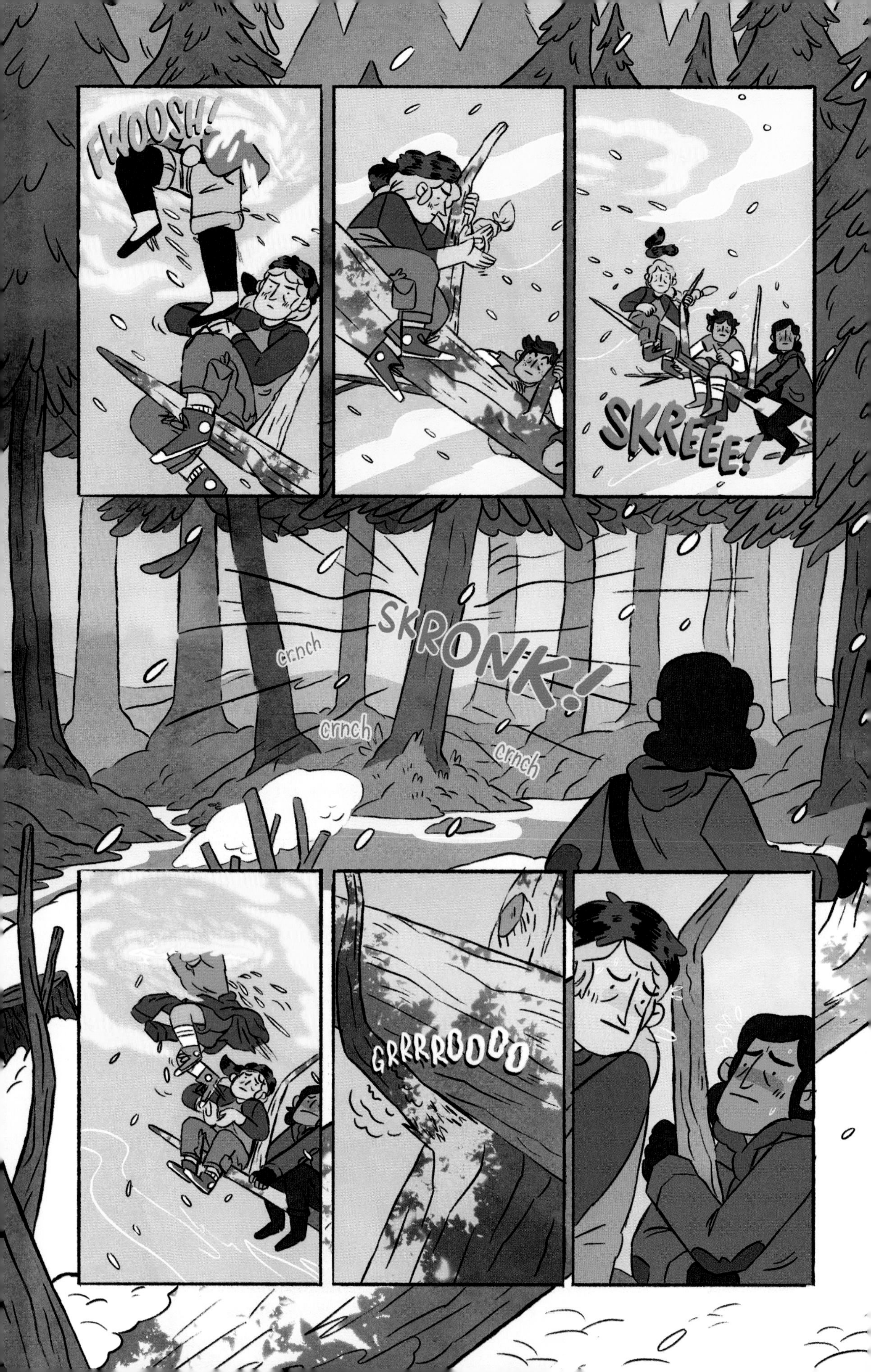
FWOOSH!
SKREEEE!
SKRONK!
crnch
crnch
crnch
GRRRROOOO

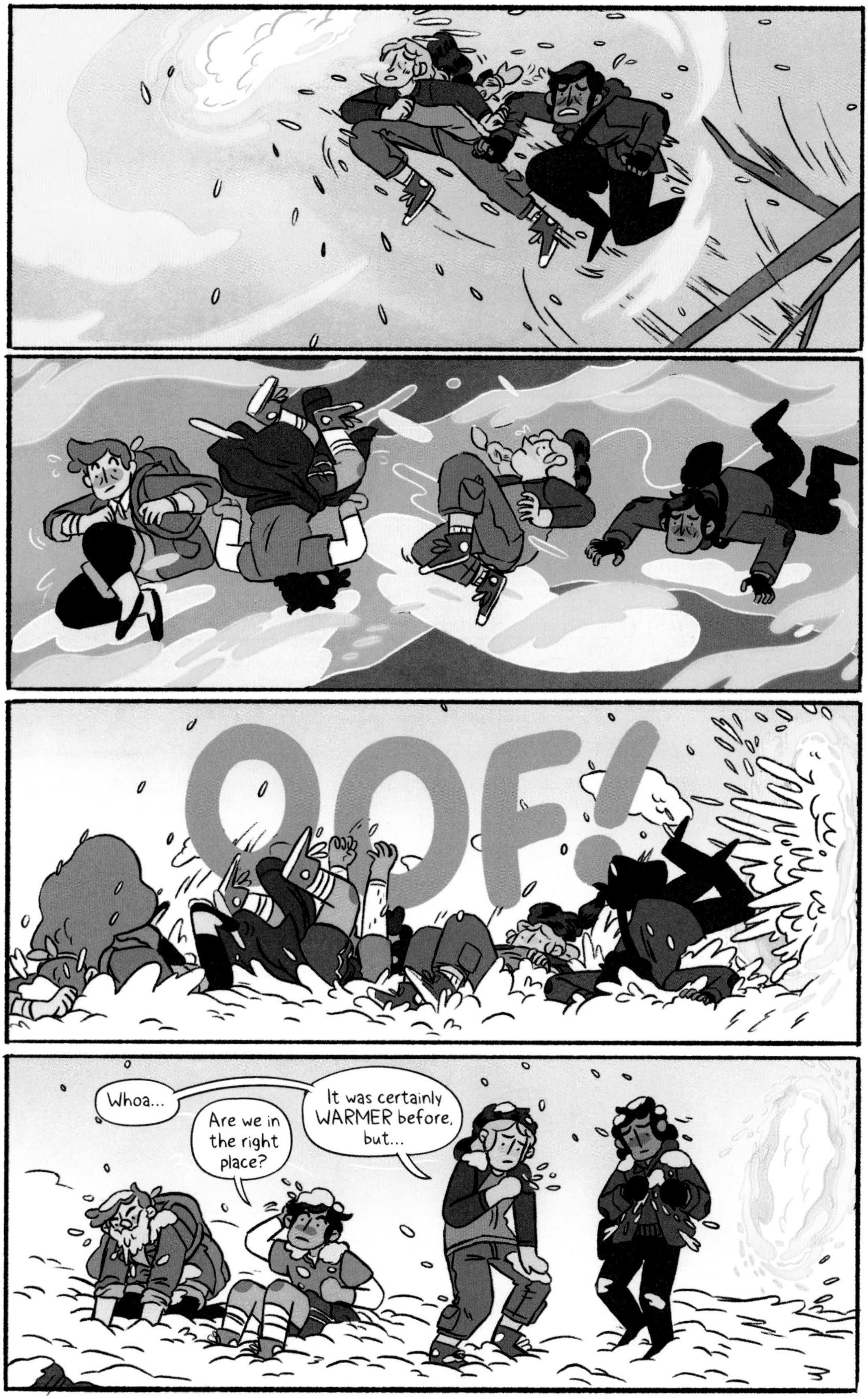
OOF!
Whoa...
Are we in the right place?
It was certainly WARMER before, but...

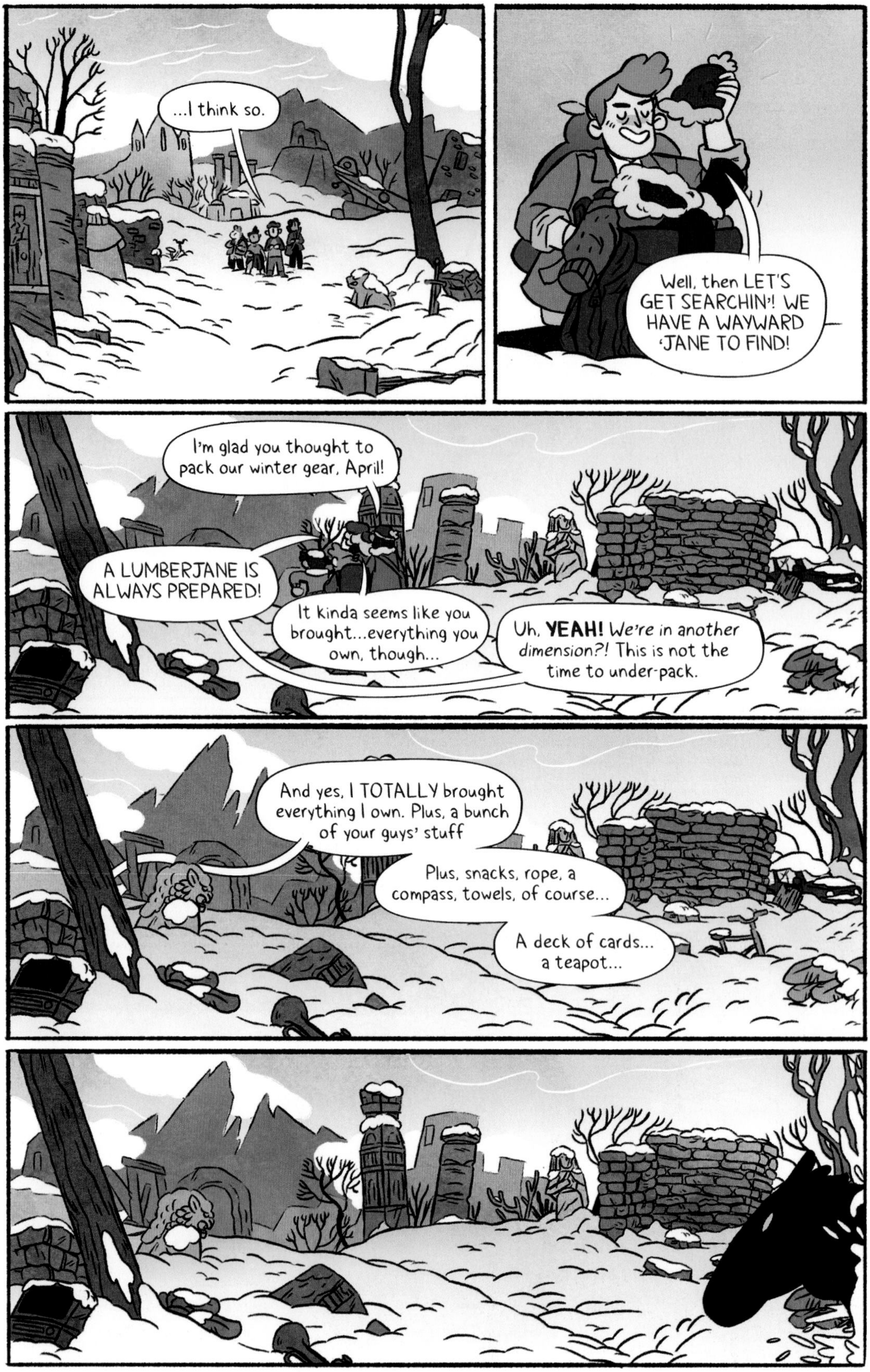
...I think so.
Well, then LET'S GET SEARCHIN'! WE HAVE A WAYWARD 'JANE TO FIND!
I'm glad you thought to pack our winter gear, April!
A LUMBERJANE IS ALWAYS PREPARED!
It kinda seems like you brought...everything you own, though...
Uh, **YEAH!** *We're in another dimension?!* This is not the time to under-pack.
And yes, I TOTALLY brought everything I own. Plus, a bunch of your guys' stuff
Plus, snacks, rope, a compass, towels, of course...
A deck of cards... a teapot...

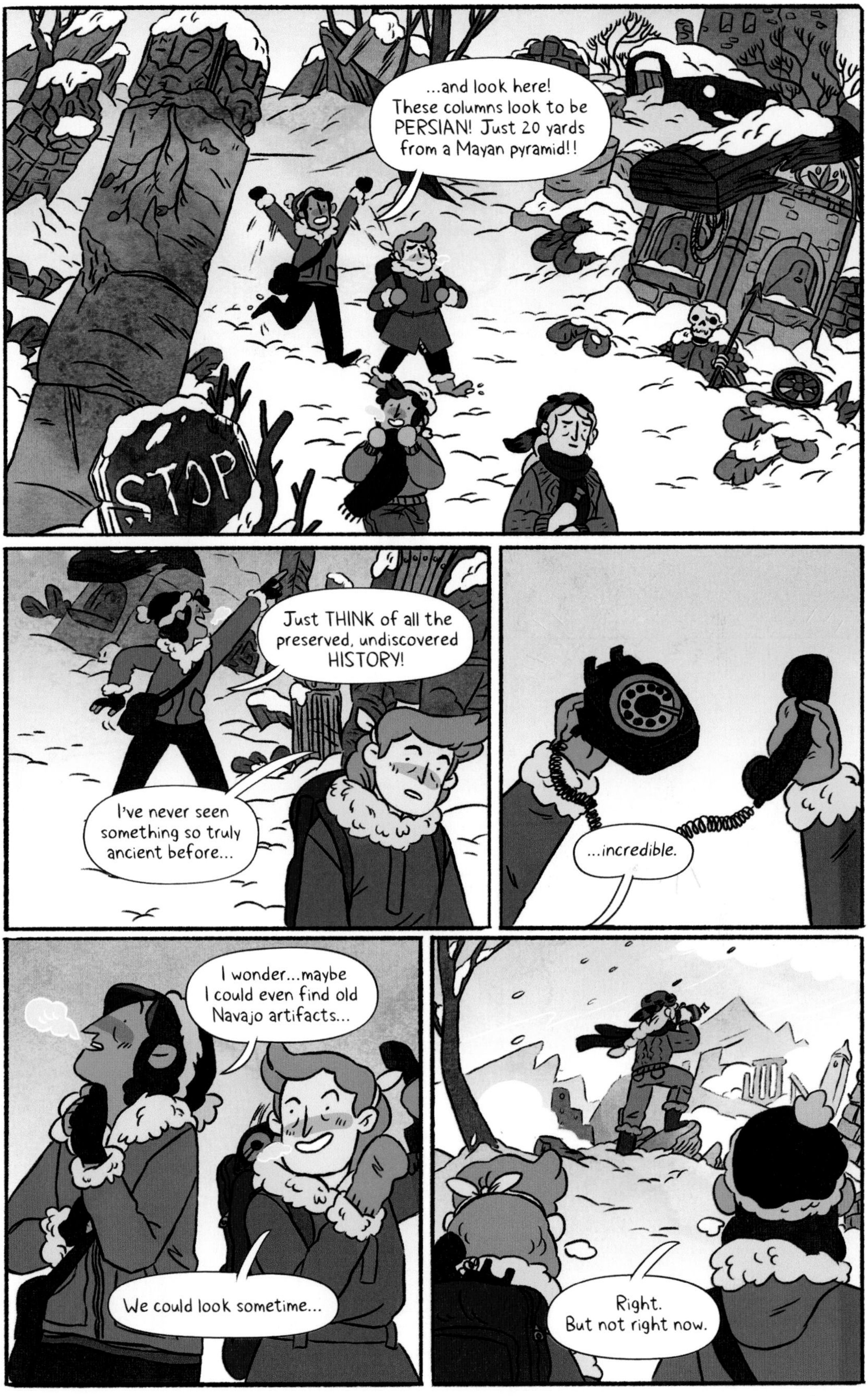

...and look here! These columns look to be PERSIAN! Just 20 yards from a Mayan pyramid!!
STOP
Just THINK of all the preserved, undiscovered HISTORY!
I've never seen something so truly ancient before...
...incredible.
I wonder...maybe I could even find old Navajo artifacts...
We could look sometime...
Right. But not right now.

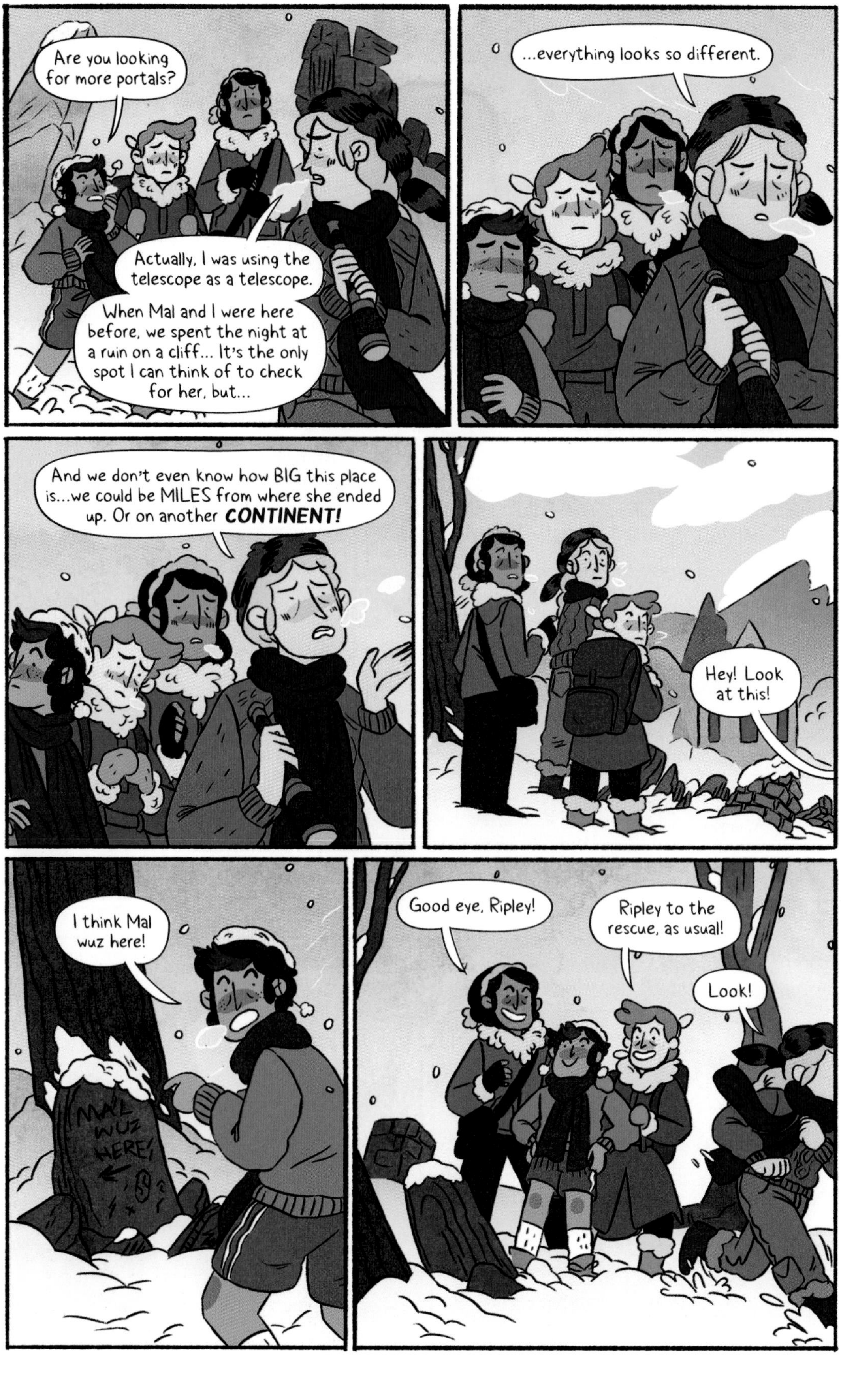

Are you looking for more portals?
Actually, I was using the telescope as a telescope.
When Mal and I were here before, we spent the night at a ruin on a cliff... It's the only spot I can think of to check for her, but...
...everything looks so different.
And we don't even know how BIG this place is...we could be MILES from where she ended up. Or on another **CONTINENT!**
Hey! Look at this!
I think Mal wuz here!
MAL WUZ HERE!
Good eye, Ripley!
Ripley to the rescue, as usual!
Look!

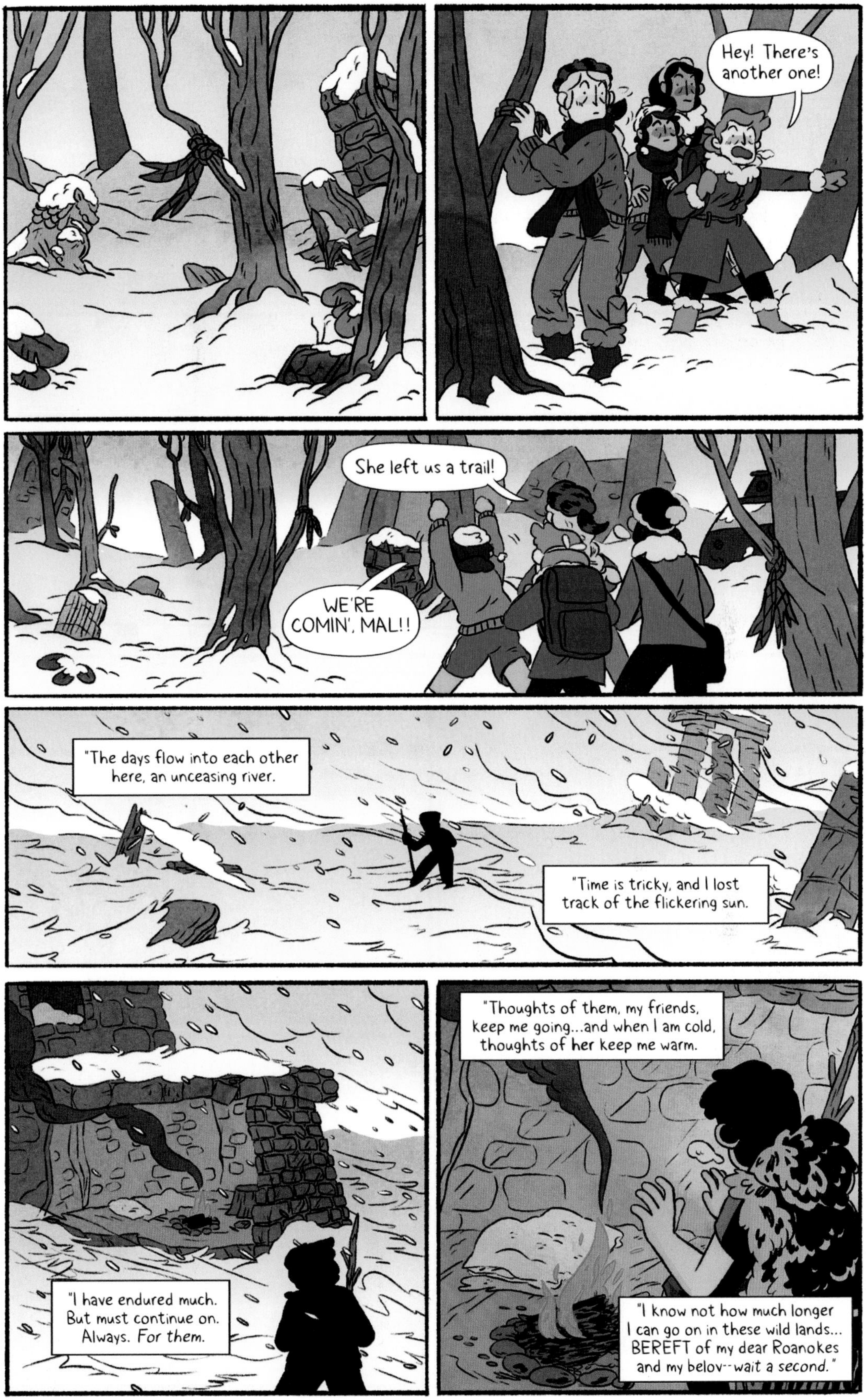
Hey! There's another one!
She left us a trail!
WE'RE COMIN', MAL!!
"The days flow into each other here, an unceasing river.
"Time is tricky, and I lost track of the flickering sun.
"I have endured much. But must continue on. Always. For them.
"Thoughts of them, my friends, keep me going...and when I am cold, thoughts of her keep me warm.
"I know not how much longer I can go on in these wild lands... BEREFT of my dear Roanokes and my belov--wait a second."

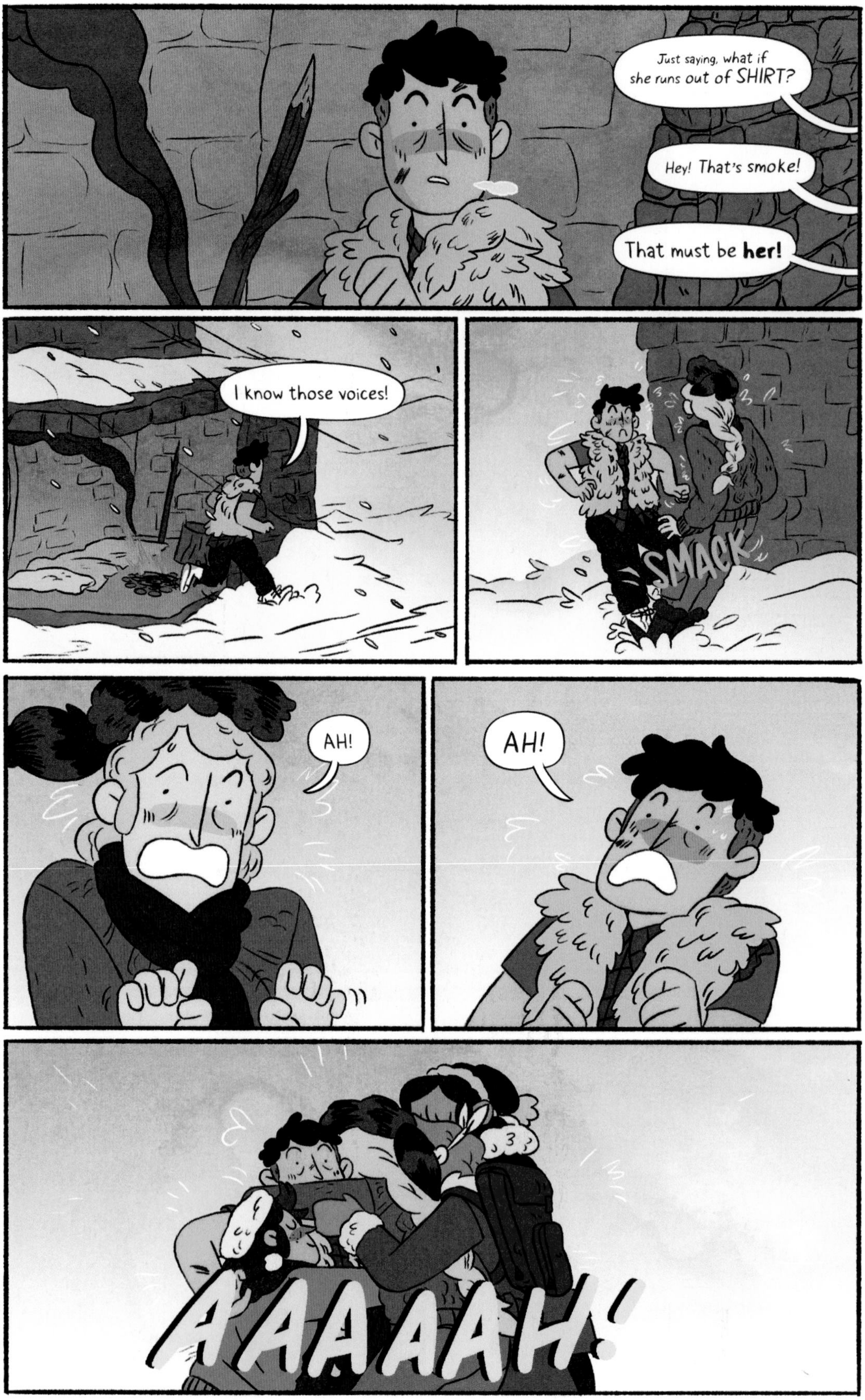
Just saying, what if she runs out of SHIRT?
Hey! That's smoke!
That must be **her!**
I know those voices!
SMACK
AH!
AH!
AAAAAH!

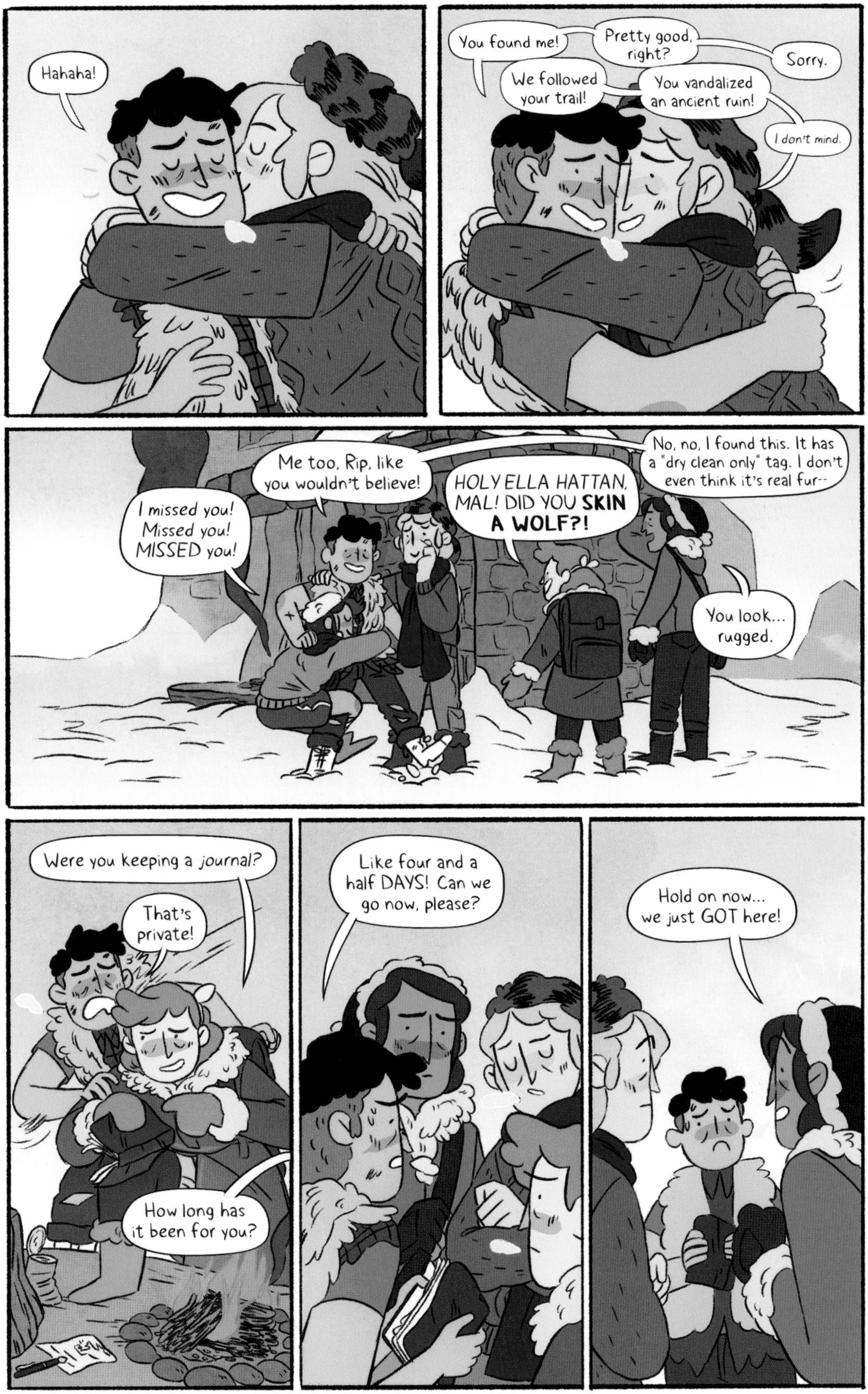

Hahaha!
You found me!
Pretty good, right?
Sorry.
We followed your trail!
You vandalized an ancient ruin!
I don't mind.
I missed you! Missed you! MISSED you!
Me too, Rip, like you wouldn't believe!
HOLY ELLA HATTAN, MAL! DID YOU SKIN A WOLF?!
No, no, I found this. It has a "dry clean only" tag. I don't even think it's real fur--
You look... rugged.
Were you keeping a journal?
That's private!
How long has it been for you?
Like four and a half DAYS! Can we go now, please?
Hold on now... we just GOT here!

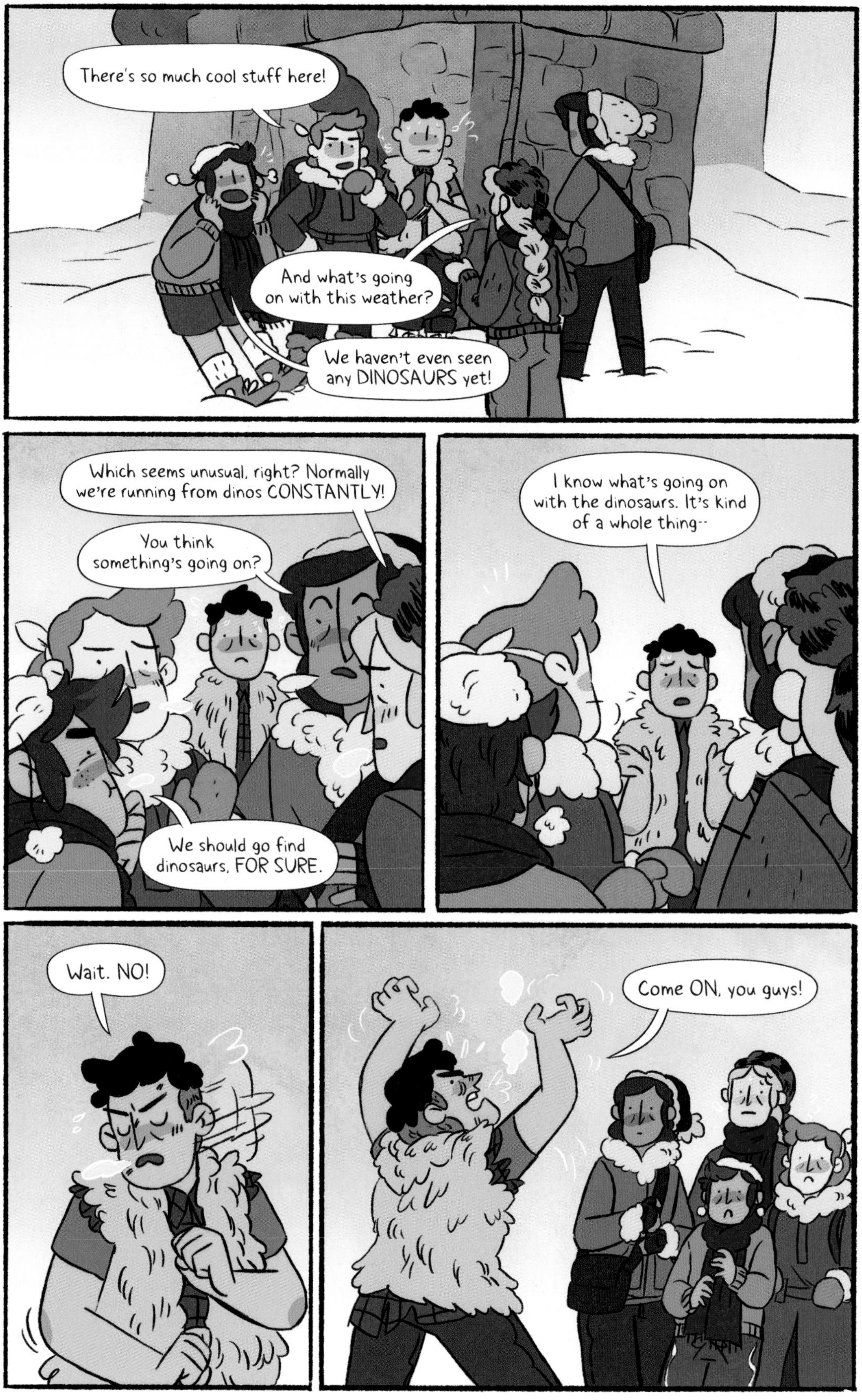
There's so much cool stuff here!
And what's going on with this weather?
We haven't even seen any DINOSAURS yet!
Which seems unusual, right? Normally we're running from dinos CONSTANTLY!
You think something's going on?
We should go find dinosaurs, FOR SURE.
I know what's going on with the dinosaurs. It's kind of a whole thing--
Wait. NO!
Come ON, you guys!

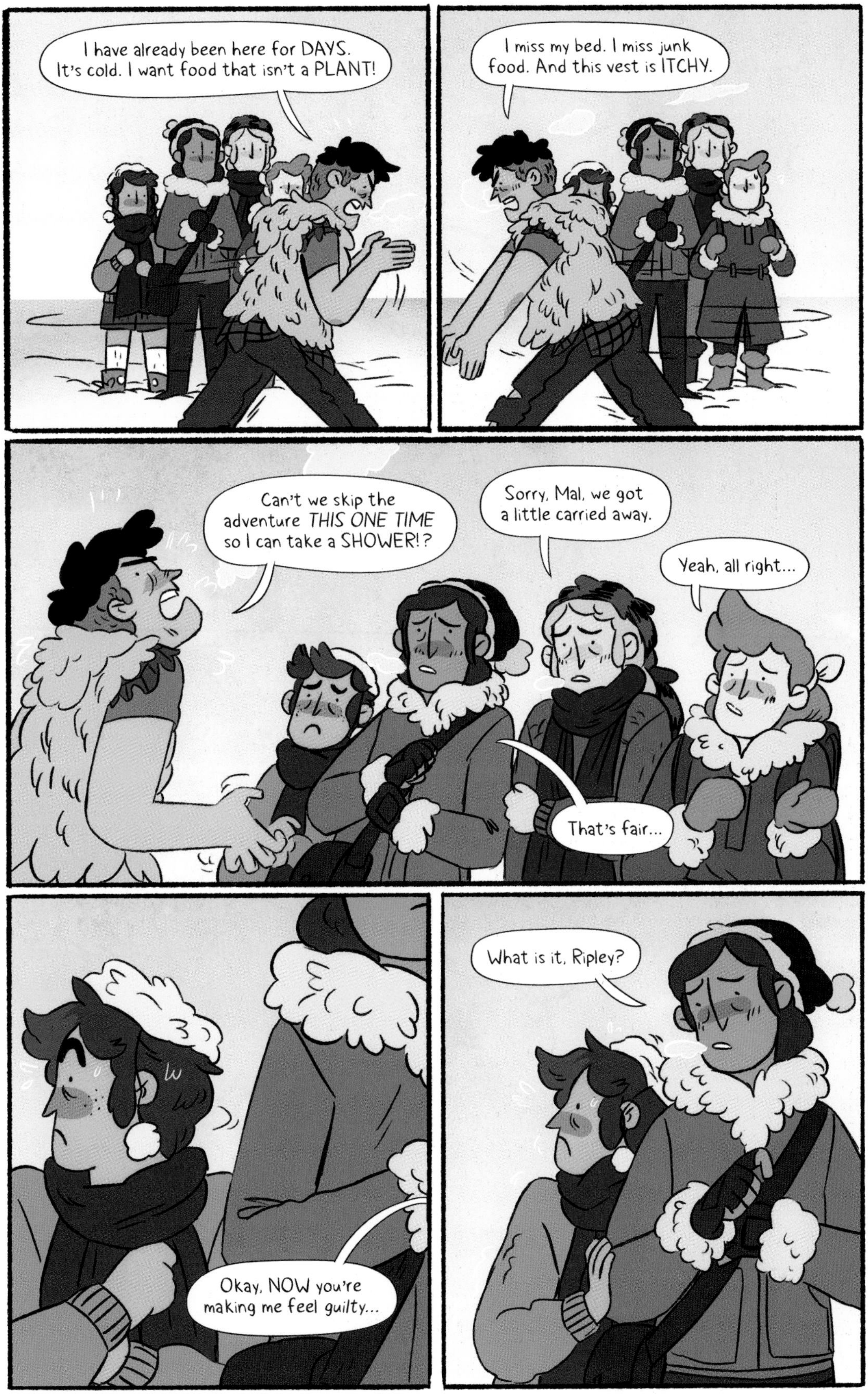

I have already been here for DAYS. It's cold. I want food that isn't a PLANT!
I miss my bed. I miss junk food. And this vest is ITCHY.
Can't we skip the adventure THIS ONE TIME so I can take a SHOWER!?
Sorry, Mal, we got a little carried away.
Yeah, all right...
That's fair...
Okay, NOW you're making me feel guilty...
What is it, Ripley?

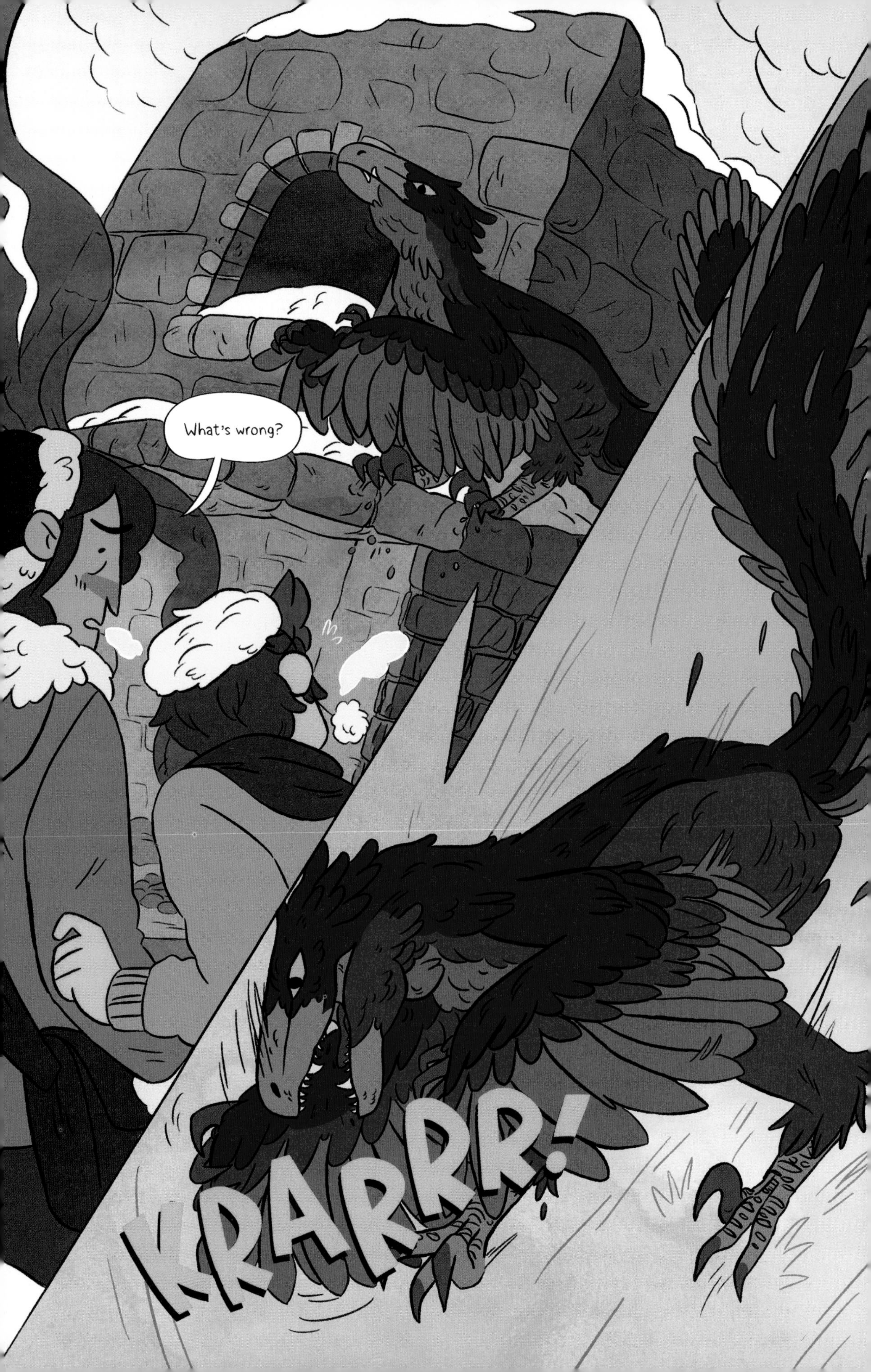
What's wrong?
KRARRR!

IT'S GOTTA BE HERE SOMEWHERE...

IT'S ALWAYS IN THE LAST PLACE YOU LOOK...

WHY CAN'T WE LOOK THERE FIRST?!

will cor...

The ur...
It helps... ...hould be worn at camp
appearan... ...vents when Lumberjanes
dress fc... ...may also be worn at other
Further... ...ions. It should be worn as a
Lumber... ...the uniform dress with
to have... ...rect shoes, and stocking or
part in...
Thiskw... ...out grows her uniform or
Hardc... ...her Lumberjane.
have... ...nsignia she has
thems... ...her
...her

The...
yellow,...
emb...
the w...
choose...
slacks,...
made or...
out-of-do...
green bere...
the colla...
Shoes ma...
heels, roun... ...ings or
socks shou... ...with the shoes or wi...
the uniform. Ne... ...s, bracelets, or other jewelry do...
belong with a Lumberjane uniform.

...feel explorer or...
...doors in just outside your door, whether...
...d or a country dweller. Get acquainted...

HOW TO WEAR THE UNIFORM

...cover how to use all the ways of getting...

To look well in a uniform demands first of...
uniform be kept in good condition—clean...
pressed. See that the skirt is the right length for your own
height and build, that the belt is adjusted to your waist,
that your shoes and stockings are in keeping with the
uniform, that you watch your posture and carry yourself
with dignity and grace. If the beret is removed indoors,
be sure that your hair is neat and kept in place with an
inconspicuous clip or ribbon. When you wear a
Lumberjane uniform you are identified as a member of
this organization and you should be doubly careful to
conduct yourself in a way that will show everyone that
courtesy and thoughtfulness are part of being a
Lumberjane. People are likely to judge a whole nation by
the selfishness of a few individuals, to criticize a whole
family because of the misconduct of one member, and to
feel unkindly toward an organization because of the

The unifor...
helps to cre...
in a group...
active life th...
another bond...
future, and pre...
in order to b...
Lumberjane pr...
Penniquiqul Thi... ...ore Lady
Types, but m... ...es will wish to have one. They
can either bu... ...he uniform, or make it themselves from
materials available at the trading post.

LUMBERJANES FIELD MANUAL

CHAPTER
SIXTY-THREE

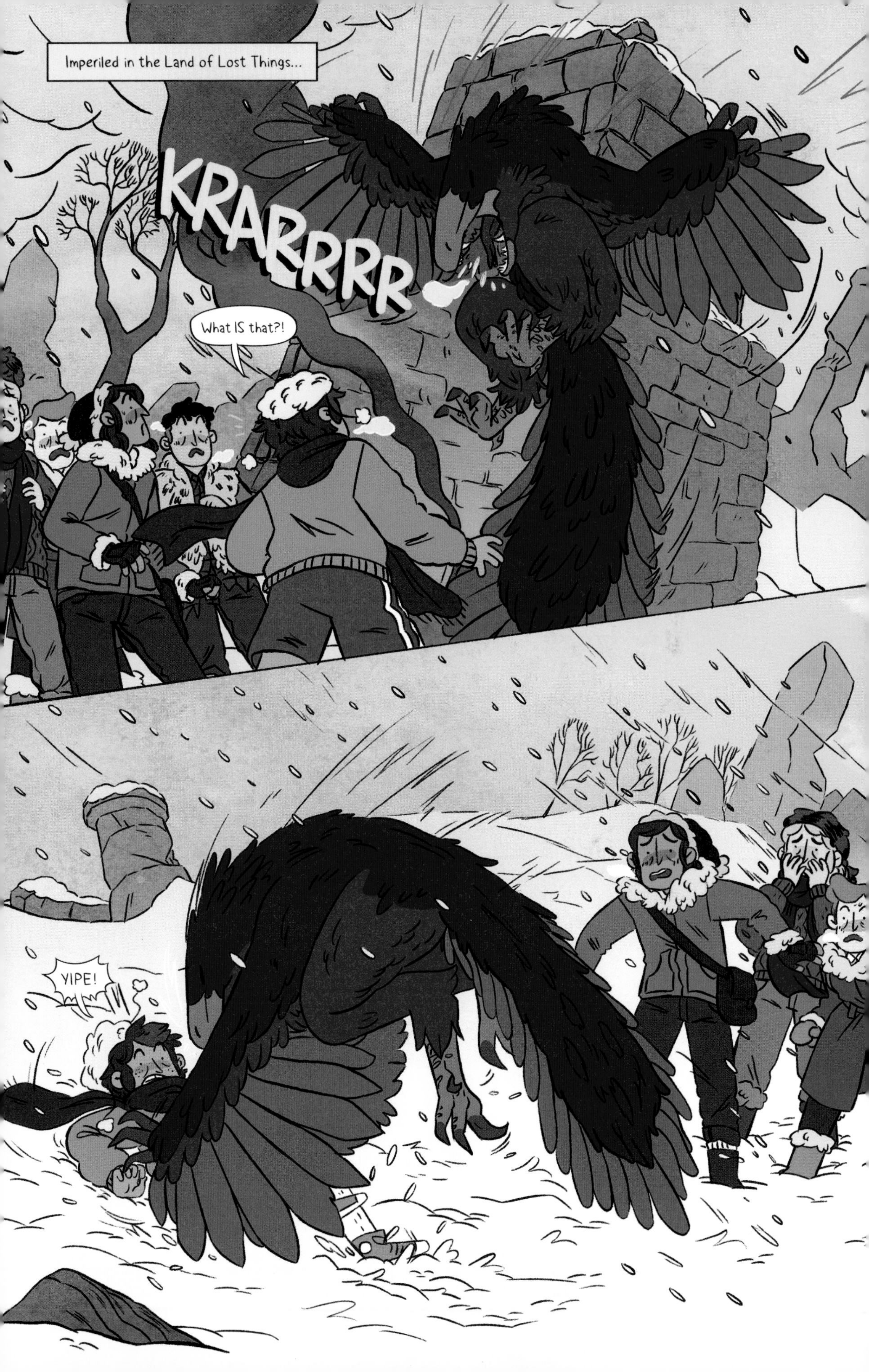
Imperiled in the Land of Lost Things...
KRARRRRR
What IS that?!
YIPE!

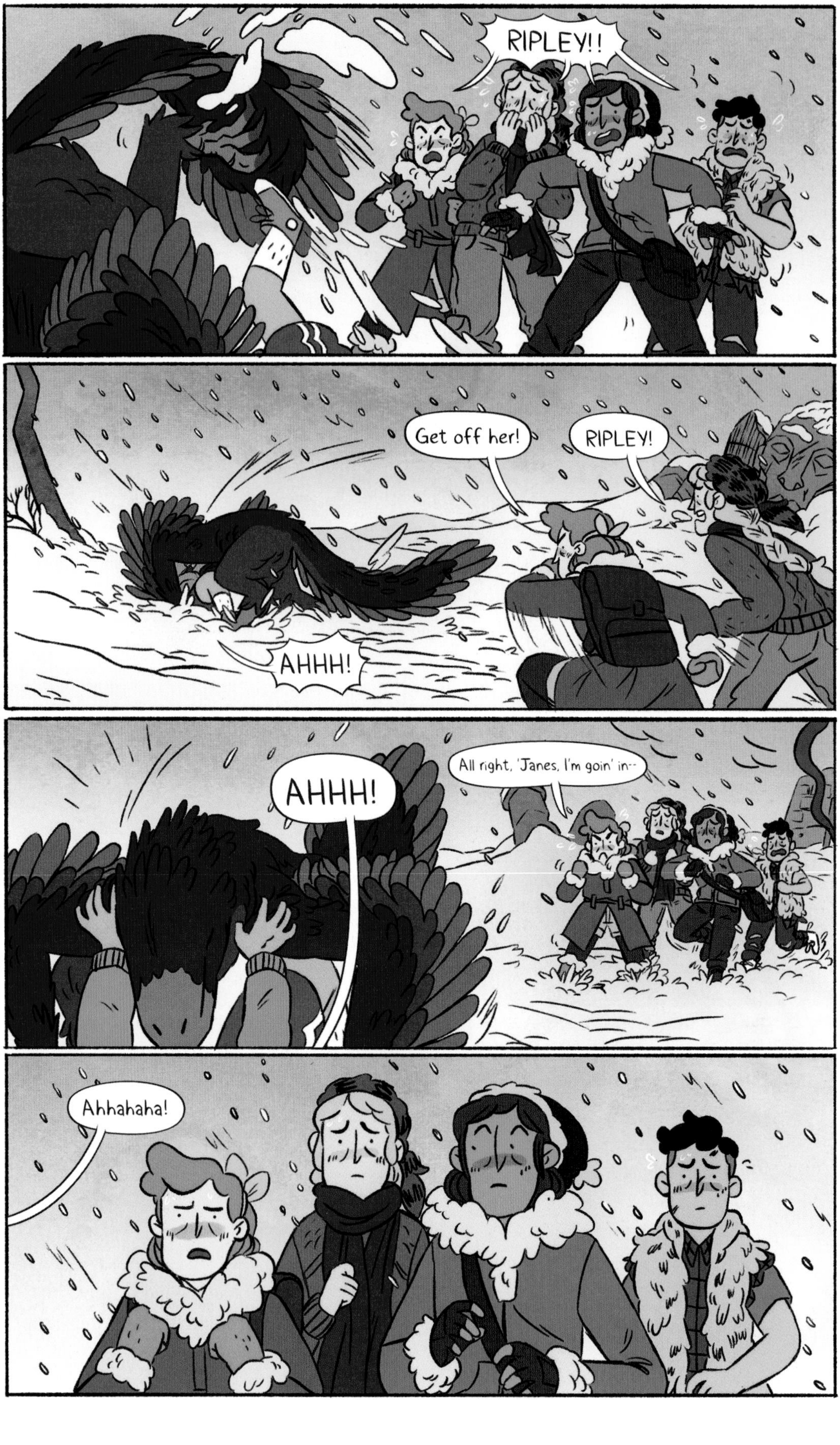

RIPLEY!!
Get off her!
RIPLEY!
AHHH!
AHHH!
All right, 'Janes, I'm goin' in--
Ahhahaha!

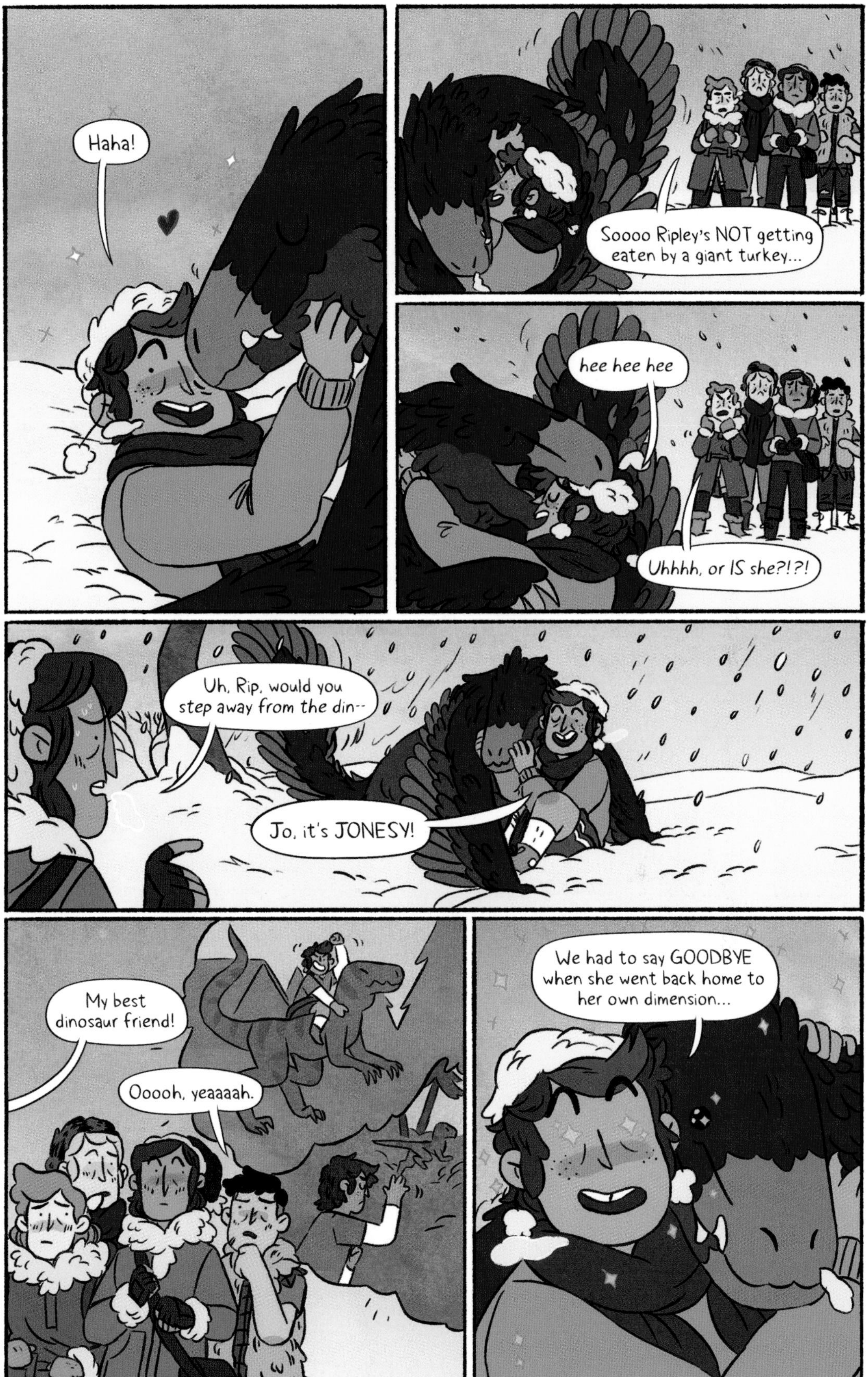
Haha!
Soooo Ripley's NOT getting eaten by a giant turkey...
hee hee hee
Uhhhh, or IS she?!?!
Uh, Rip, would you step away from the din--
Jo, it's JONESY!
My best dinosaur friend!
Ooooh, yeaaaah.
We had to say GOODBYE when she went back home to her own dimension...

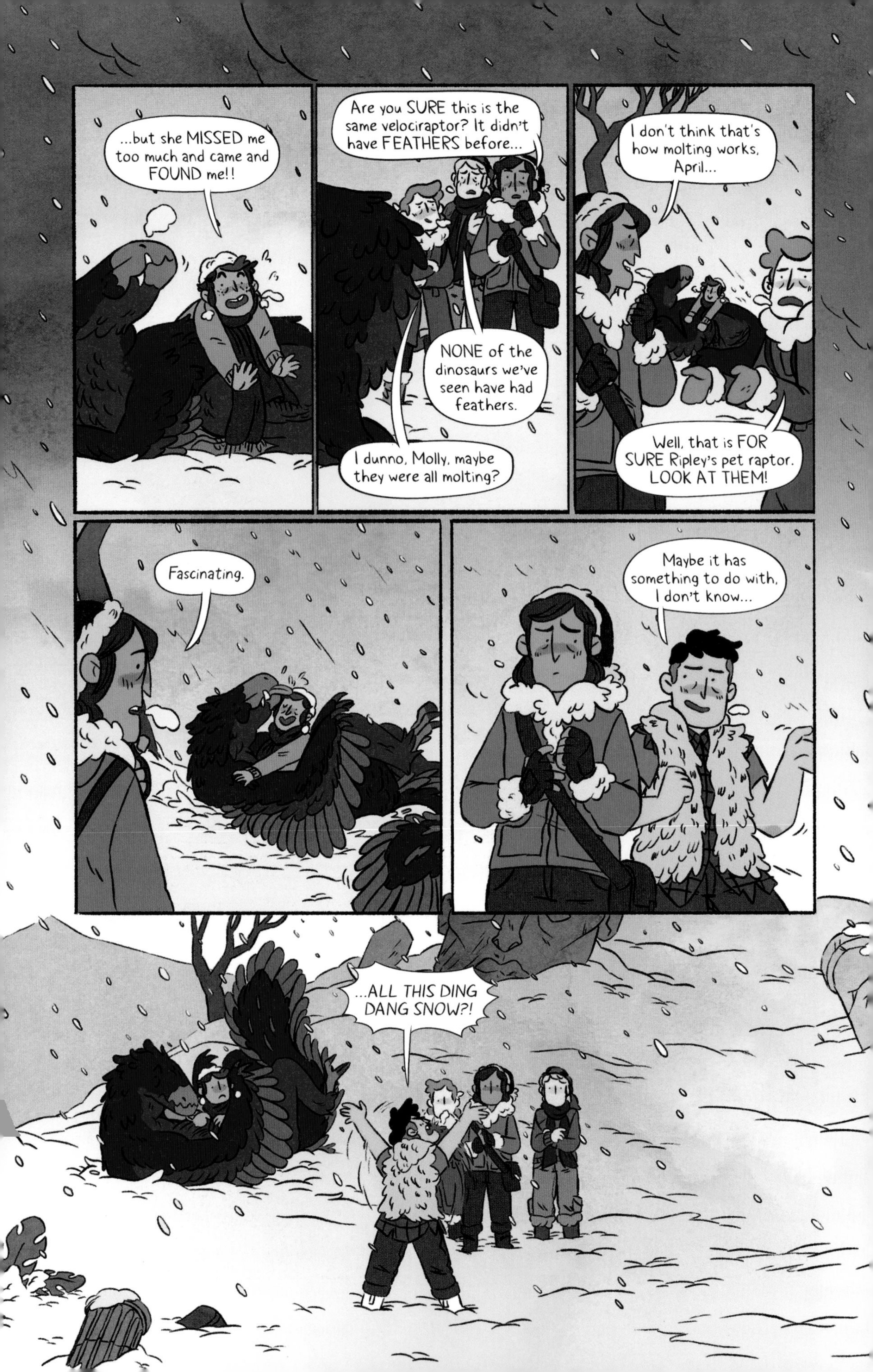
...but she MISSED me too much and came and FOUND me!!
Are you SURE this is the same velociraptor? It didn't have FEATHERS before...
NONE of the dinosaurs we've seen have had feathers.
I dunno, Molly, maybe they were all molting?
I don't think that's how molting works, April...
Well, that is FOR SURE Ripley's pet raptor. LOOK AT THEM!
Fascinating.
Maybe it has something to do with, I don't know...
...ALL THIS DING DANG SNOW?!

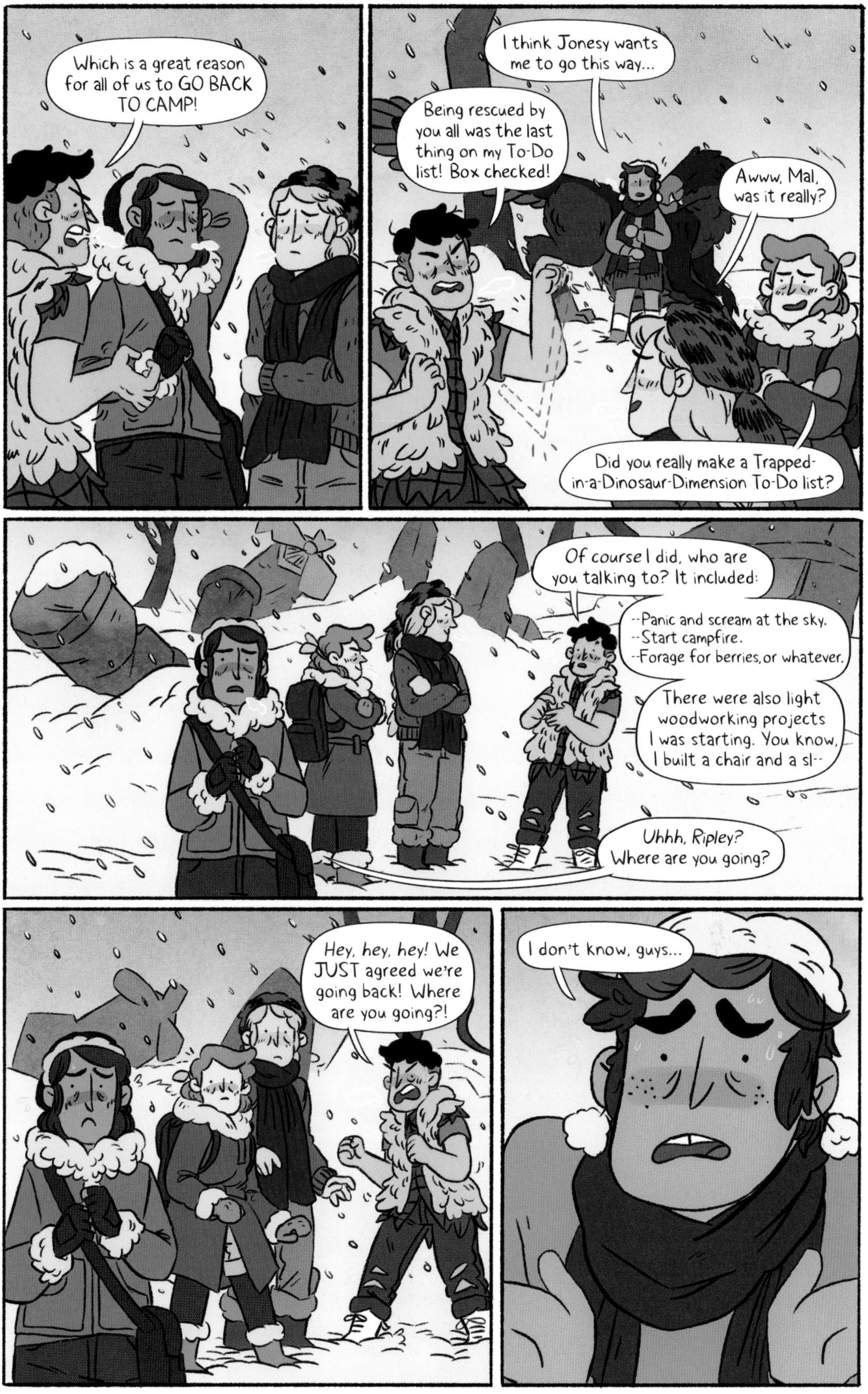
Which is a great reason for all of us to GO BACK TO CAMP!
I think Jonesy wants me to go this way...
Being rescued by you all was the last thing on my To-Do list! Box checked!
Awww, Mal, was it really?
Did you really make a Trapped-in-a-Dinosaur-Dimension To-Do list?
Of course I did, who are you talking to? It included:
--Panic and scream at the sky.
--Start campfire.
--Forage for berries, or whatever.
There were also light woodworking projects I was starting. You know, I built a chair and a sl--
Uhhh, Ripley? Where are you going?
Hey, hey, hey! We JUST agreed we're going back! Where are you going?!
I don't know, guys...

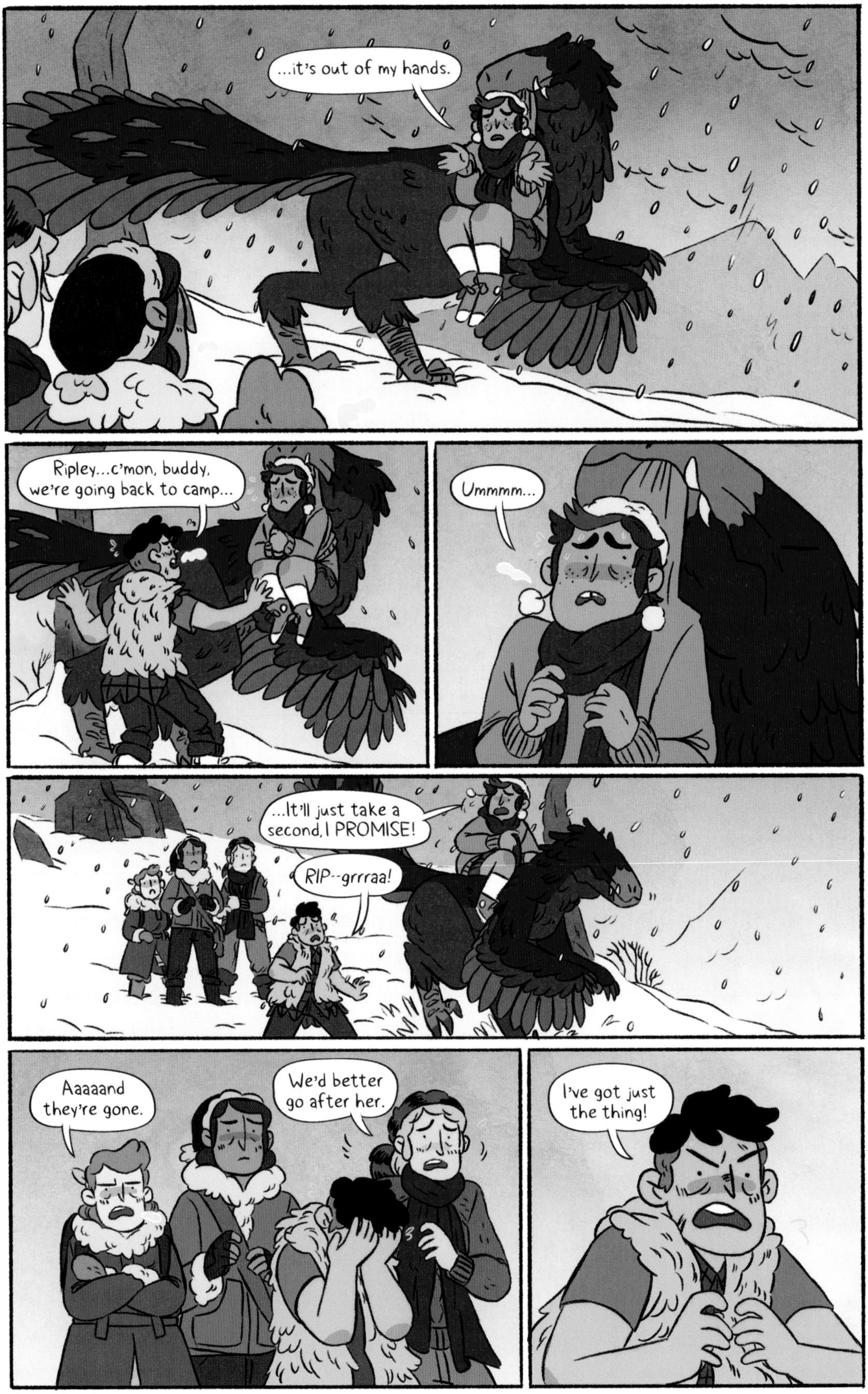
...it's out of my hands.
Ripley...c'mon, buddy, we're going back to camp...
Ummmm...
...It'll just take a second, I PROMISE!
RIP--grrraa!
Aaaaand they're gone.
We'd better go after her.
I've got just the thing!

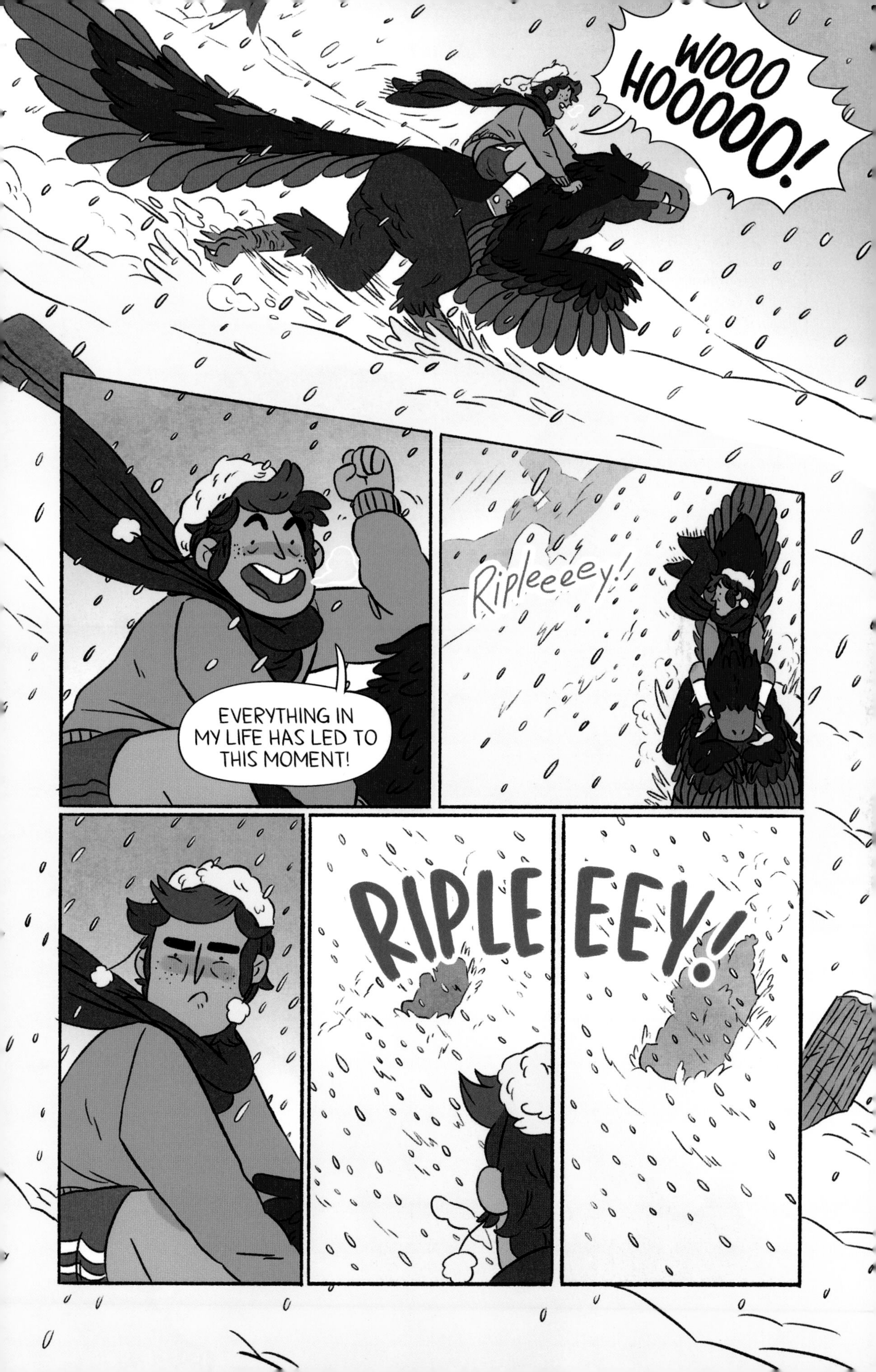
WOOO HOOOOOO!
EVERYTHING IN MY LIFE HAS LED TO THIS MOMENT!
Ripleeeey!
RIPLEEEY!

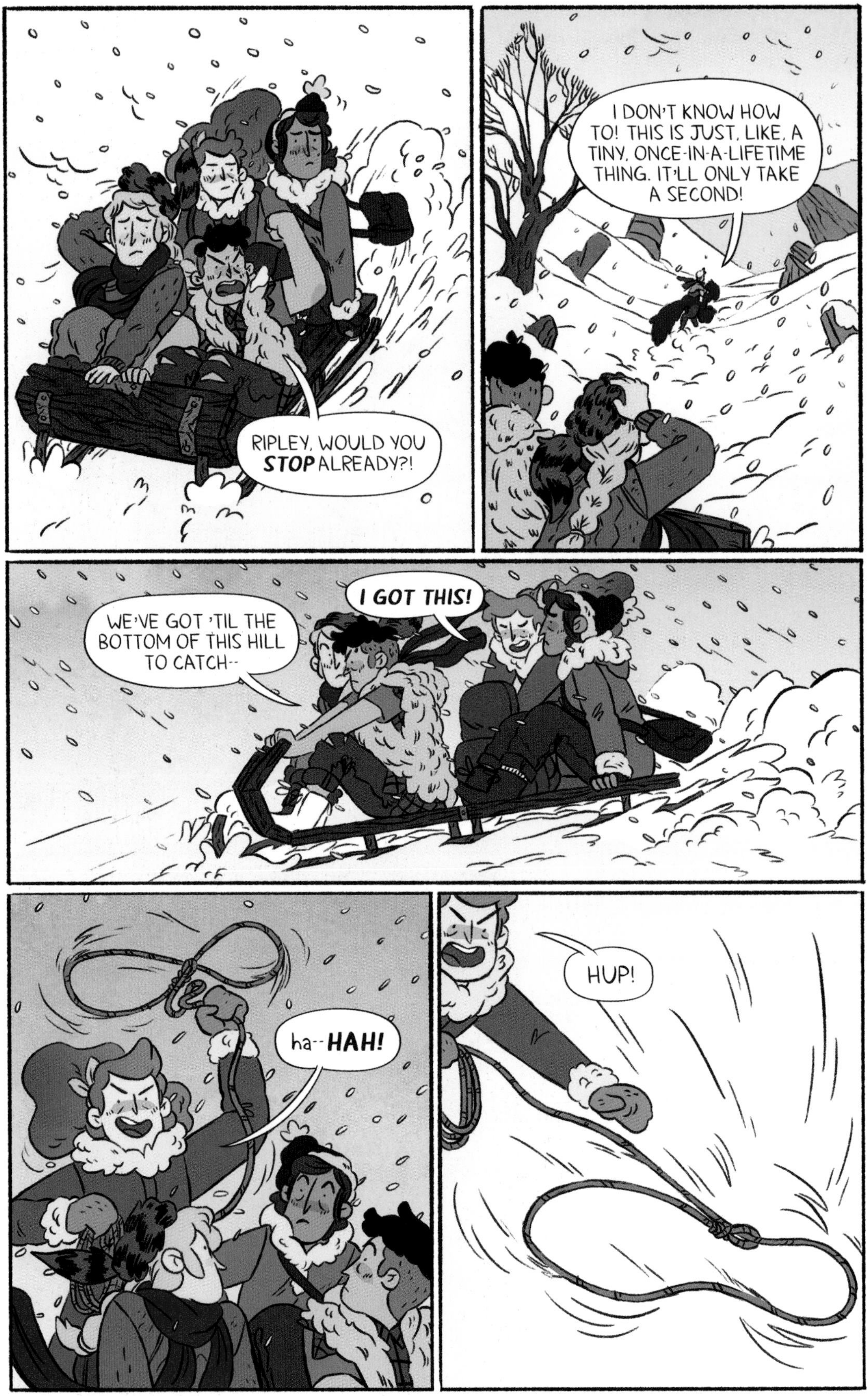
RIPLEY, WOULD YOU STOP ALREADY?!
I DON'T KNOW HOW TO! THIS IS JUST, LIKE, A TINY, ONCE-IN-A-LIFETIME THING. IT'LL ONLY TAKE A SECOND!
WE'VE GOT 'TIL THE BOTTOM OF THIS HILL TO CATCH--
I GOT THIS!
ha--HAH!
HUP!

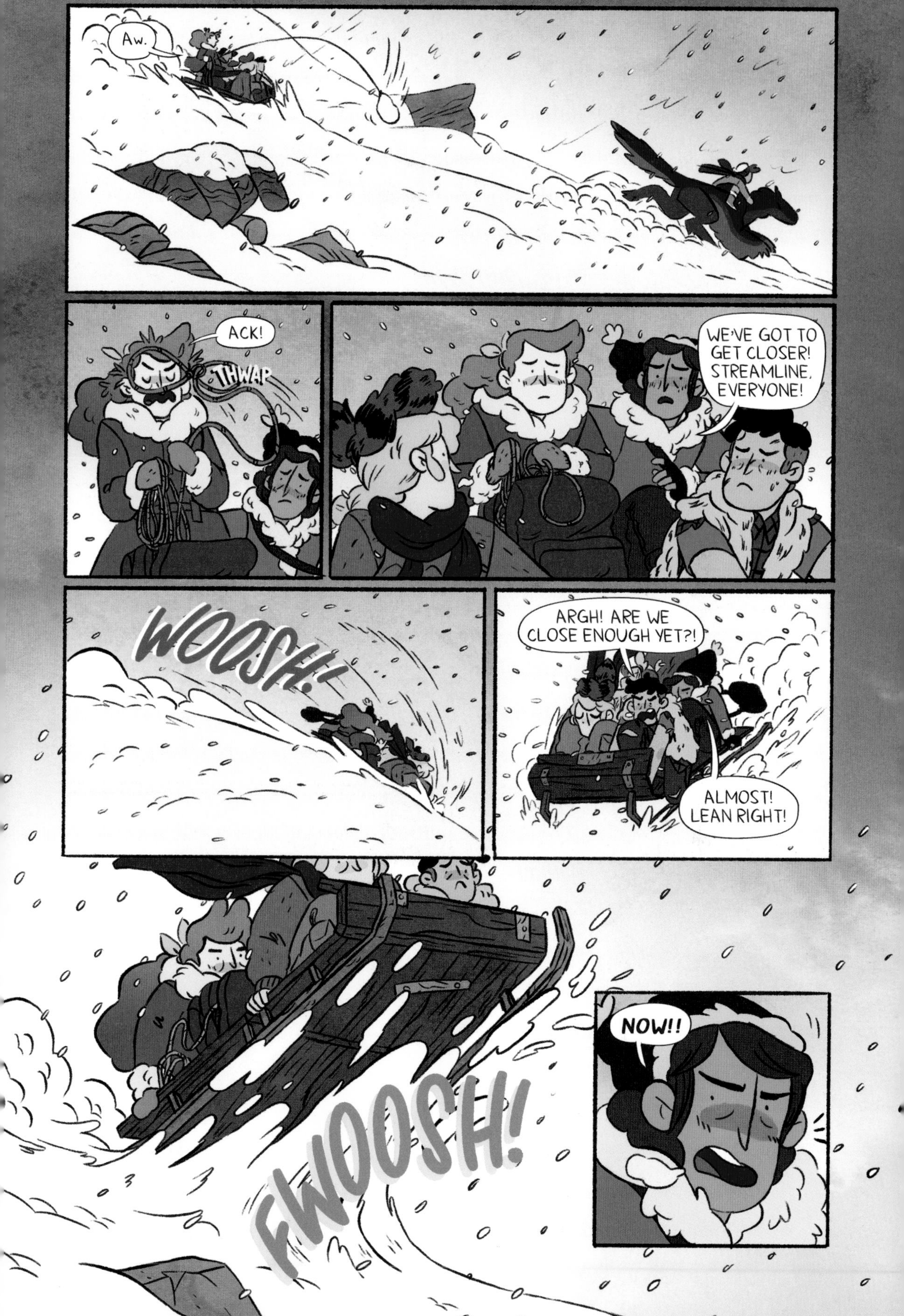

Aw.
ACK!
THWAP
WE'VE GOT TO GET CLOSER! STREAMLINE, EVERYONE!
WOOSH!
ARGH! ARE WE CLOSE ENOUGH YET?!
ALMOST! LEAN RIGHT!
FWOOSH!
NOW!!

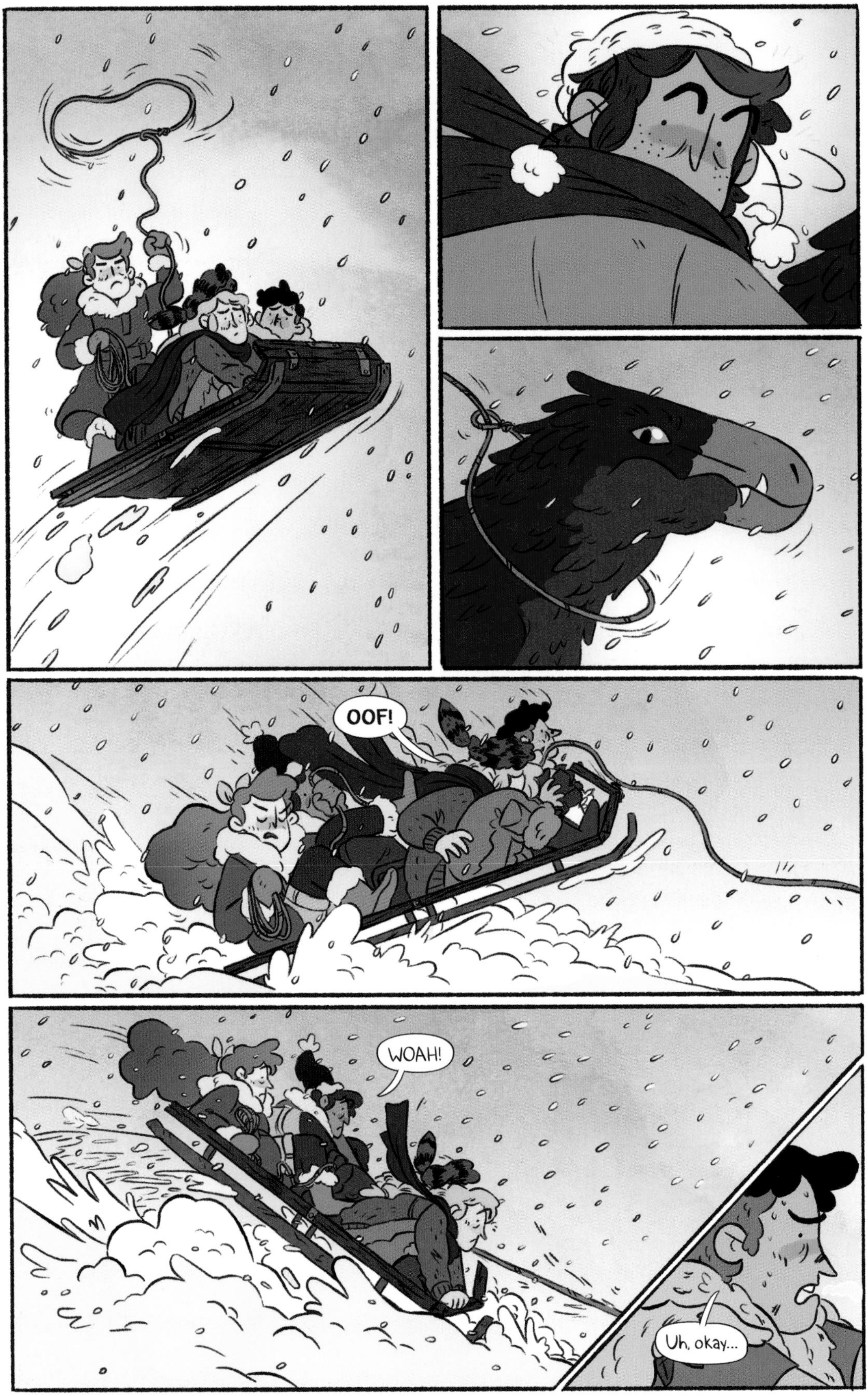
OOF!
WOAH!
Uh, okay...

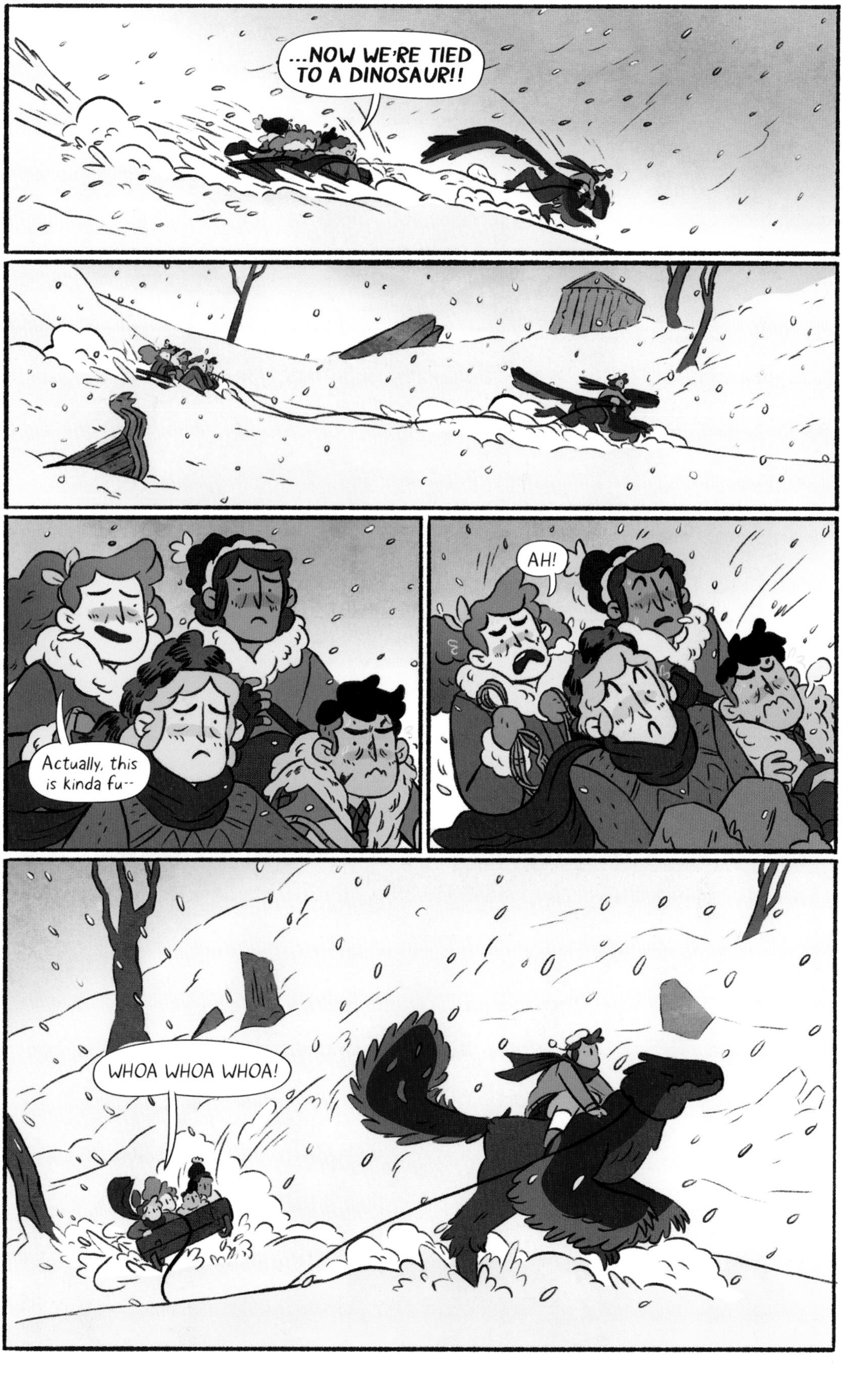
...NOW WE'RE TIED TO A DINOSAUR!!
Actually, this is kinda fu--
AH!
WHOA WHOA WHOA!

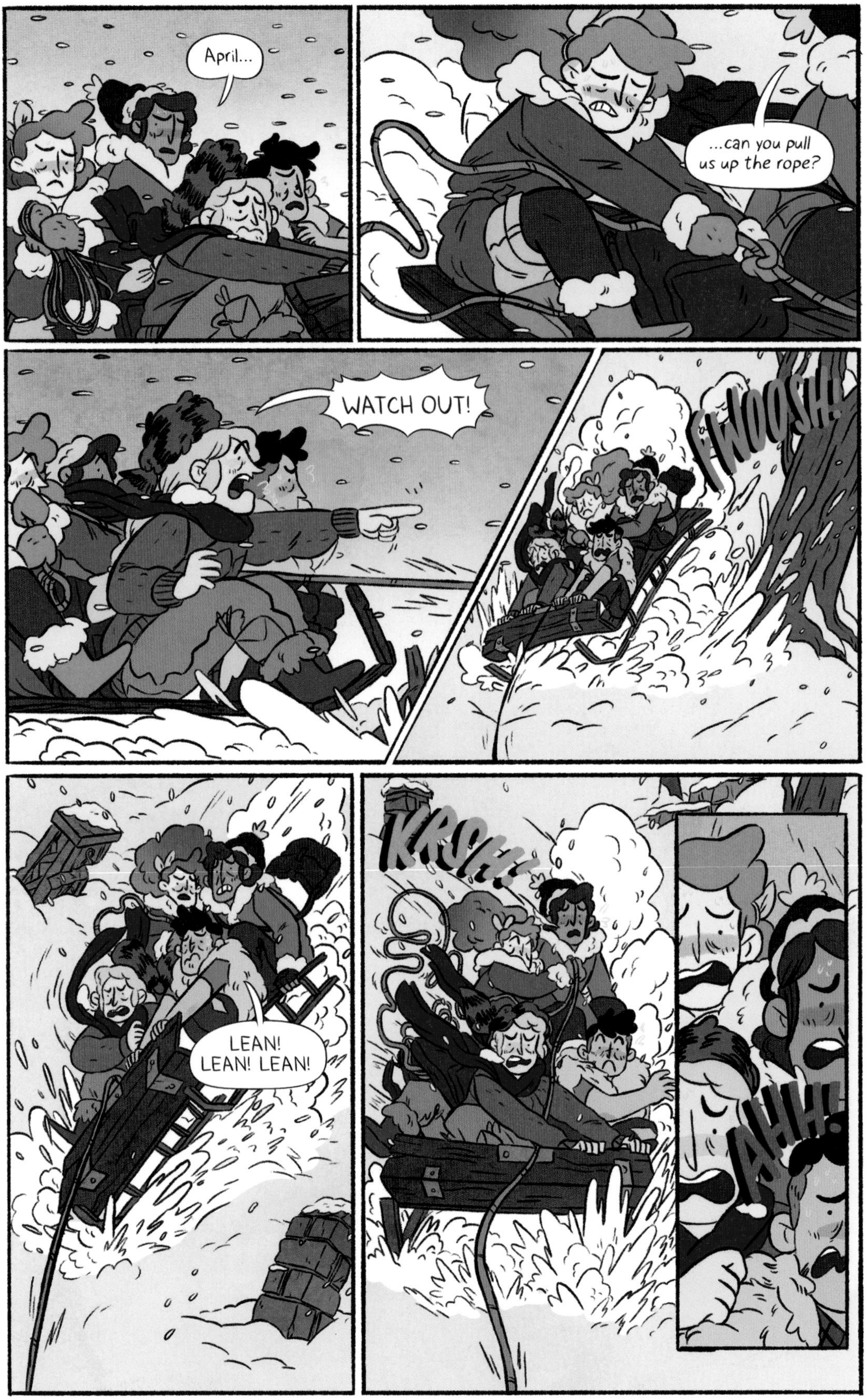
April...
...can you pull us up the rope?
WATCH OUT!
FWOOSH!
LEAN! LEAN! LEAN!
KRSH!
AHH!

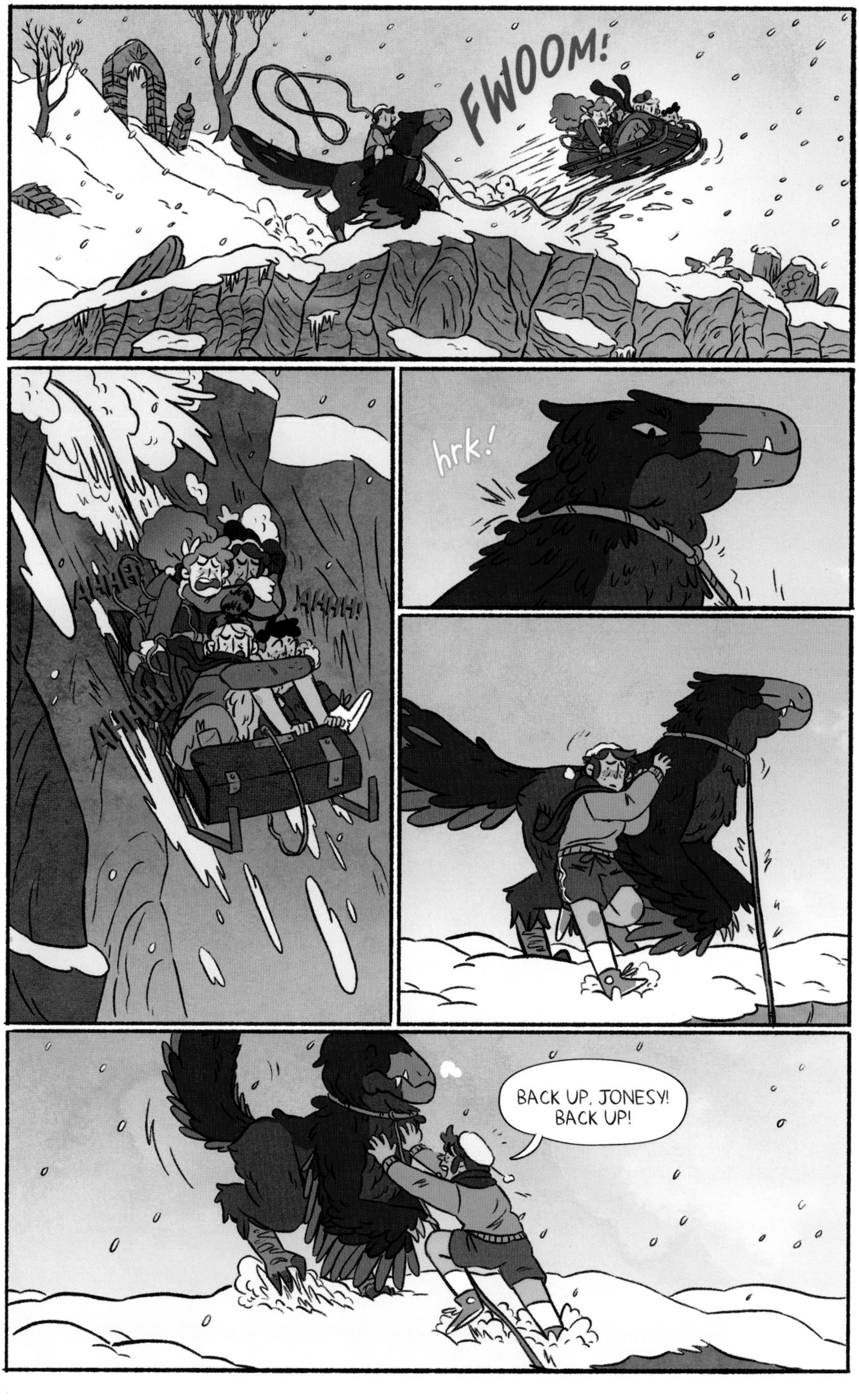
FWOOM!
AHHH!
AHHH!
AHHH!
hrk!
BACK UP, JONESY! BACK UP!

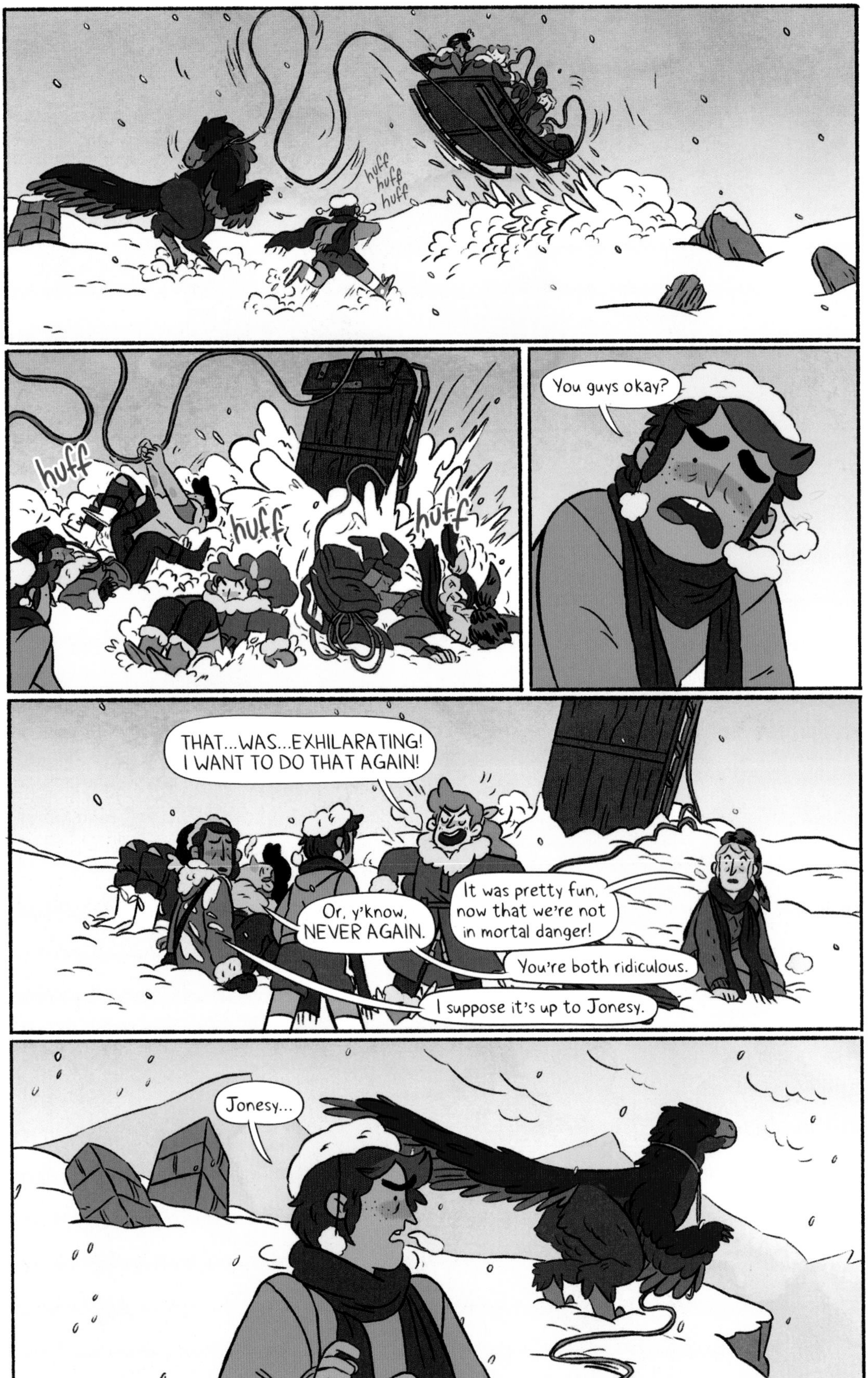
huff
huff
huff
huff
huff
huff
You guys okay?
THAT...WAS...EXHILARATING!
I WANT TO DO THAT AGAIN!
Or, y'know,
NEVER AGAIN.
It was pretty fun,
now that we're not
in mortal danger!
You're both ridiculous.
I suppose it's up to Jonesy.
Jonesy...

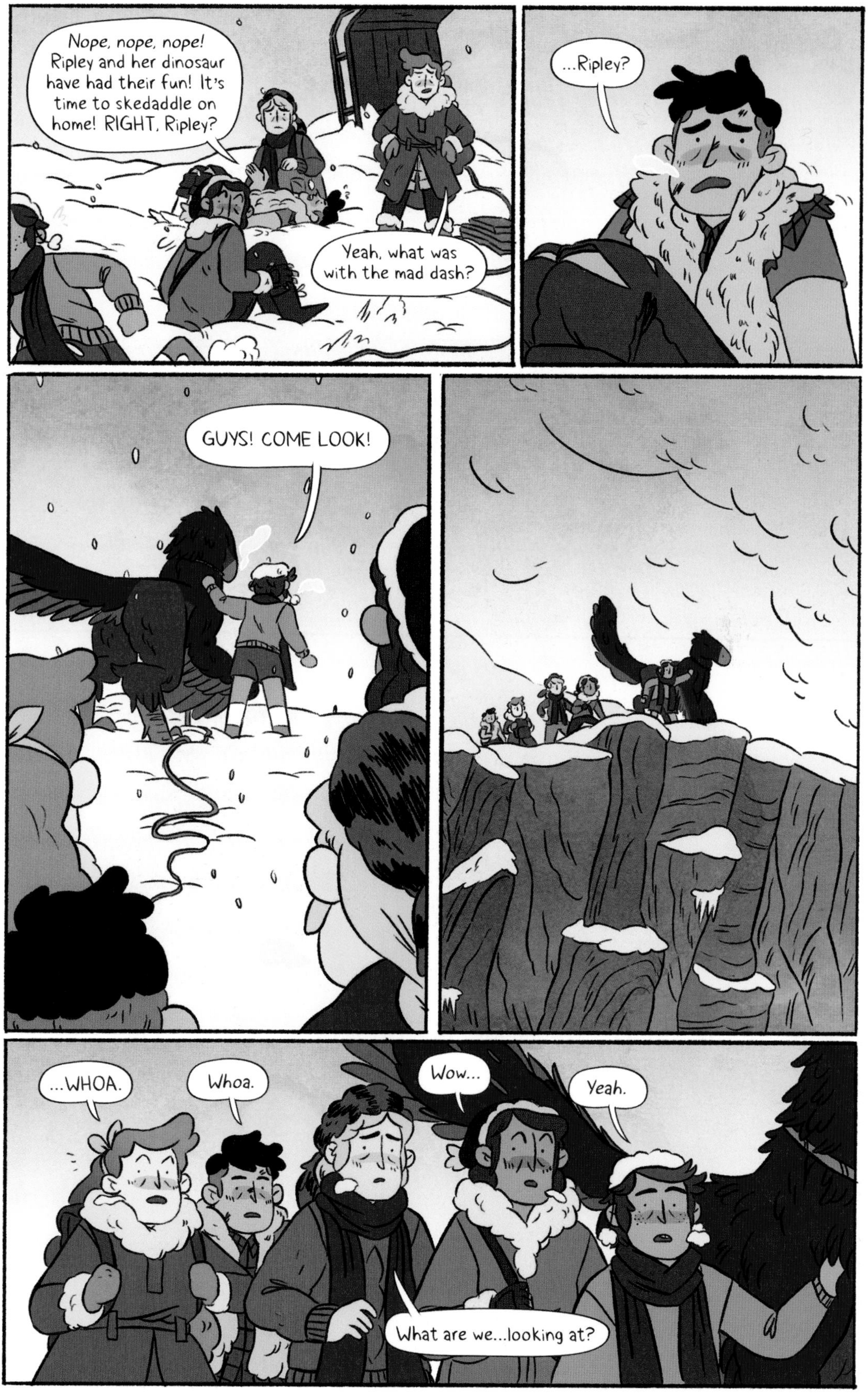
Nope, nope, nope! Ripley and her dinosaur have had their fun! It's time to skedaddle on home! RIGHT, Ripley?
Yeah, what was with the mad dash?
...Ripley?
GUYS! COME LOOK!
...WHOA.
Whoa.
Wow...
Yeah.
What are we...looking at?

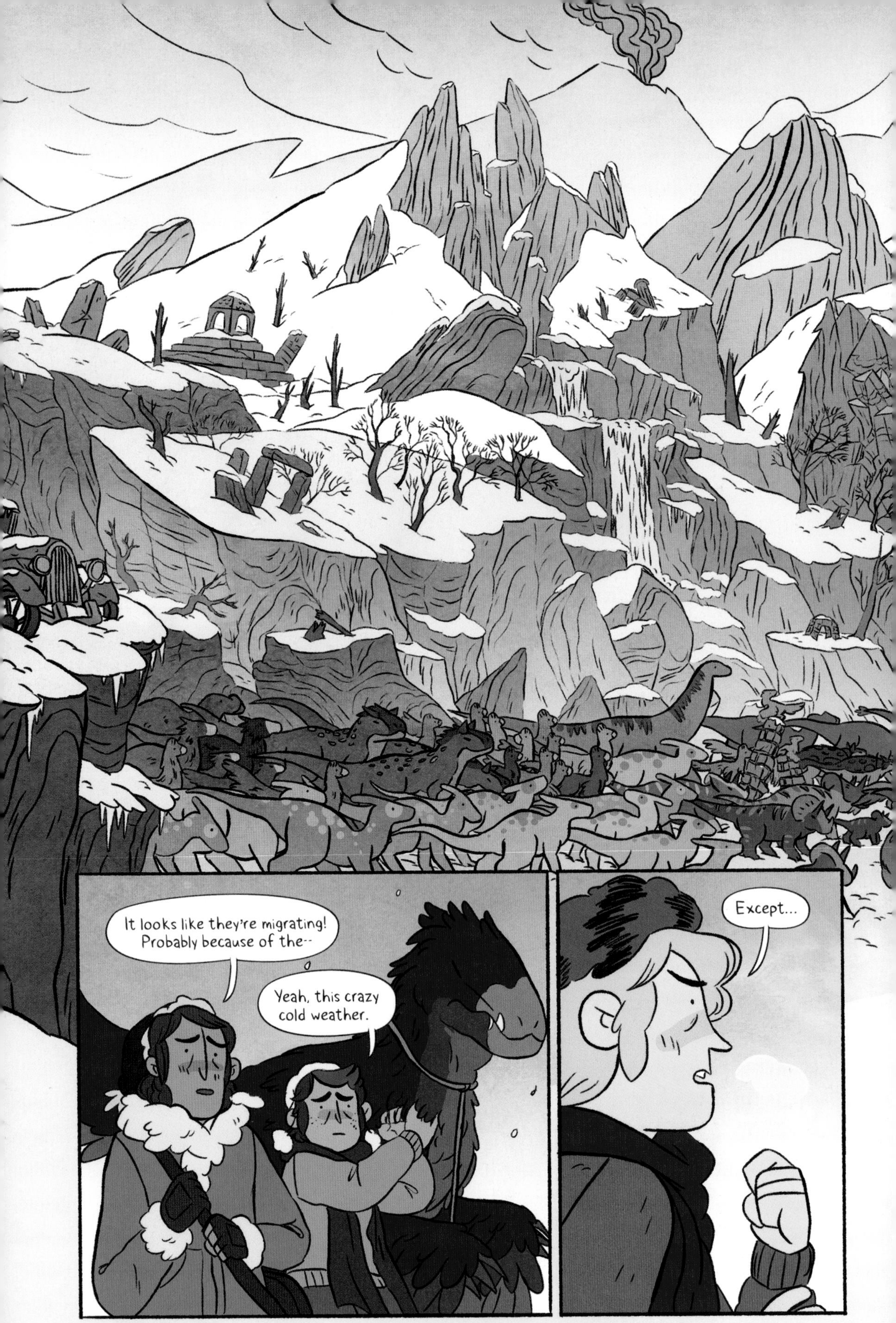
It looks like they're migrating! Probably because of the--
Yeah, this crazy cold weather.
Except...

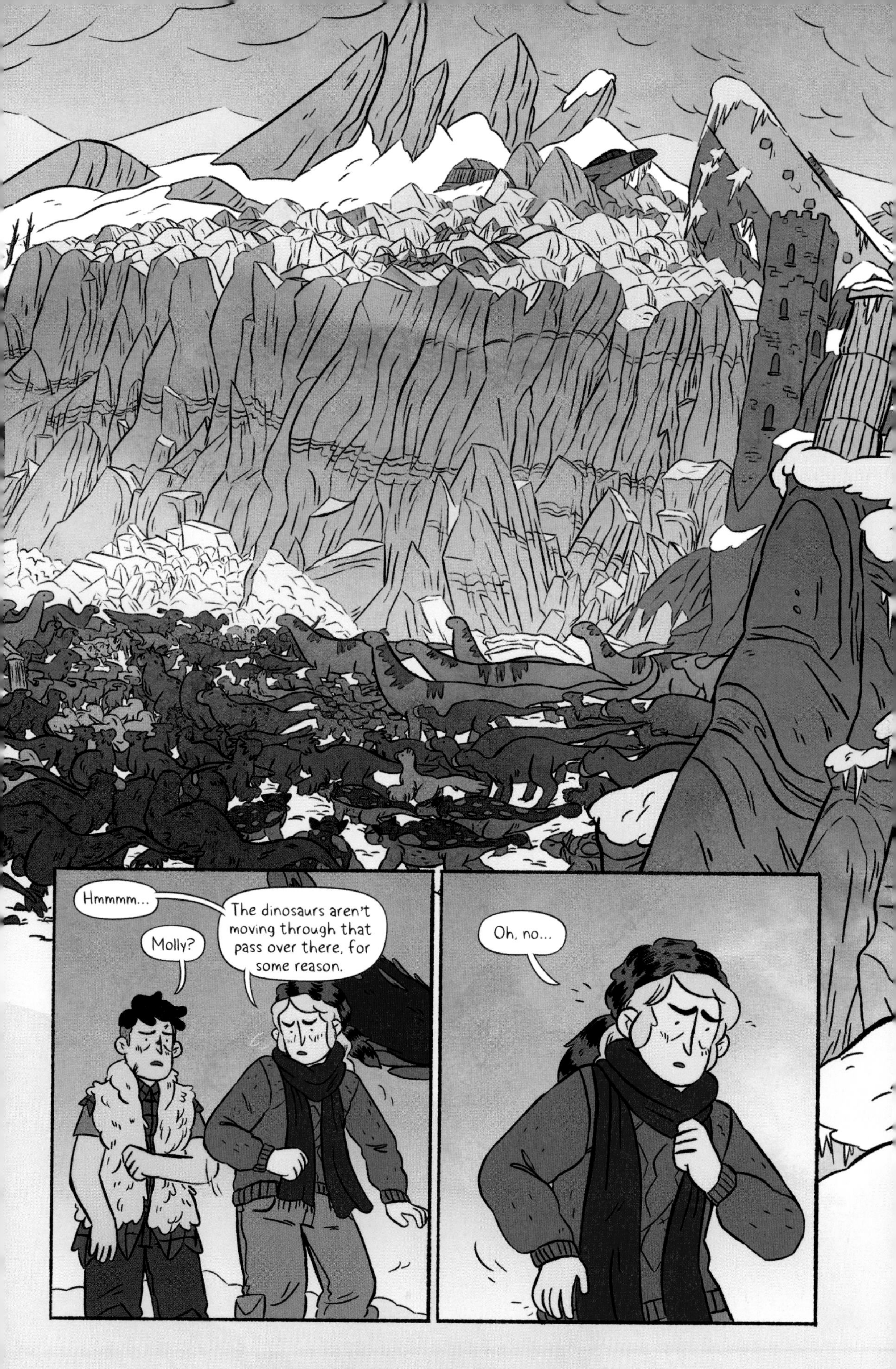
Hmmmm...
Molly?
The dinosaurs aren't moving through that pass over there, for some reason.
Oh, no...

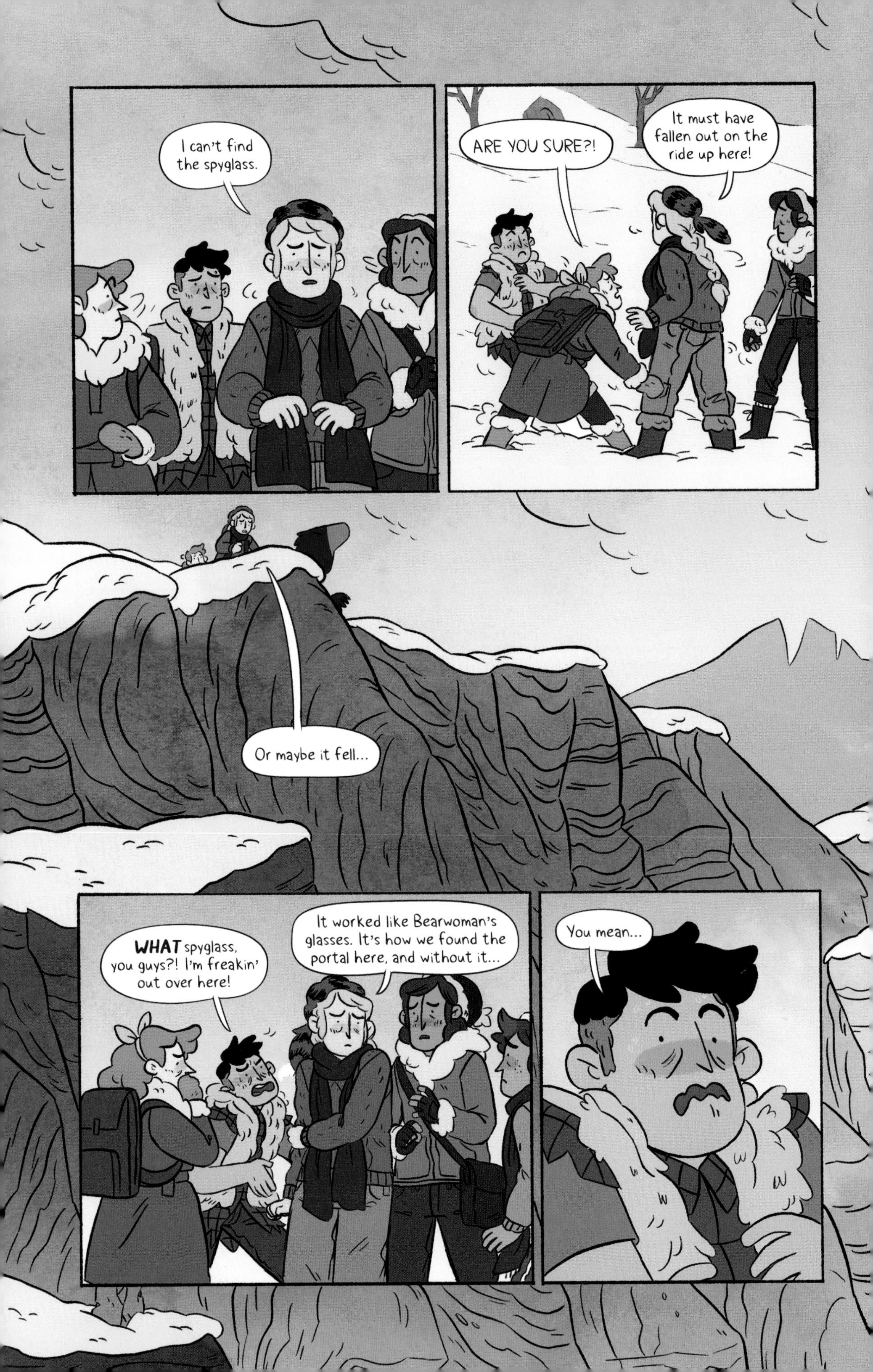
I can't find the spyglass.
ARE YOU SURE?!
It must have fallen out on the ride up here!
Or maybe it fell...
WHAT spyglass, you guys?! I'm freakin' out over here!
It worked like Bearwoman's glasses. It's how we found the portal here, and without it...
You mean...

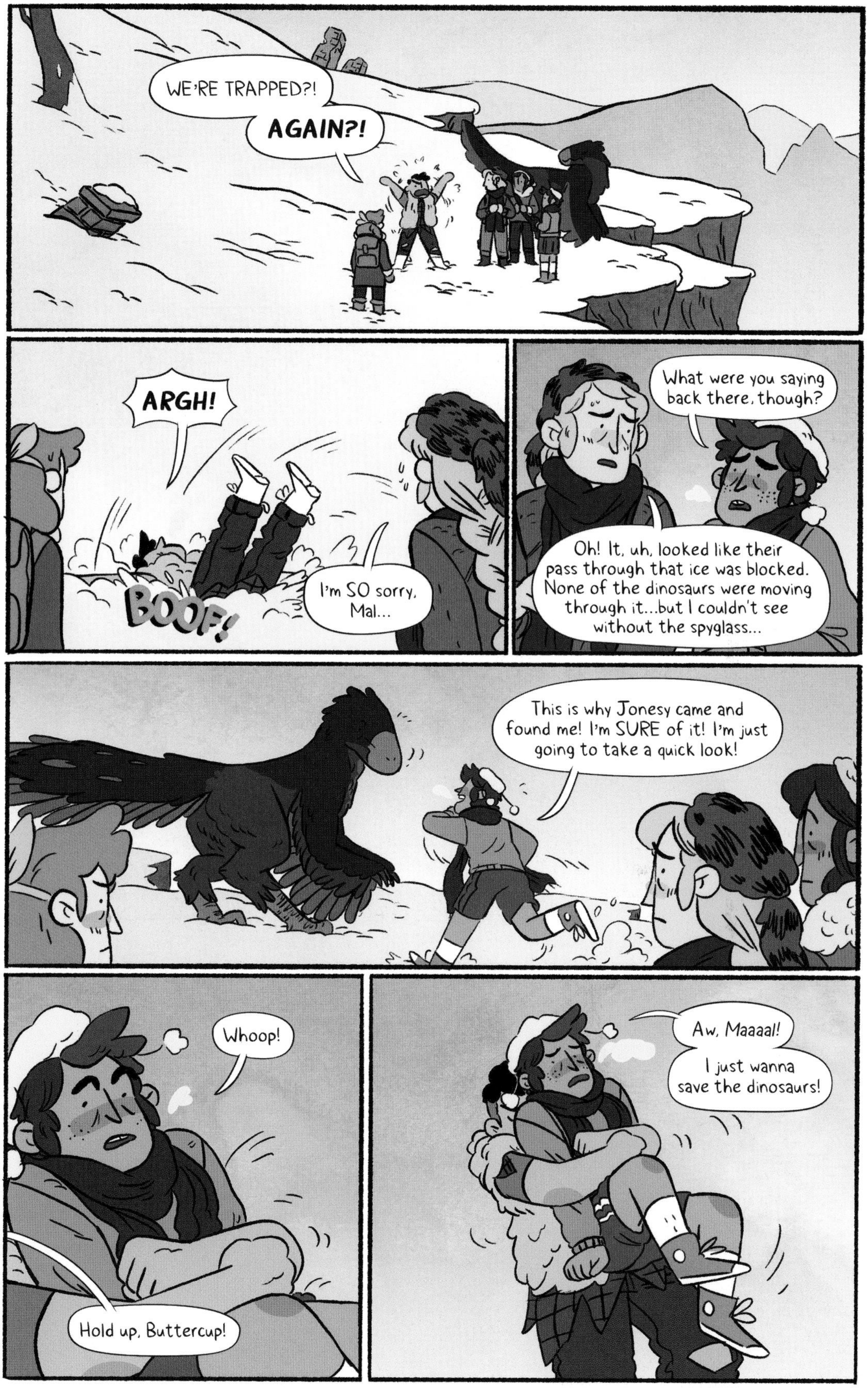
WE'RE TRAPPED?!
AGAIN?!
ARGH!
BOOF!
I'm SO sorry, Mal...
What were you saying back there, though?
Oh! It, uh, looked like their pass through that ice was blocked. None of the dinosaurs were moving through it...but I couldn't see without the spyglass...
This is why Jonesy came and found me! I'm SURE of it! I'm just going to take a quick look!
Whoop!
Hold up, Buttercup!
Aw, Maaaal!
I just wanna save the dinosaurs!

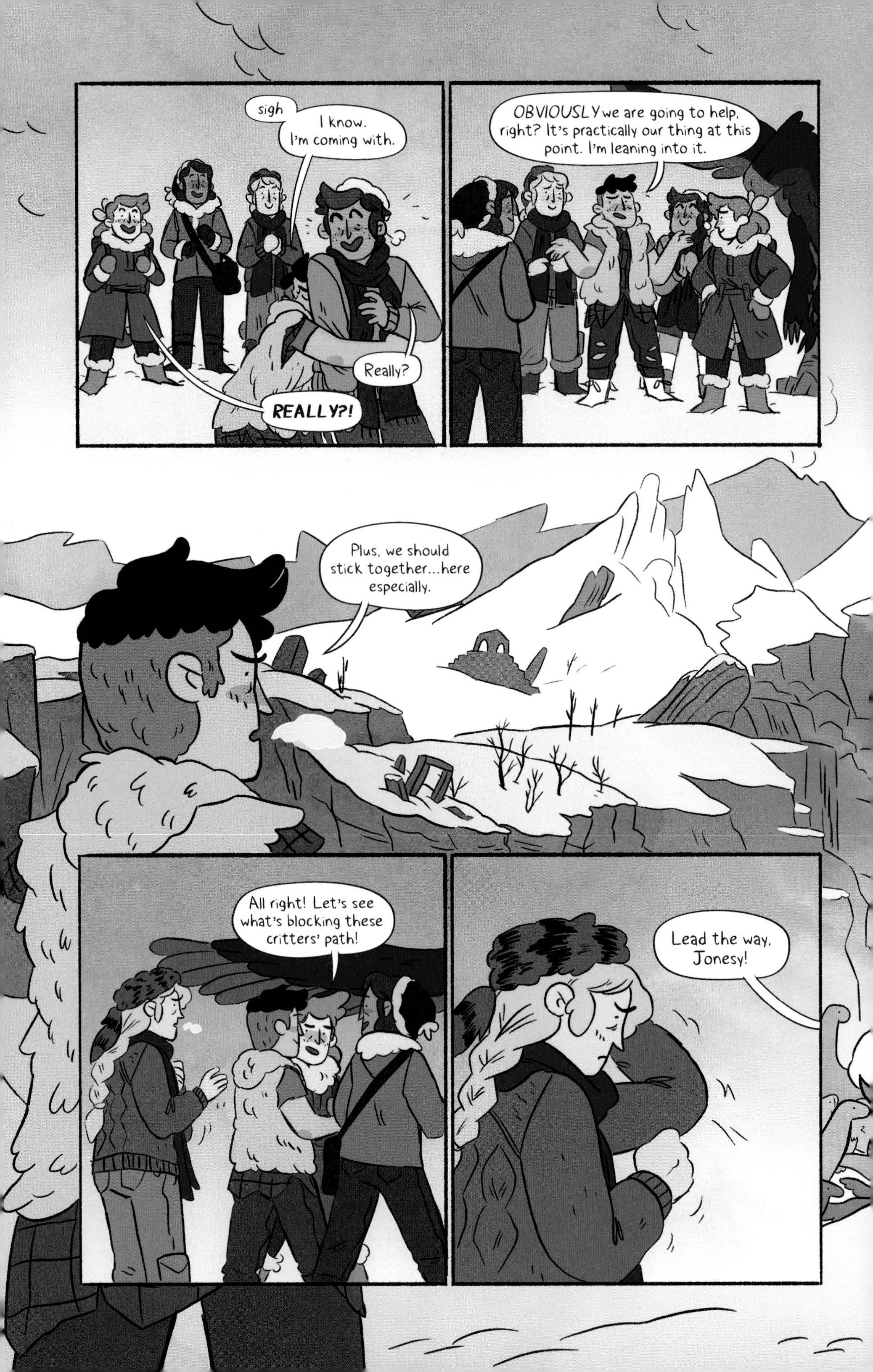
sigh
I know. I'm coming with.
Really?
REALLY?!
OBVIOUSLY we are going to help, right? It's practically our thing at this point. I'm leaning into it.
Plus, we should stick together...here especially.
All right! Let's see what's blocking these critters' path!
Lead the way, Jonesy!

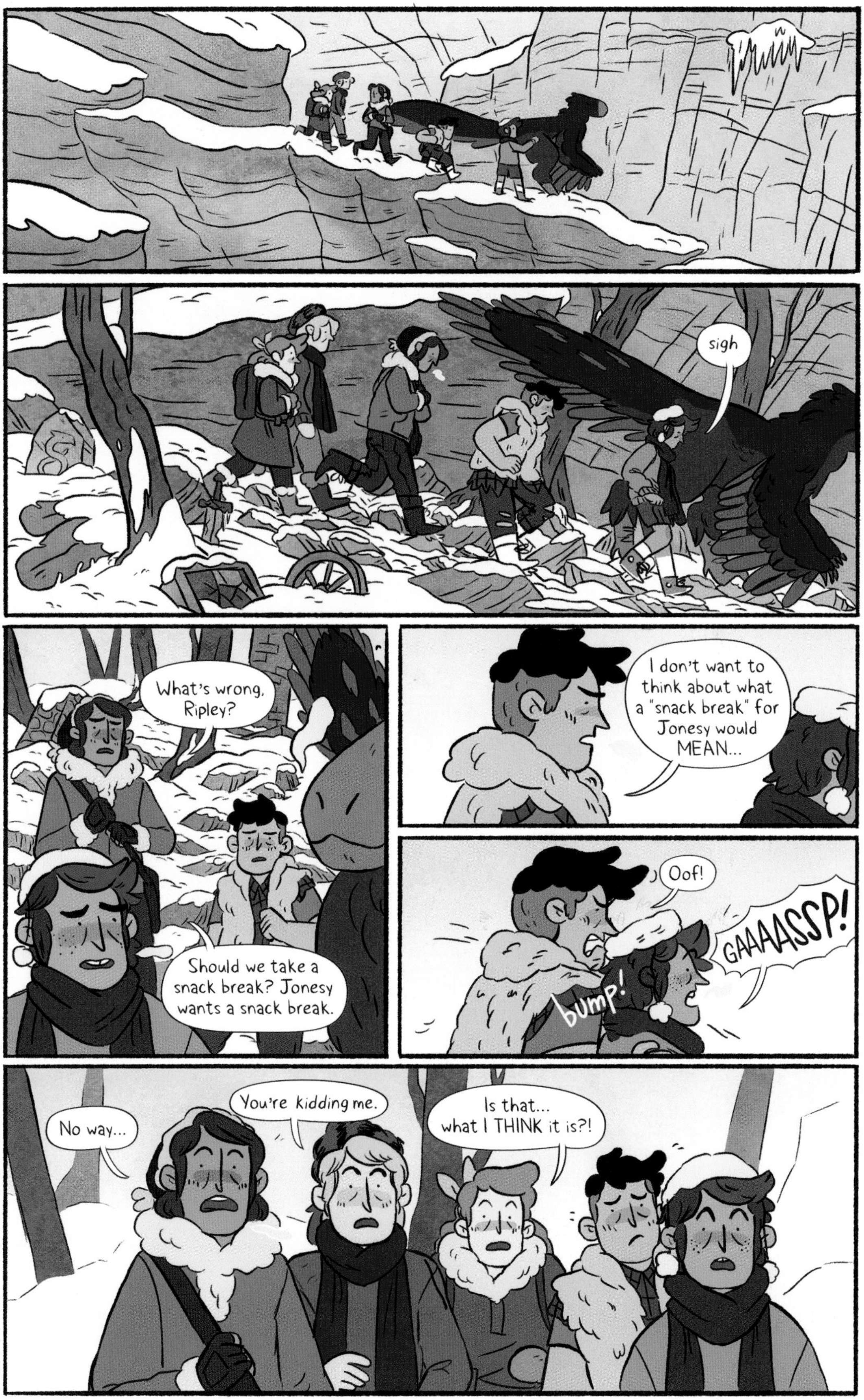
sigh
What's wrong, Ripley?
Should we take a snack break? Jonesy wants a snack break.
I don't want to think about what a "snack break" for Jonesy would MEAN...
Oof!
GAAAASSP!
bump!
No way...
You're kidding me.
Is that... what I THINK it is?!

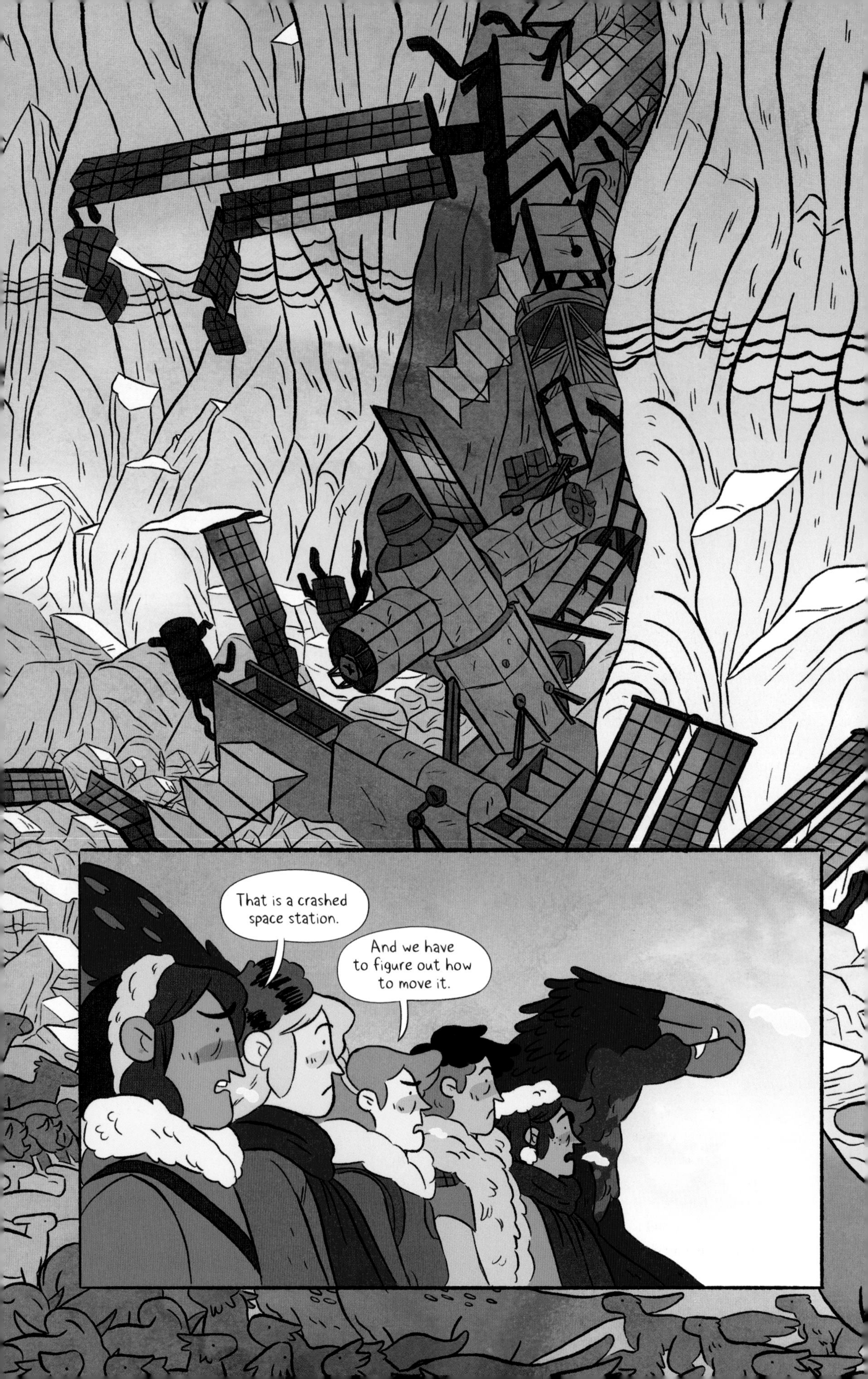

That is a crashed space station.
And we have to figure out how to move it.

will co

The

It helps
appearan
dress fo
Further
Lumber
to have
part in
Thiskv
Hardc
have
them

THE UNIFORM

hould be worn at camp
events when Lumberjanes
n may also be worn at other
ions. It should be worn as a
the uniform dress with
rect shoes, and stocking or

ut grows her uniform or
ther Lumberjane.
ia she has
her
her

ALL THIS DING-DANG SNOW!

The
yellow, short sl
emb
the w
choose
slacks,
made o
out-of-do
green bere
the colla
Shoes ma
heels, round
socks shoul
the uniform. Ne bracelets, or other jewelry do
belong with a Lumberjane uniform.

HOW TO WEAR THE UNIFORM

To look well in a uniform demands first of
uniform be kept in good condition—clean
pressed. See that the skirt is the right length for your own
height and build, that the belt is adjusted to your waist,
that your shoes and stockings are in keeping with the
uniform, that you watch your posture and carry yourself
with dignity and grace. If the beret is removed indoors,
be sure that your hair is neat and kept in place with an
inconspicuous clip or ribbon. When you wear a
Lumberjane uniform you are identified as a member of
this organization and you should be doubly careful to
conduct yourself in a way that will show everyone that
courtesy and thoughtfulness are part of being a
Lumberjane. People are likely to judge a whole nation by
the selfishness of a few individuals, to criticize a whole
family because of the misconduct of one member, and to
feel unkindly toward an organization because of the

The unifor
helps to cre
in a group.
active life th
another bond
future, and pr
in order to b
Lumberjane pr
Penniquiqul Thi
Types, but m
can either b he uniform, or make it themselves from
materials available at the trading post.

WHOA WHOA WHOA!!!

LUMBERJANES FIELD MANUAL

CHAPTER
SIXTY-FOUR

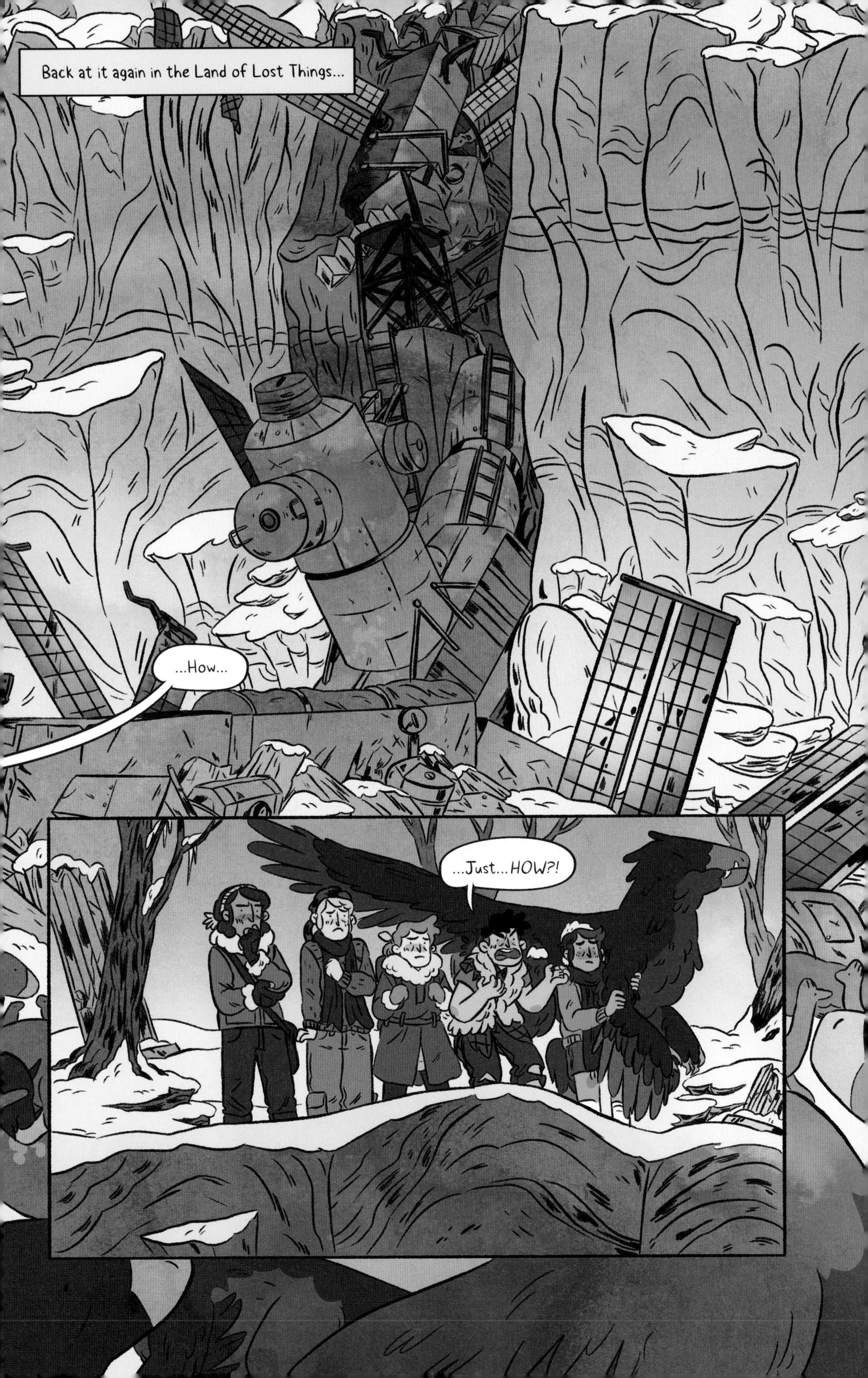
Back at it again in the Land of Lost Things...
...How...
...Just...HOW?!

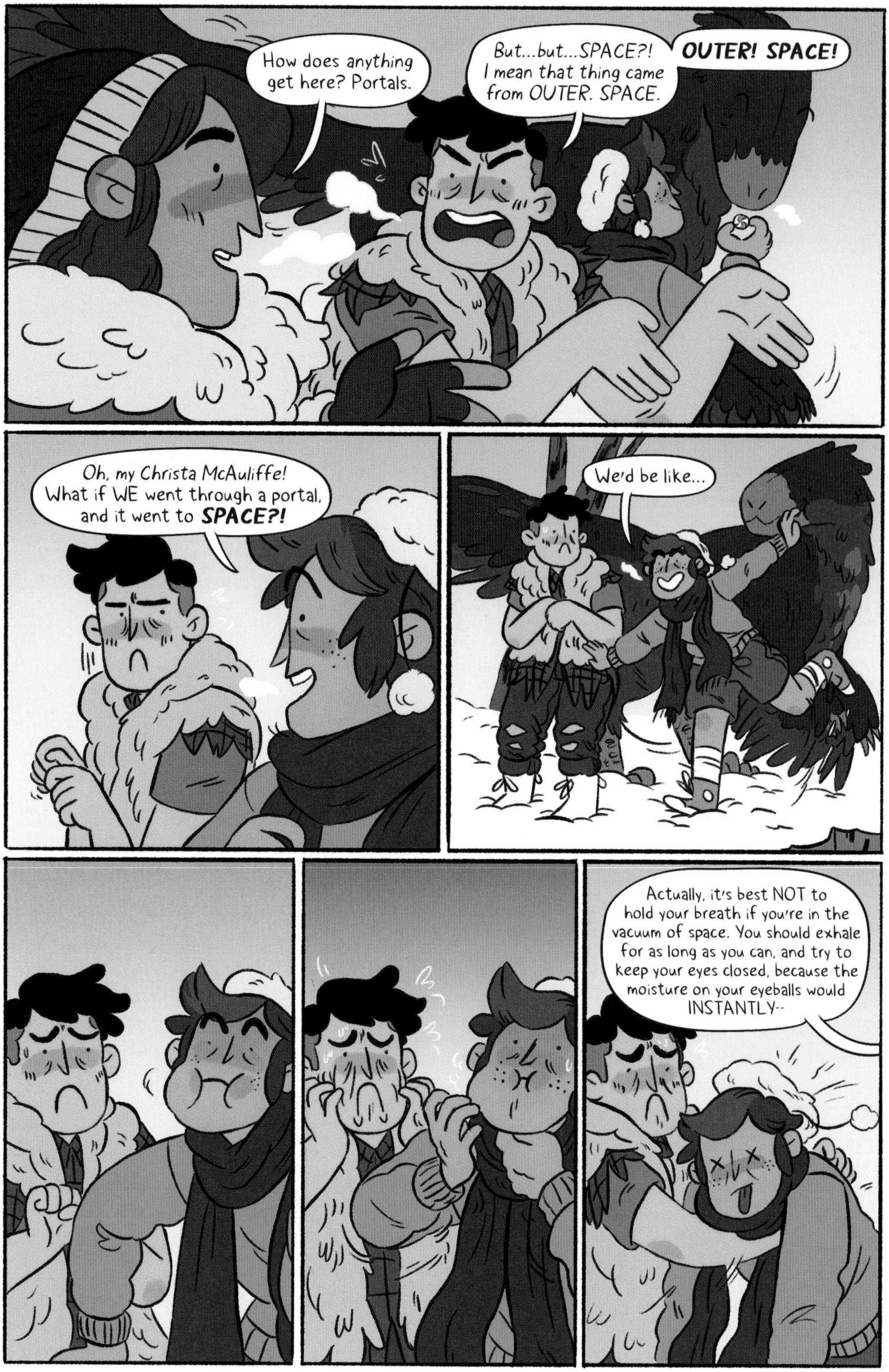
How does anything get here? Portals.
But...but...SPACE?! I mean that thing came from OUTER. SPACE.
OUTER! SPACE!
Oh, my Christa McAuliffe! What if WE went through a portal, and it went to SPACE?!
We'd be like...
Actually, it's best NOT to hold your breath if you're in the vacuum of space. You should exhale for as long as you can, and try to keep your eyes closed, because the moisture on your eyeballs would INSTANTLY--

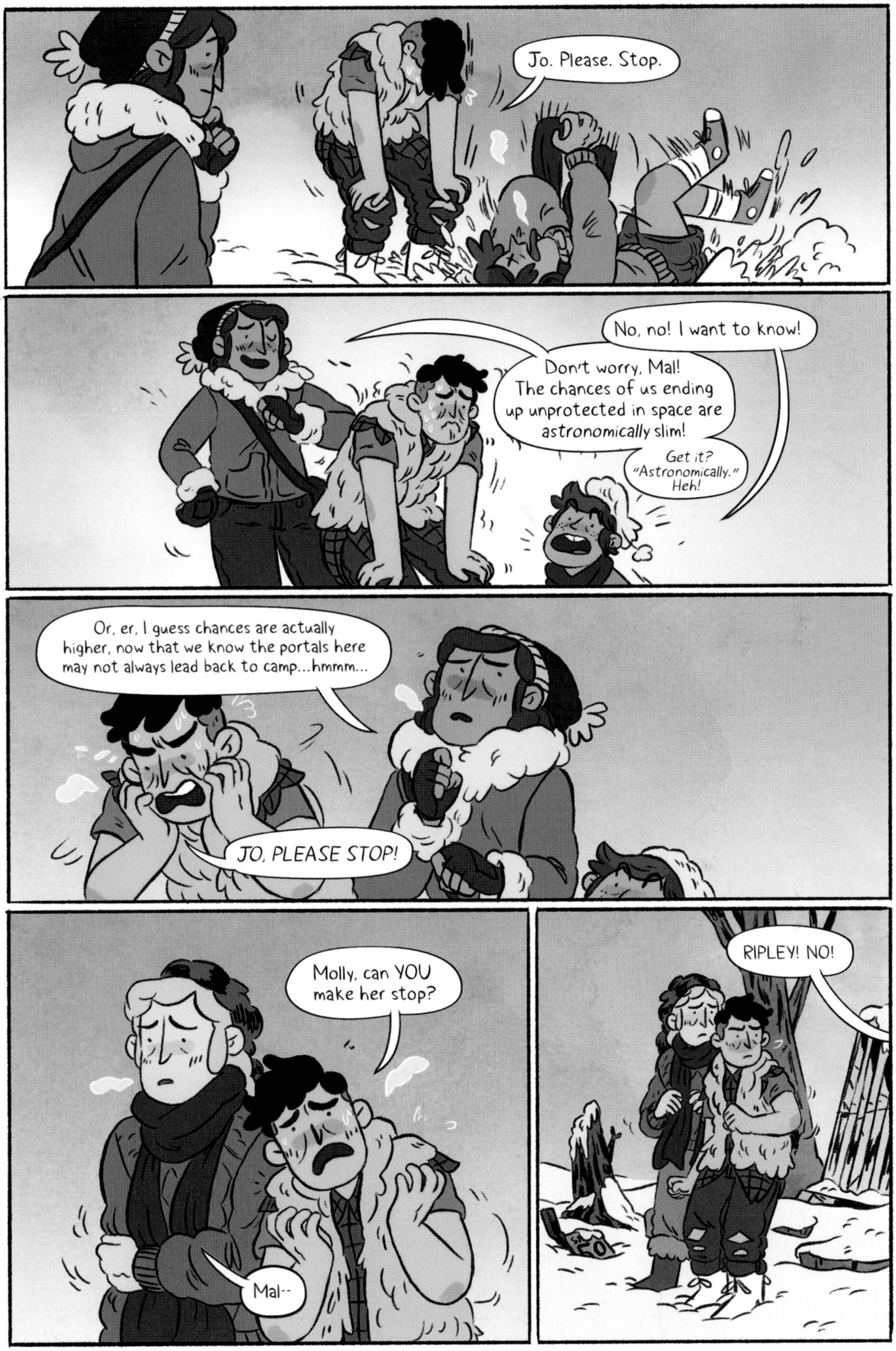
Jo. Please. Stop.
No, no! I want to know!
Don't worry, Mal! The chances of us ending up unprotected in space are astronomically slim!
Get it? "Astronomically." Heh!
Or, er, I guess chances are actually higher, now that we know the portals here may not always lead back to camp...hmmm...
JO, PLEASE STOP!
Molly, can YOU make her stop?
Mal--
RIPLEY! NO!

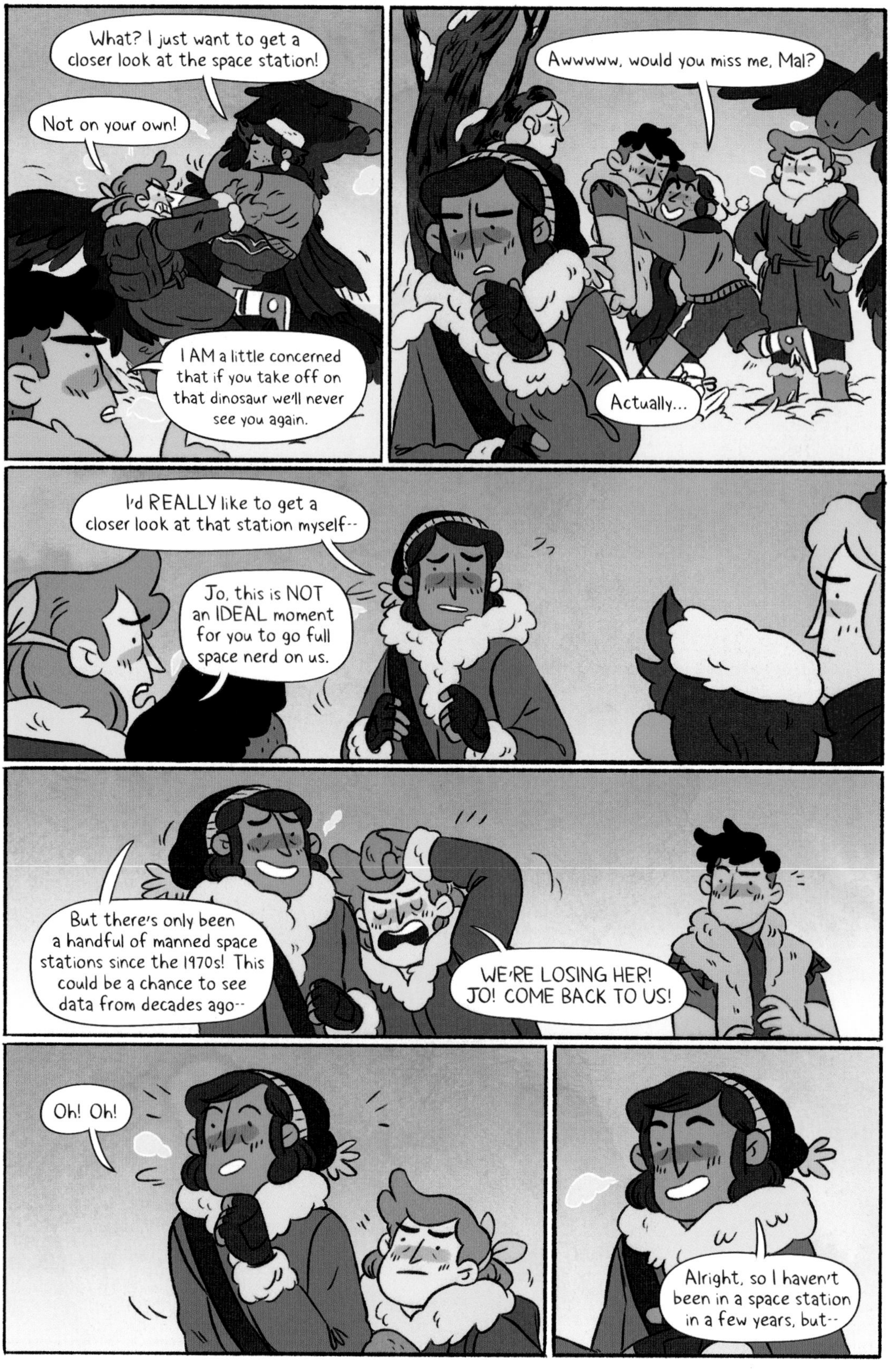
What? I just want to get a closer look at the space station!
Not on your own!
I AM a little concerned that if you take off on that dinosaur we'll never see you again.
Awwwww, would you miss me, Mal?
Actually...
I'd REALLY like to get a closer look at that station myself--
Jo, this is NOT an IDEAL moment for you to go full space nerd on us.
But there's only been a handful of manned space stations since the 1970s! This could be a chance to see data from decades ago--
WE'RE LOSING HER! JO! COME BACK TO US!
Oh! Oh!
Alright, so I haven't been in a space station in a few years, but--

...What?

Are you secretly a SPACE PERSON? FROM SPACE?!?!

My dads are rocket scientists, you guys! I saw the stations when they were still on earth!

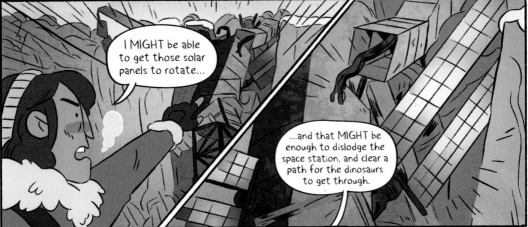

GASP! DO YOU KNOW HOW TO FLY IT?!

Space stations don't fly. They get brought to space with rockets.

Buuut?

I MIGHT be able to get those solar panels to rotate...

...and that MIGHT be enough to dislodge the space station, and clear a path for the dinosaurs to get through.

You really think that'll do it?

I'd say it's worth a try!

You're not just saying this 'cause you want to get a closer look at that thing, are you?

Wh--Can't it be BOTH?!

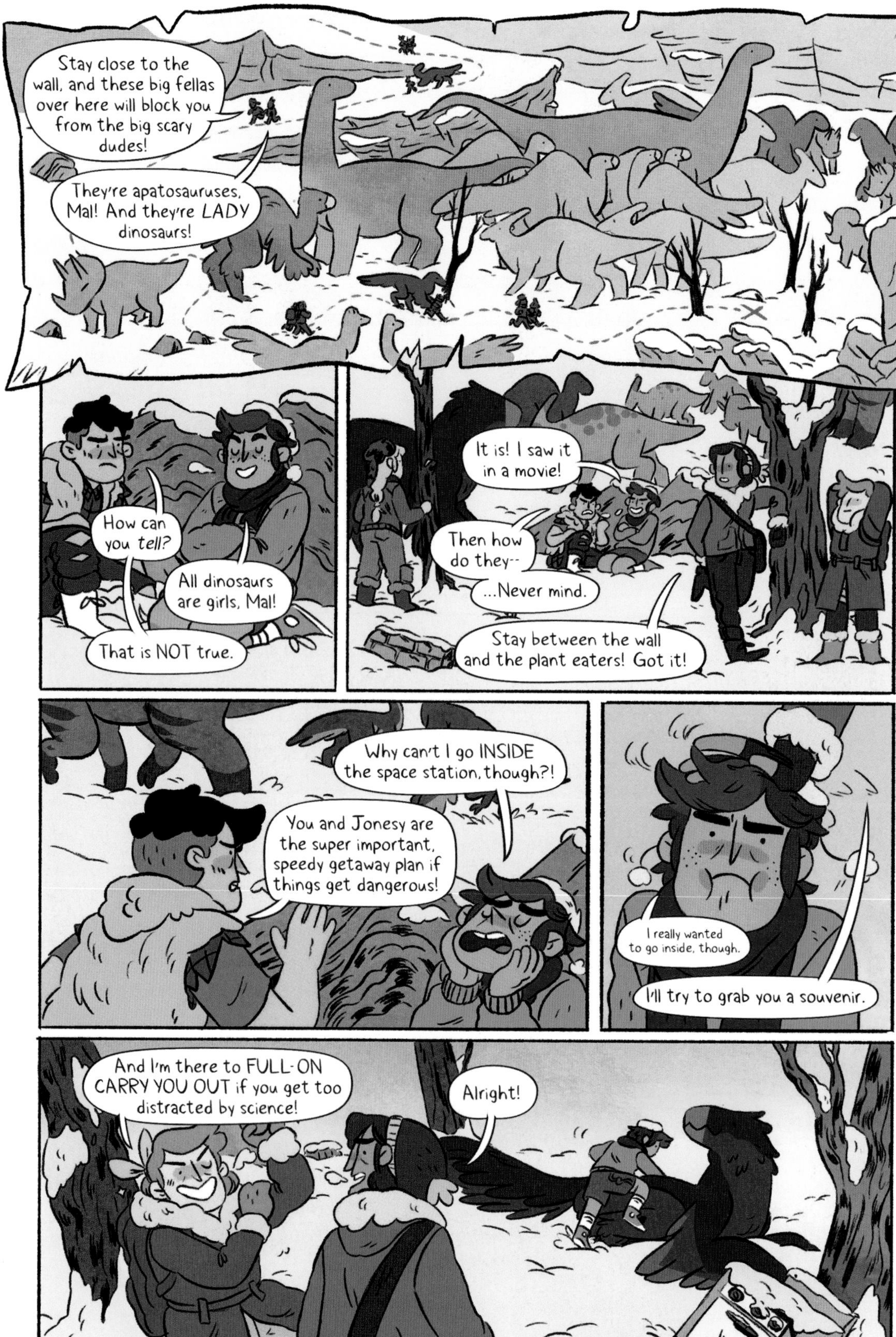
Stay close to the wall, and these big fellas over here will block you from the big scary dudes!
They're apatosauruses, Mal! And they're LADY dinosaurs!
How can you tell?
All dinosaurs are girls, Mal!
That is NOT true.
It is! I saw it in a movie!
Then how do they--
...Never mind.
Stay between the wall and the plant eaters! Got it!
Why can't I go INSIDE the space station, though?!
You and Jonesy are the super important, speedy getaway plan if things get dangerous!
I really wanted to go inside, though.
I'll try to grab you a souvenir.
And I'm there to FULL-ON CARRY YOU OUT if you get too distracted by science!
Alright!

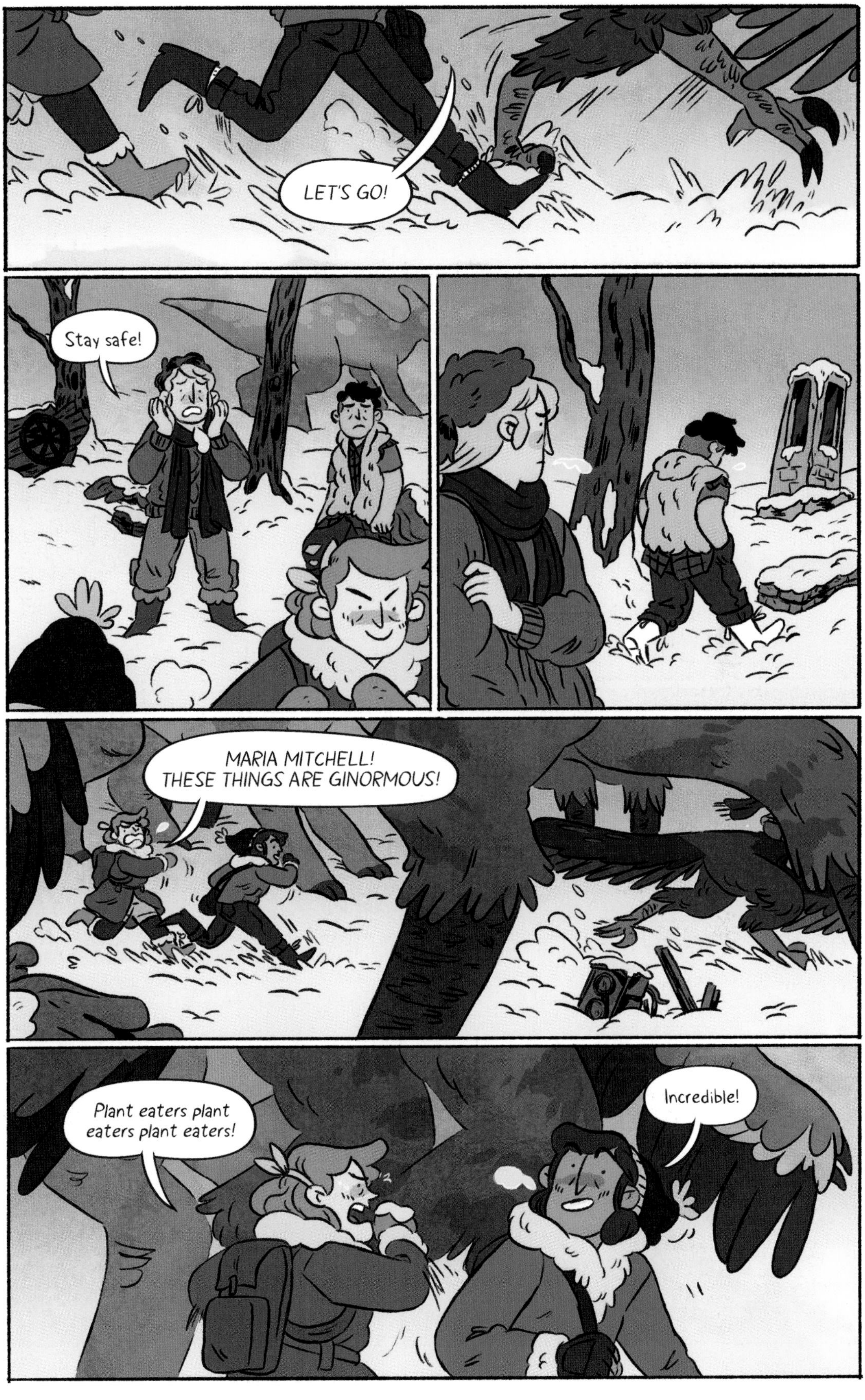
LET'S GO!
Stay safe!
MARIA MITCHELL! THESE THINGS ARE GINORMOUS!
Plant eaters plant eaters plant eaters!
Incredible!

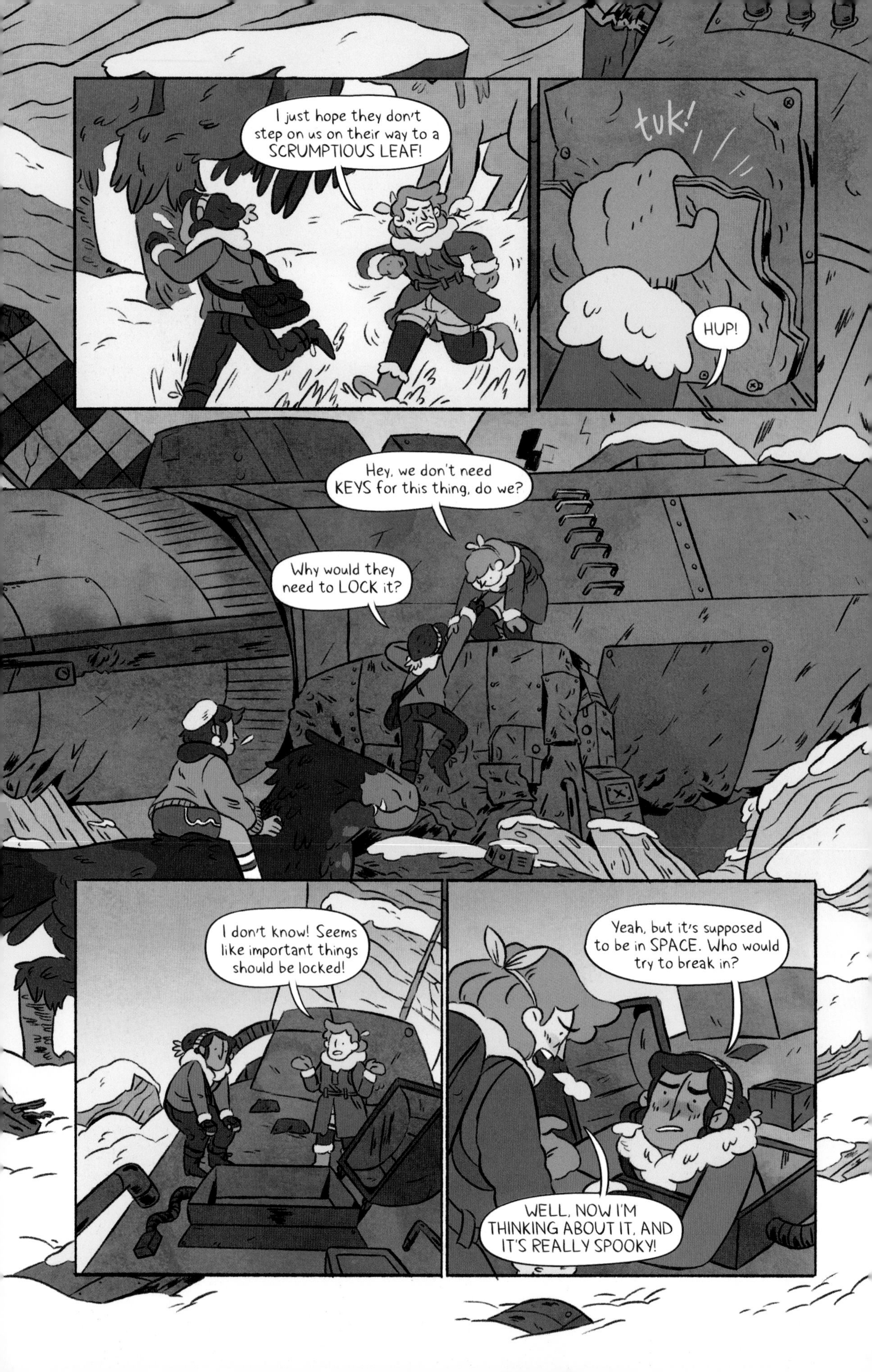

I just hope they don't step on us on their way to a SCRUMPTIOUS LEAF!
tuk!
HUP!
Hey, we don't need KEYS for this thing, do we?
Why would they need to LOCK it?
I don't know! Seems like important things should be locked!
Yeah, but it's supposed to be in SPACE. Who would try to break in?
WELL, NOW I'M THINKING ABOUT IT, AND IT'S REALLY SPOOKY!

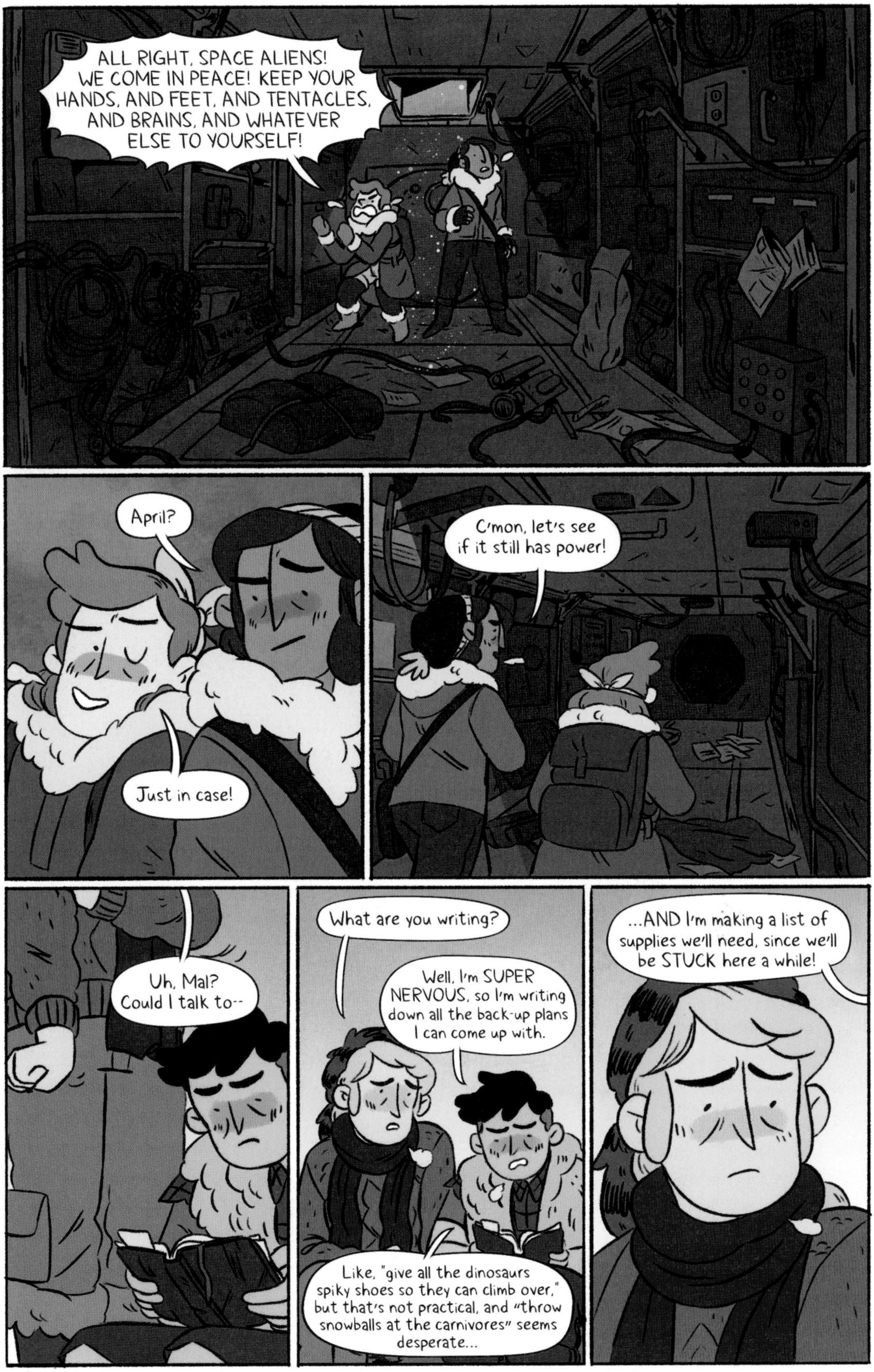
ALL RIGHT, SPACE ALIENS! WE COME IN PEACE! KEEP YOUR HANDS, AND FEET, AND TENTACLES, AND BRAINS, AND WHATEVER ELSE TO YOURSELF!
April?
Just in case!
C'mon, let's see if it still has power!
Uh, Mal? Could I talk to--
What are you writing?
Well, I'm SUPER NERVOUS, so I'm writing down all the back-up plans I can come up with.
Like, "give all the dinosaurs spiky shoes so they can climb over," but that's not practical, and "throw snowballs at the carnivores" seems desperate...
...AND I'm making a list of supplies we'll need, since we'll be STUCK here a while!

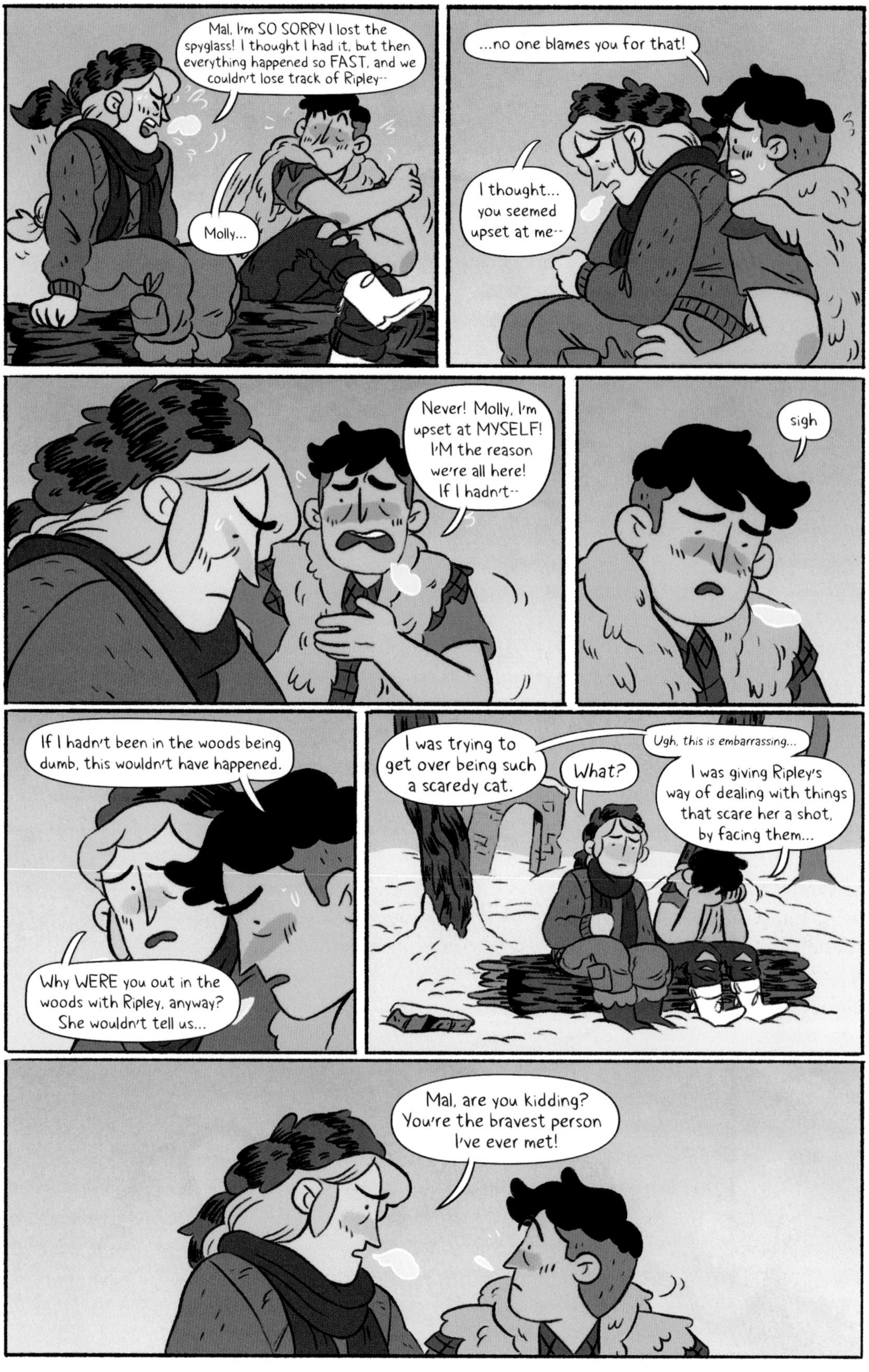
Mal, I'm SO SORRY I lost the spyglass! I thought I had it, but then everything happened so FAST, and we couldn't lose track of Ripley--
Molly...
...no one blames you for that!
I thought... you seemed upset at me--
Never! Molly, I'm upset at MYSELF! I'M the reason we're all here! If I hadn't--
sigh
If I hadn't been in the woods being dumb, this wouldn't have happened.
Why WERE you out in the woods with Ripley, anyway? She wouldn't tell us...
I was trying to get over being such a scaredy cat.
Ugh, this is embarrassing...
What?
I was giving Ripley's way of dealing with things that scare her a shot, by facing them...
Mal, are you kidding? You're the bravest person I've ever met!

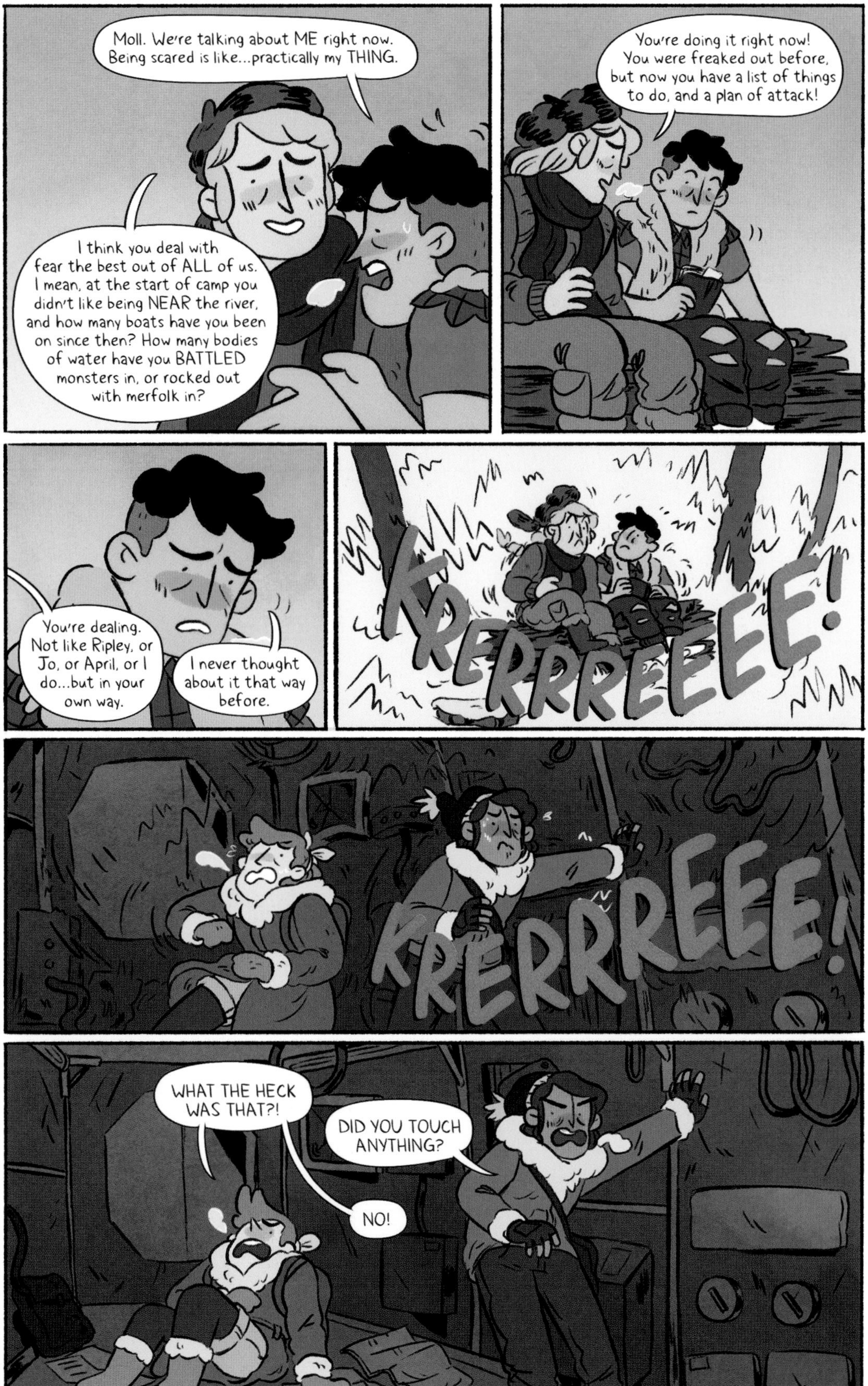
Moll. We're talking about ME right now. Being scared is like...practically my THING.
I think you deal with fear the best out of ALL of us. I mean, at the start of camp you didn't like being NEAR the river, and how many boats have you been on since then? How many bodies of water have you BATTLED monsters in, or rocked out with merfolk in?
You're doing it right now! You were freaked out before, but now you have a list of things to do, and a plan of attack!
You're dealing. Not like Ripley, or Jo, or April, or I do...but in your own way.
I never thought about it that way before.
KRERRREEEE!
KRERRREEE!
WHAT THE HECK WAS THAT?!
DID YOU TOUCH ANYTHING?
NO!

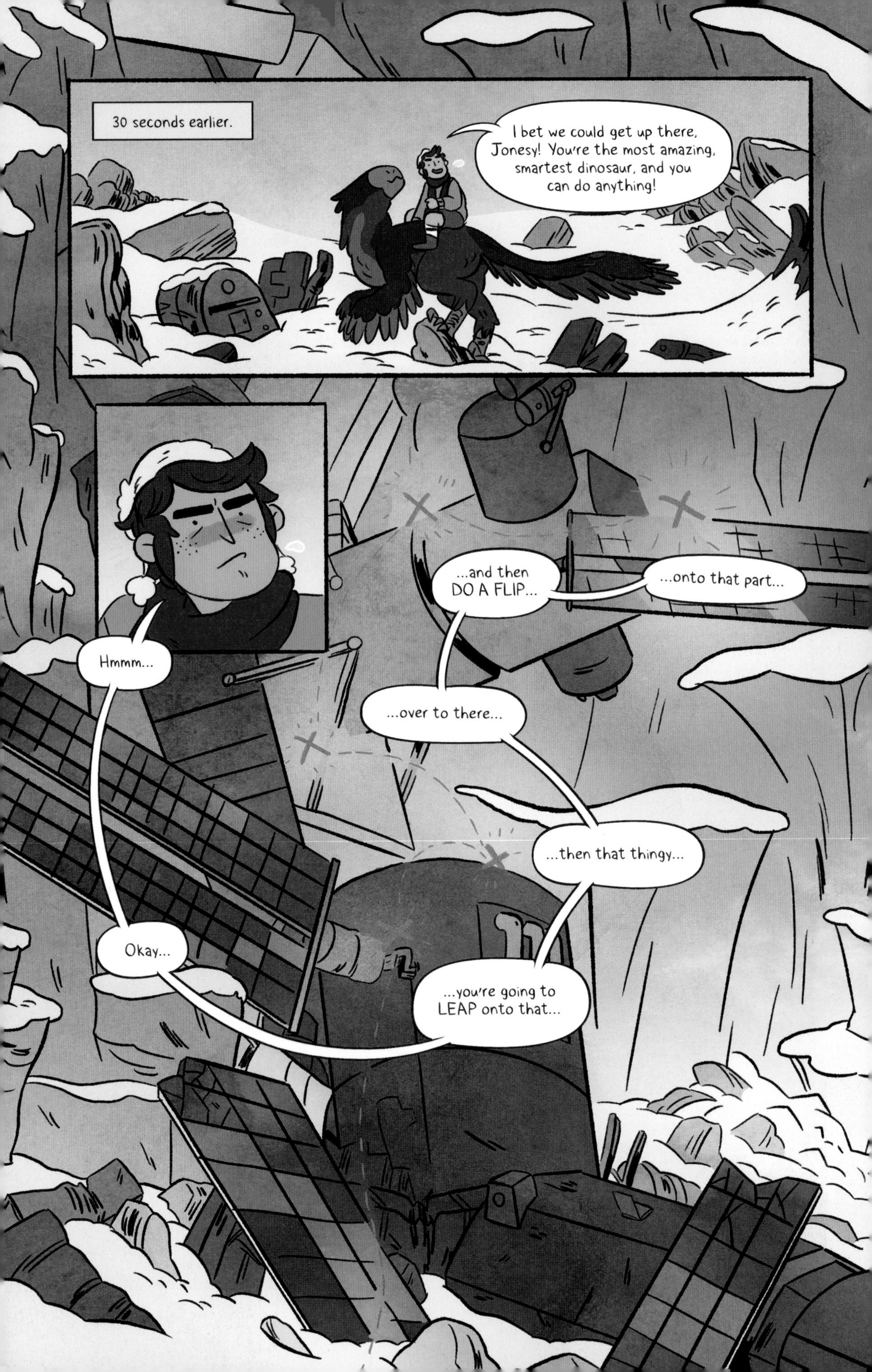
30 seconds earlier.
I bet we could get up there, Jonesy! You're the most amazing, smartest dinosaur, and you can do anything!
Hmmm...
Okay...
...you're going to LEAP onto that...
...then that thingy...
...over to there...
...and then DO A FLIP...
...onto that part...

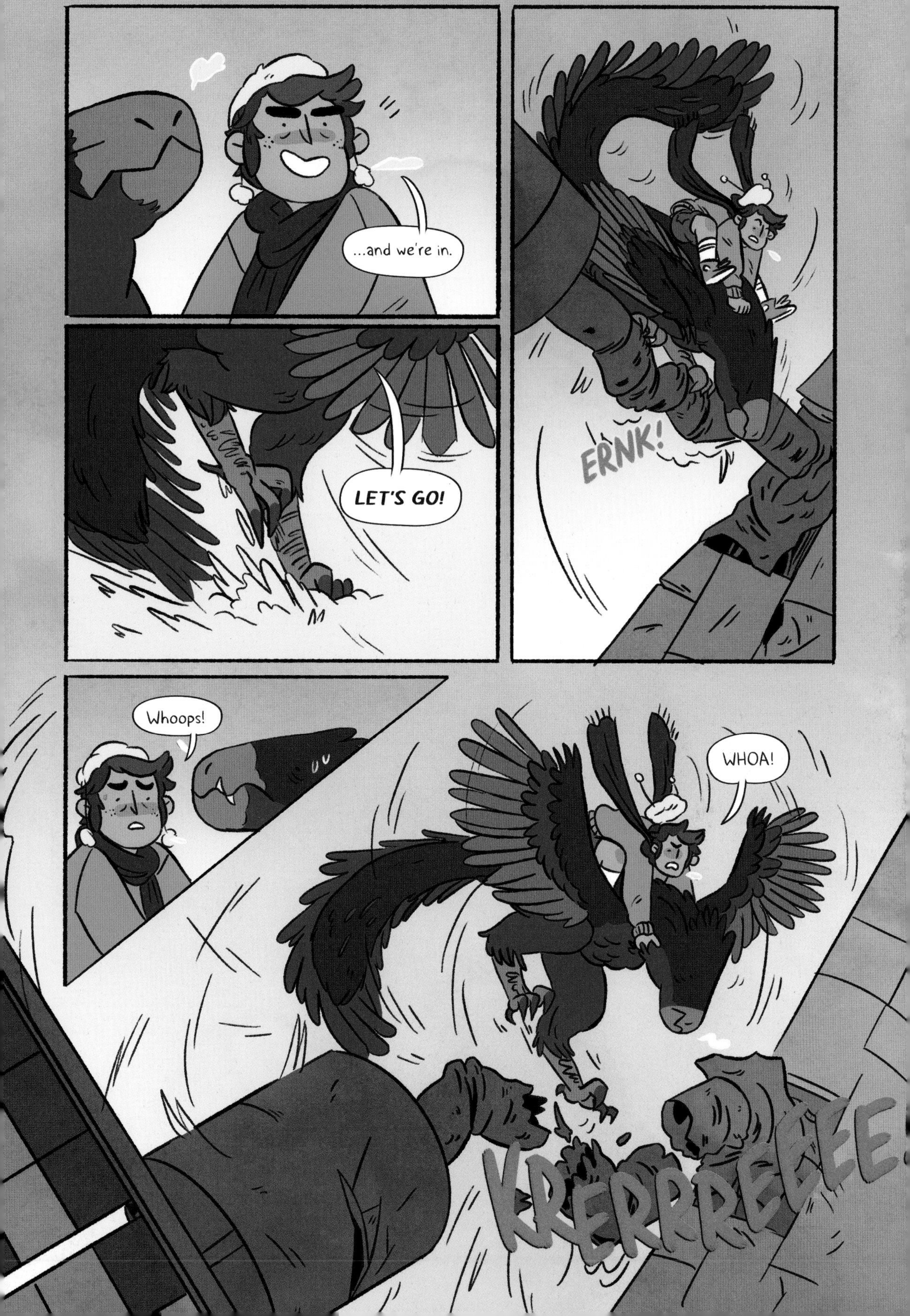
...and we're in.
LET'S GO!
ERNK!
Whoops!
WHOA!
KERRREEEE!

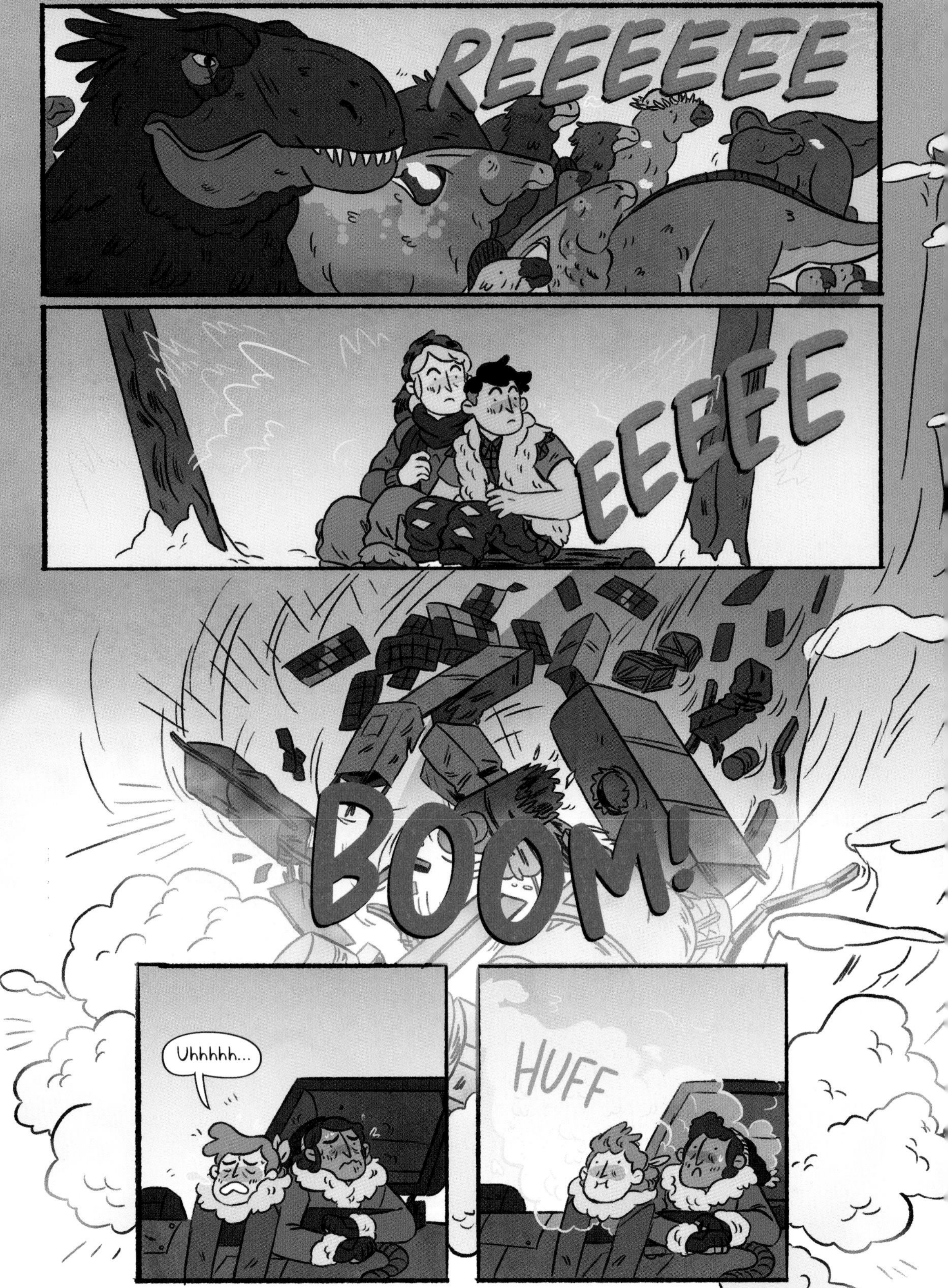
REEEEEEE
EEEEE
BOOM!
Uhhhhh...
HUFF

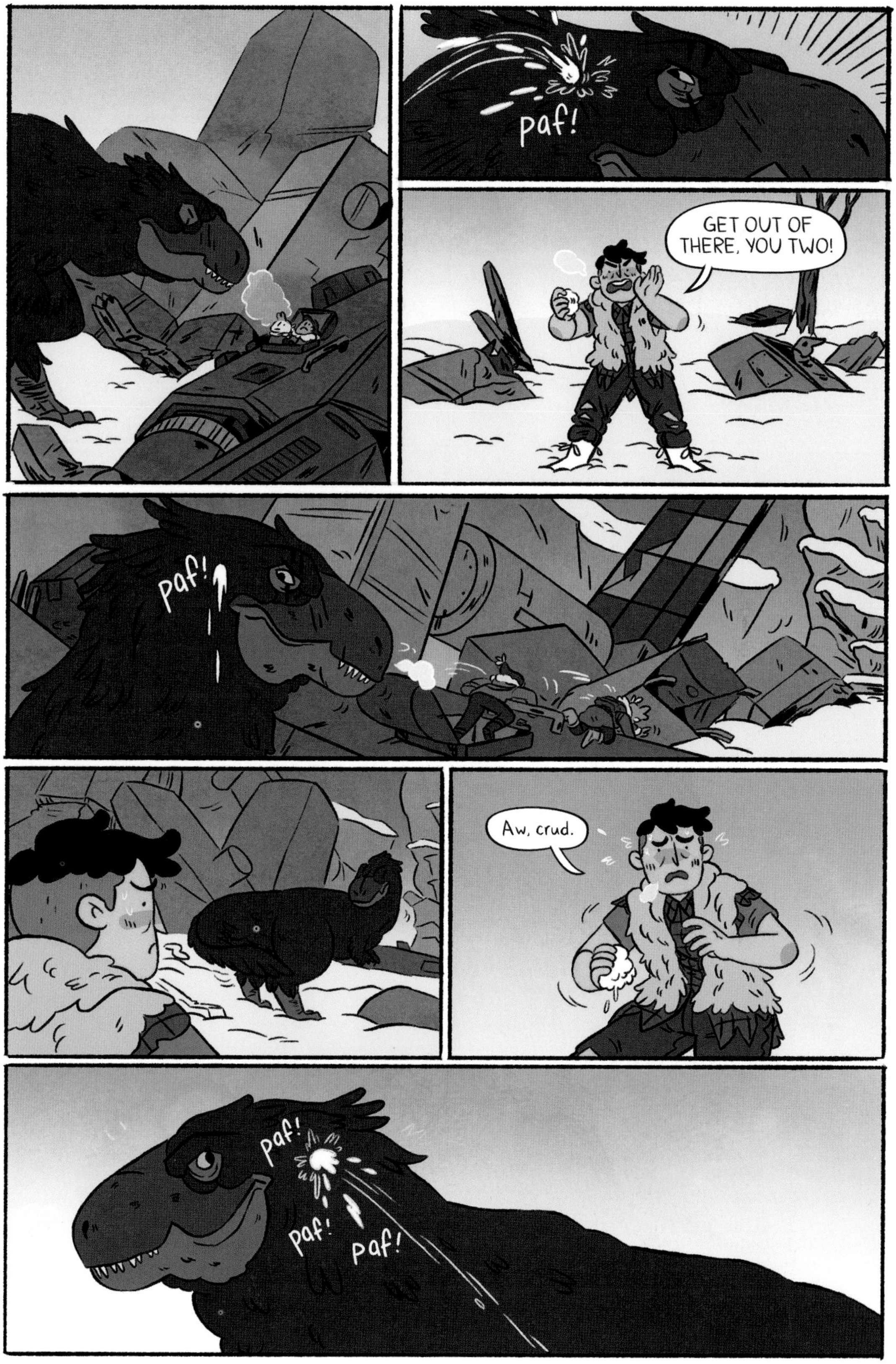
paf!
GET OUT OF THERE, YOU TWO!
paf!
Aw, crud.
paf!
paf!
paf!

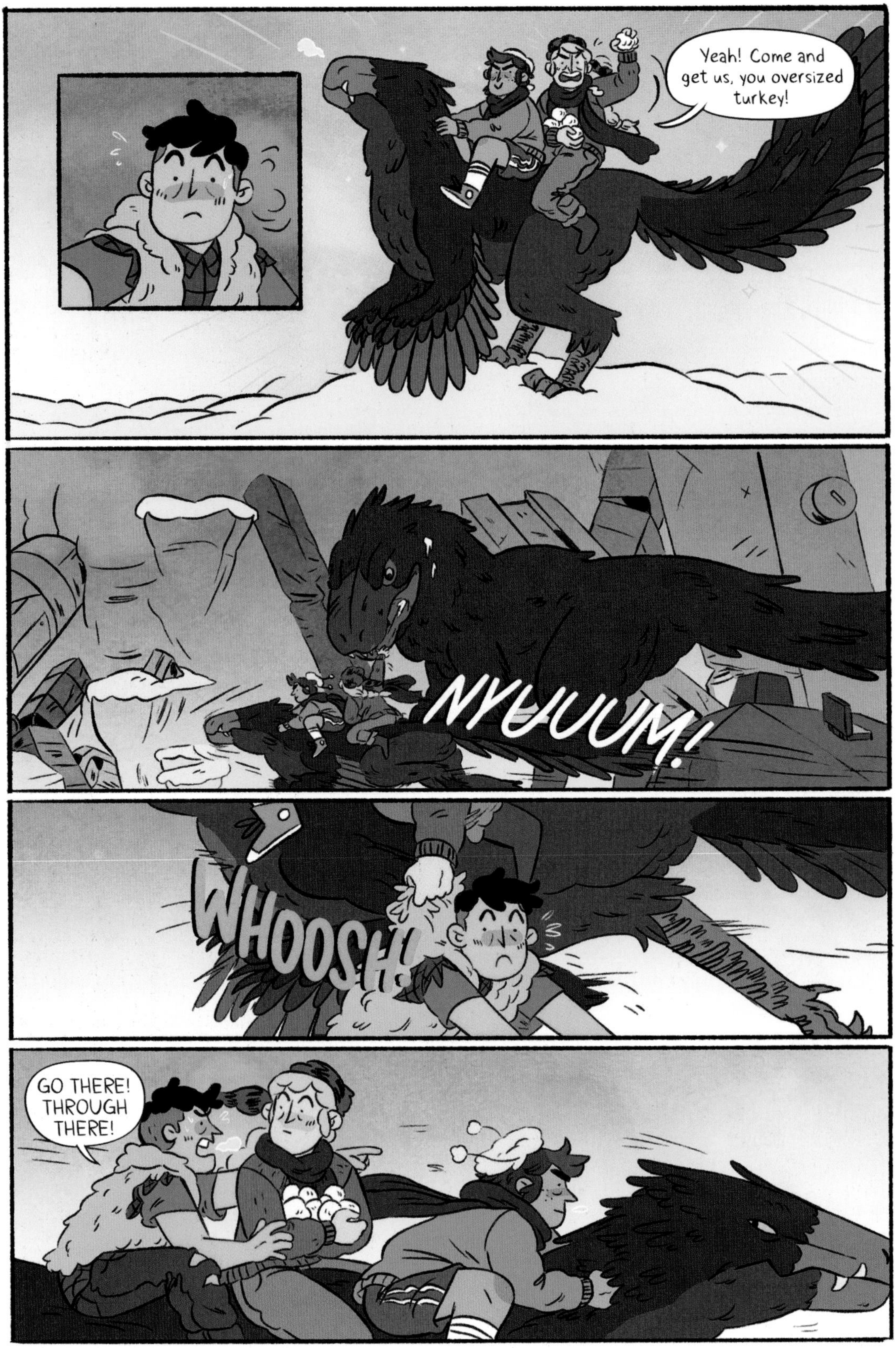
Yeah! Come and get us, you oversized turkey!
NYUUUM!
WHOOSH!
GO THERE! THROUGH THERE!

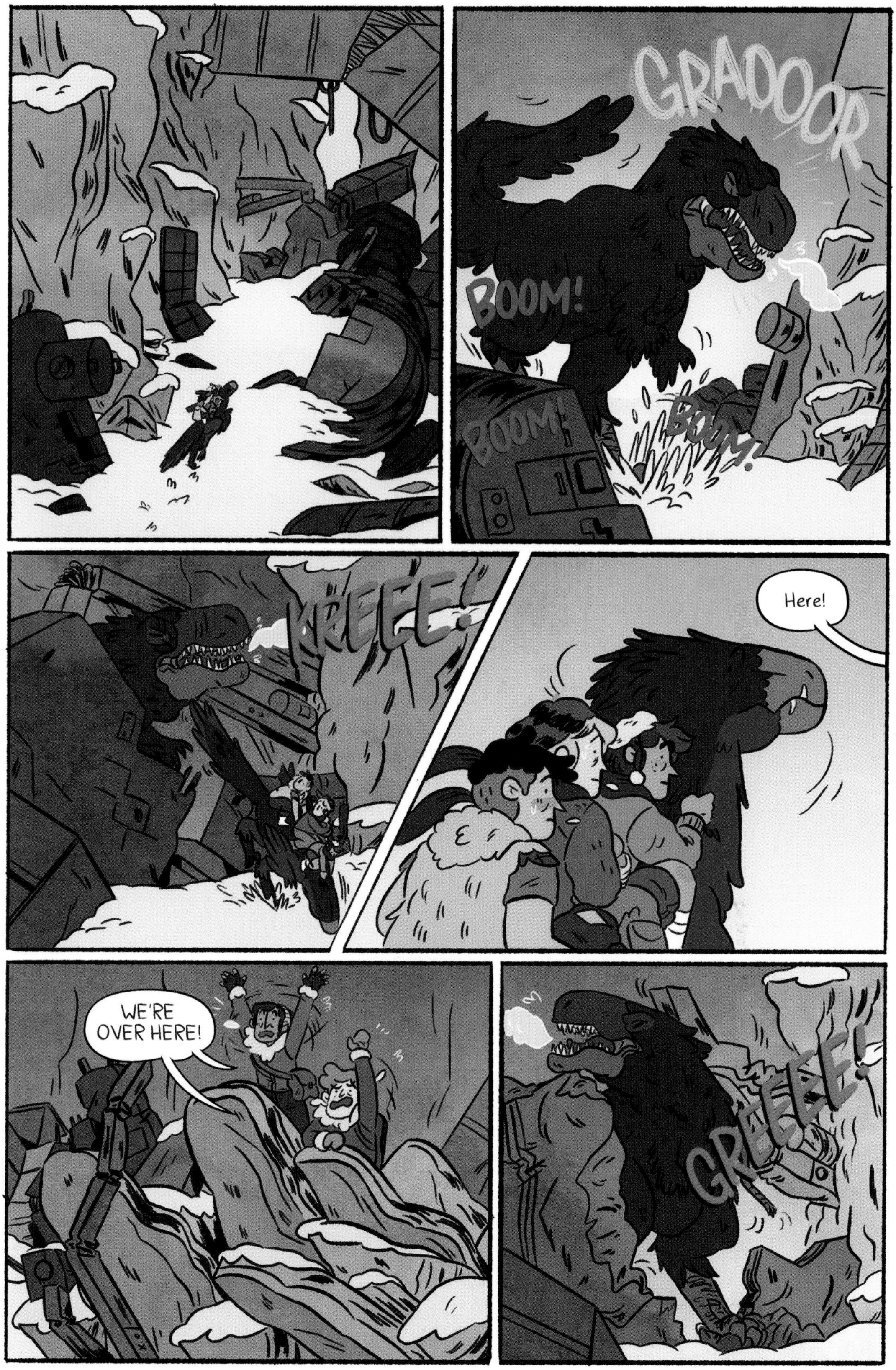
GRADOOOR
BOOM!
BOOM!
BOOM!
KREEE!
Here!
WE'RE OVER HERE!
GREEEE!

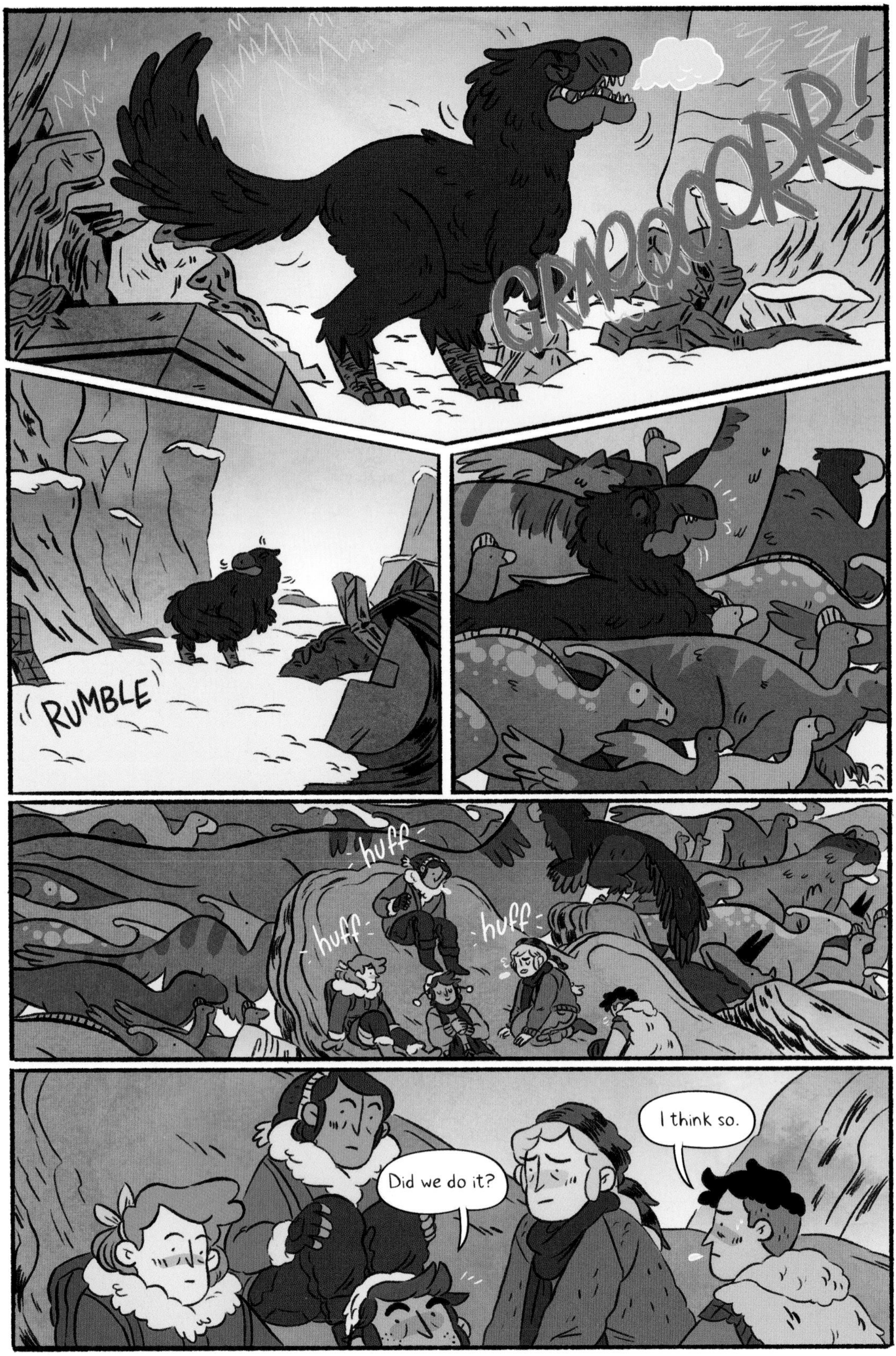
GRAOOOORR!
RUMBLE
huff
huff
huff
Did we do it?
I think so.

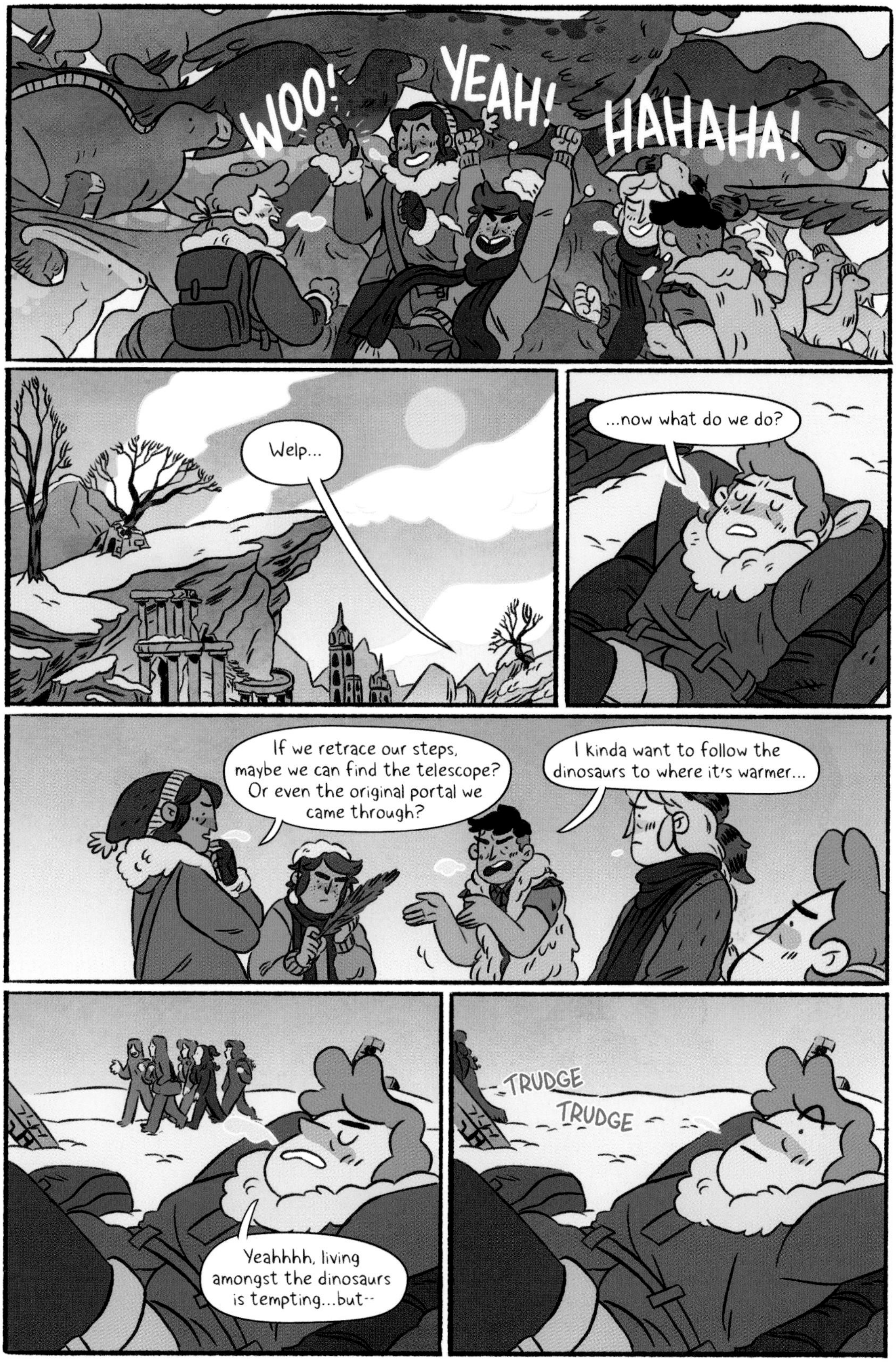
WOO!
YEAH!
HAHAHA!
Welp...
...now what do we do?
If we retrace our steps, maybe we can find the telescope? Or even the original portal we came through?
I kinda want to follow the dinosaurs to where it's warmer...
Yeahhhh, living amongst the dinosaurs is tempting...but--
TRUDGE
TRUDGE

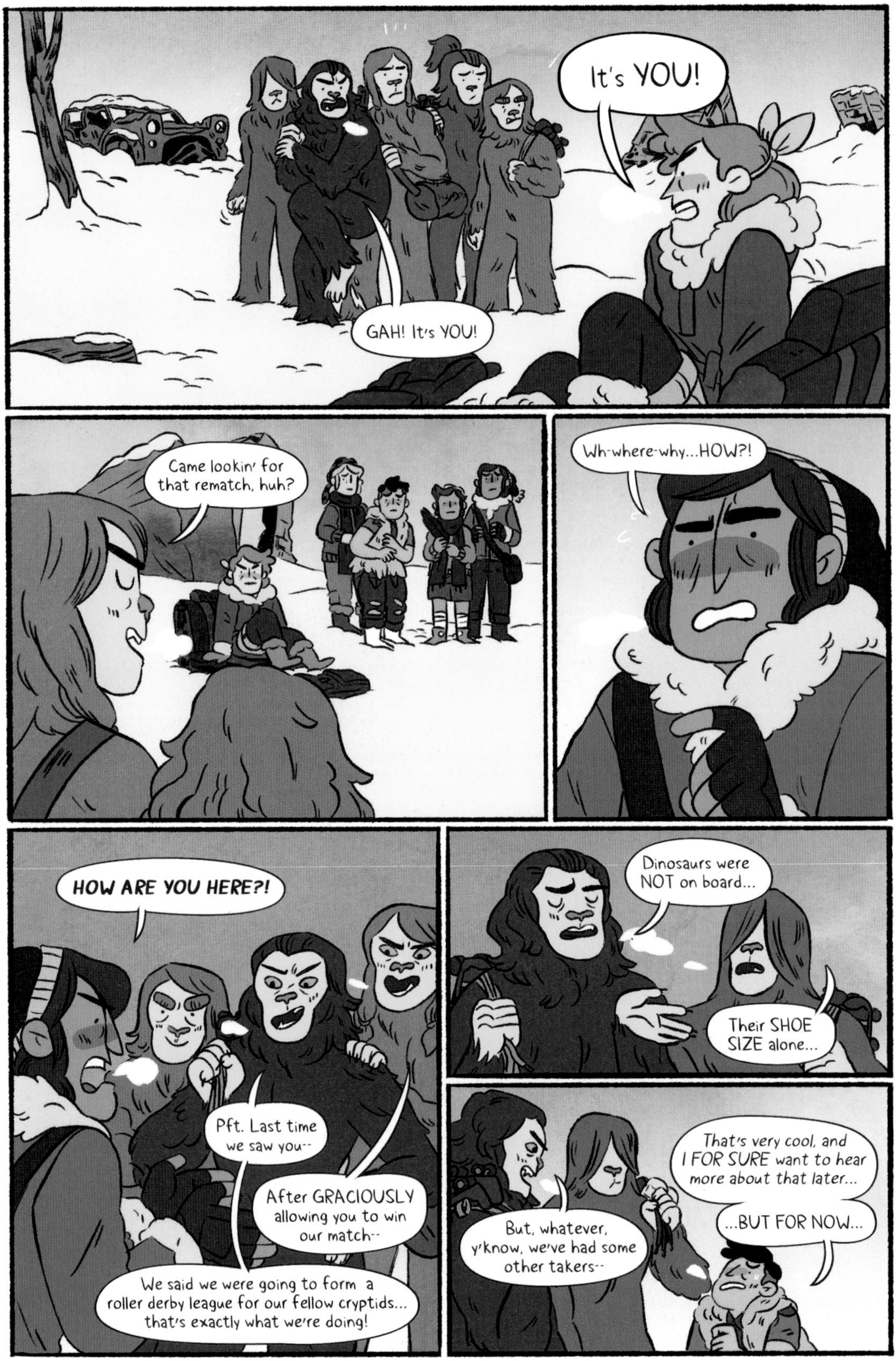
It's YOU!
GAH! It's YOU!
Came lookin' for that rematch, huh?
Wh-where-why...HOW?!
HOW ARE YOU HERE?!
Pft. Last time we saw you--
After GRACIOUSLY allowing you to win our match--
We said we were going to form a roller derby league for our fellow cryptids... that's exactly what we're doing!
Dinosaurs were NOT on board...
Their SHOE SIZE alone...
But, whatever, y'know, we've had some other takers--
That's very cool, and I FOR SURE want to hear more about that later...
...BUT FOR NOW...

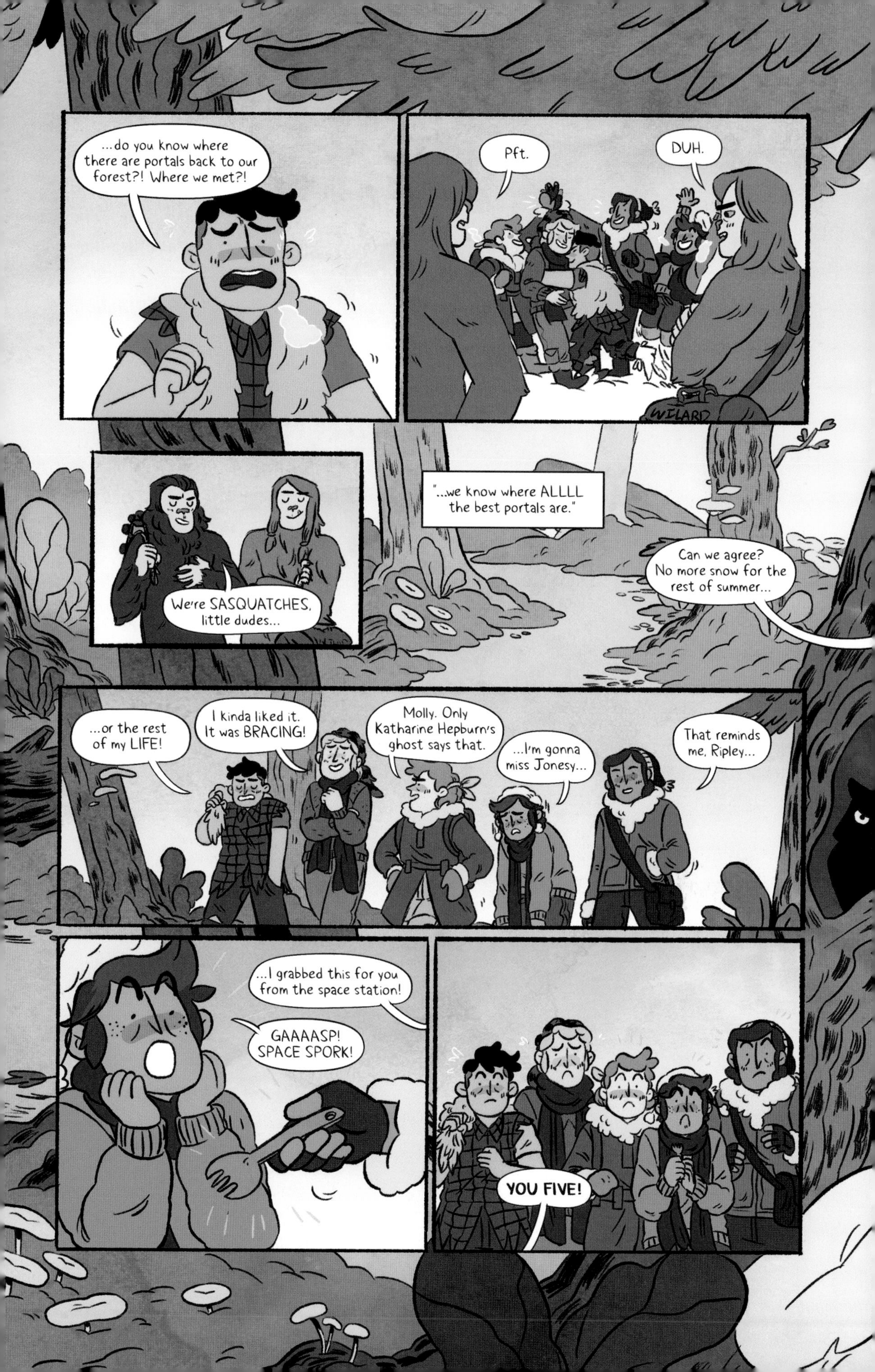
...do you know where there are portals back to our forest?! Where we met?!
Pft.
DUH.
WILARD
We're SASQUATCHES, little dudes...
"...we know where ALLLL the best portals are."
Can we agree? No more snow for the rest of summer...
...or the rest of my LIFE!
I kinda liked it. It was BRACING!
Molly. Only Katharine Hepburn's ghost says that.
...I'm gonna miss Jonesy...
That reminds me, Ripley...
...I grabbed this for you from the space station!
GAAAASP! SPACE SPORK!
YOU FIVE!

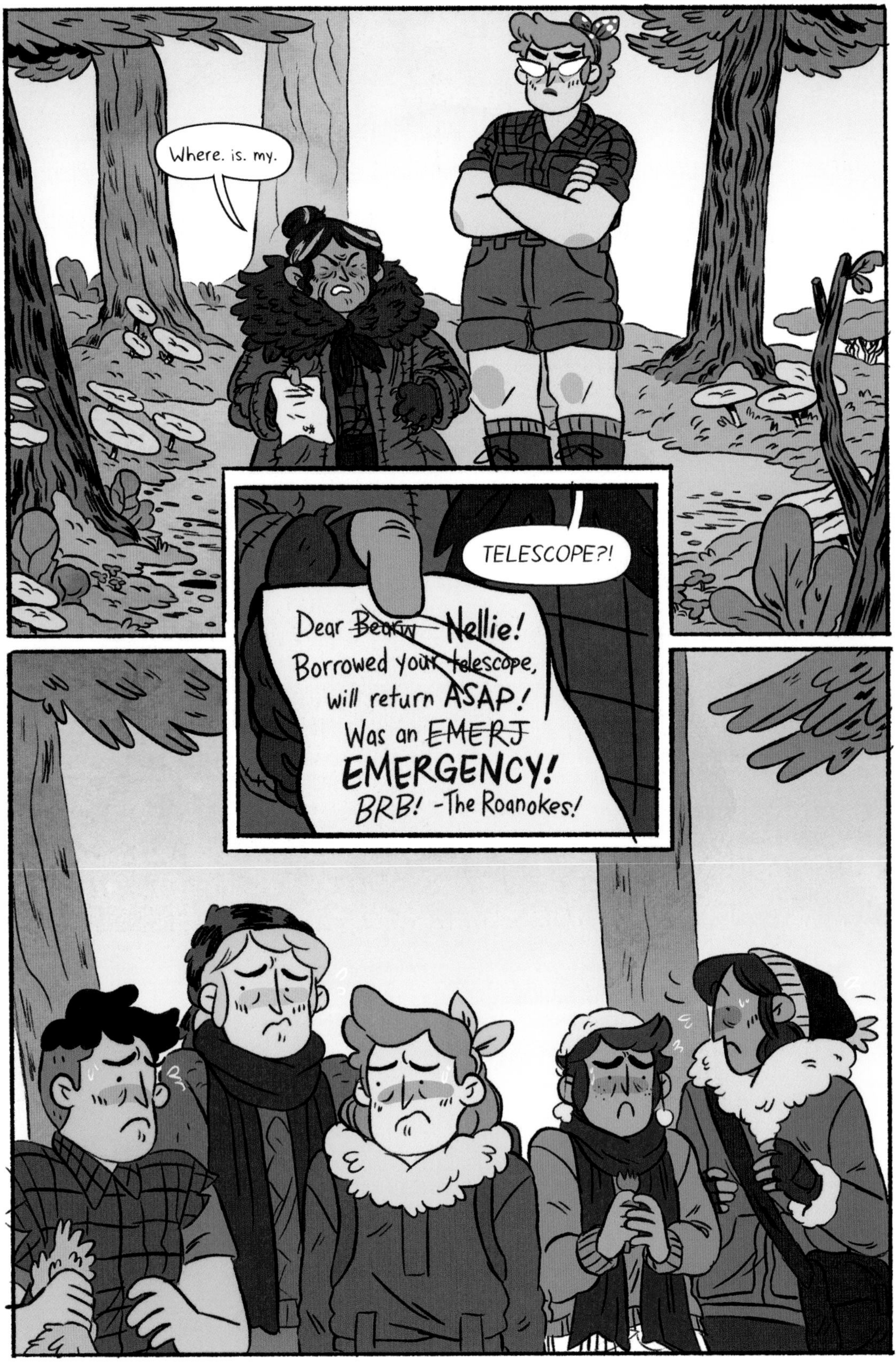
Where. is. my.
TELESCOPE?!
Dear ~~Beary~~ Nellie!
Borrowed your ~~telescope~~ telescope,
will return ASAP!
Was an ~~EMERJ~~
EMERGENCY!
BRB! -The Roanokes!

NEXT: IT'S A MYTH-TERY!

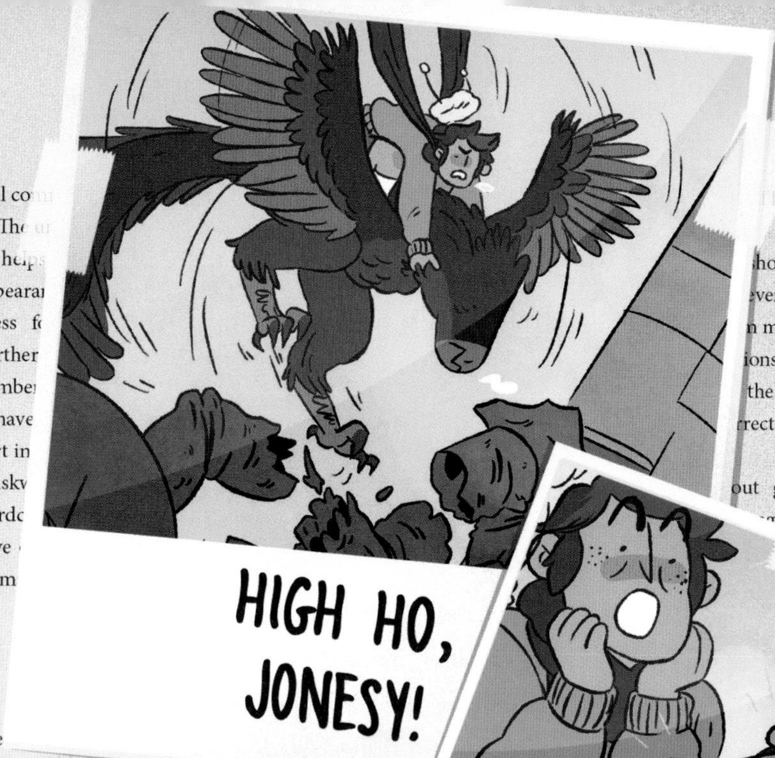
HIGH HO, JONESY!

will co...

The u...
It helps...
appeara...
dress f...
Further...
Lumbe...
to have...
part in...
Thiskv...
Hardc...
have...
them...

...HE UNIFORM

...hould be worn at camp ...events when Lumberjanes ...n may also be worn at other ...ions. It should be worn as a ... the uniform dress with ...rrect shoes, and stocking or

...out grows her uniform or ...another Lumberjane. ...insignia she has ... her ... her

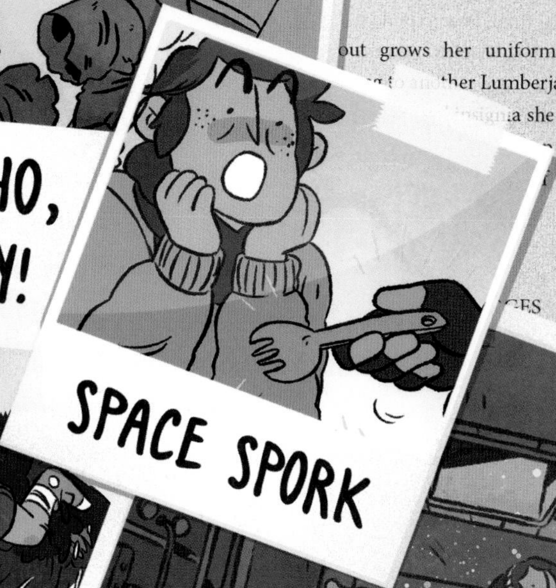
SPACE SPORK

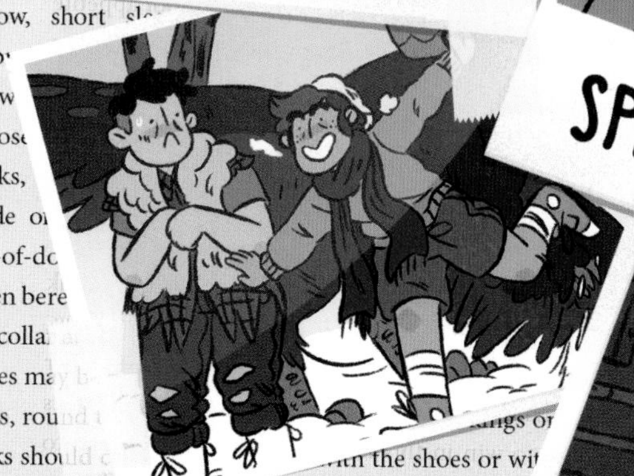

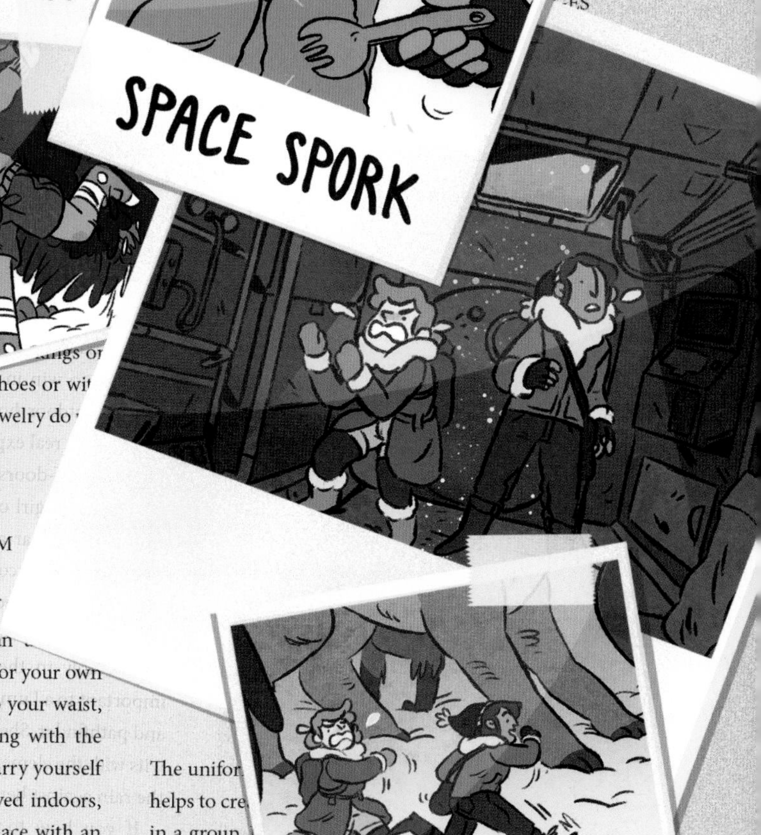

The...
yellow, short sl...
emb...
the w...
choos...
slacks, ...
made o...
out-of-do...
green bere...
the colla...
Shoes may b...
heels, rou... ...ngs or
socks shou... ...th the shoes or wi...
the uniform. Ne... ...es, bracelets, or other jewelry do...
belong with a Lumberjane uniform.

HOW TO WEAR THE UNIFORM

To look well in a uniform demands first of ... uniform be kept in good condition—clean ... pressed. See that the skirt is the right length for your own height and build, that the belt is adjusted to your waist, that your shoes and stockings are in keeping with the uniform, that you watch your posture and carry yourself with dignity and grace. If the beret is removed indoors, be sure that your hair is neat and kept in place with an inconspicuous clip or ribbon. When you wear a Lumberjane uniform you are identified as a member of this organization and you should be doubly careful to conduct yourself in a way that will show everyone that courtesy and thoughtfulness are part of being a Lumberjane. People are likely to judge a whole nation by the selfishness of a few individuals, to criticize a whole family because of the misconduct of one member, and to feel unkindly toward an organization because of the

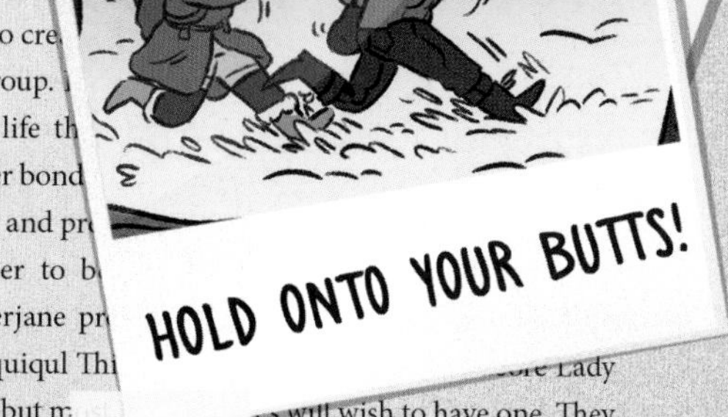
HOLD ONTO YOUR BUTTS!

The unifor...
helps to cre...
in a group. ...
active life th...
another bond...
future, and pr...
in order to b...
Lumberjane pr...
Penniquiqul Thi... ...ore Lady
Types, but m... ...s will wish to have one. They can either bu... the uniform, or make it themselves from materials available at the trading post.

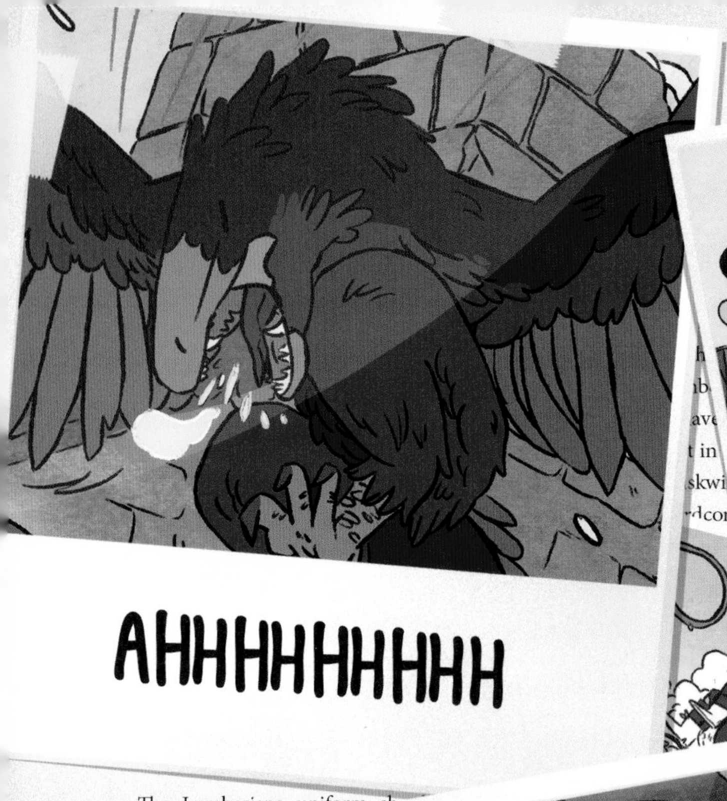
AHHHHHHHHH

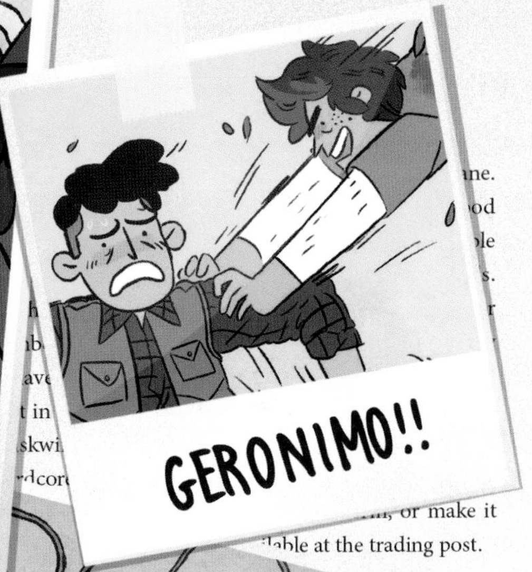
GERONIMO!!

ane.
ood
ple
s.
r

...m, or make it
...ilable at the trading post.

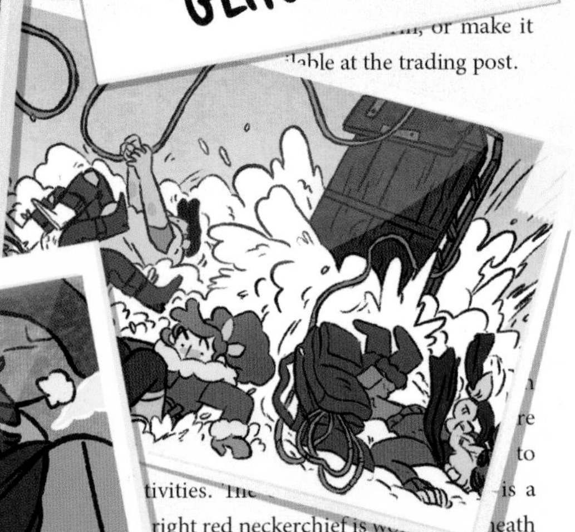

The Lumberjane uniform ...
meetings...

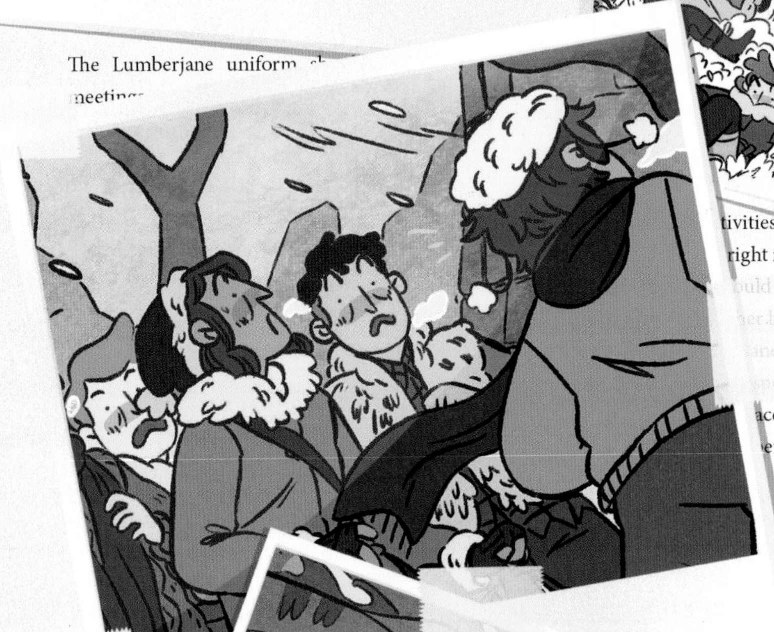

...tivities. The ... is a
...right red neckerchief is wo... neath
...uld be tied in a simple friendship knot.
...black or brown and should have flat
...a straight inner line. Stockings or
...nd in color with the shoes or with
...aces, bracelets, or other jewelry do not
...erjane uniform.

...WEAR THE UNIFORM

...orm demands first of all that the
...ood condition—clean and well
...t is the right length for your own
...e belt is adjusted to your waist,
...kings are in keeping with the
...our posture and carry yourself
...dignity and grace. If the beret is removed indoors,
...e sure that your hair is neat and kept in place with an inconspicuous clip or ribbon. When you wear a Lumberjane uniform you are identified as a member of this organization and you should be doubly careful to conduct yourself in a way that will show everyone that courtesy and thoughtfulness are part of being a Lumberjane. People are likely to judge a whole nation by the selfishness of a few individuals, to criticize a whole family because of the misconduct of one member, and to feel unkindly toward an organization because of the

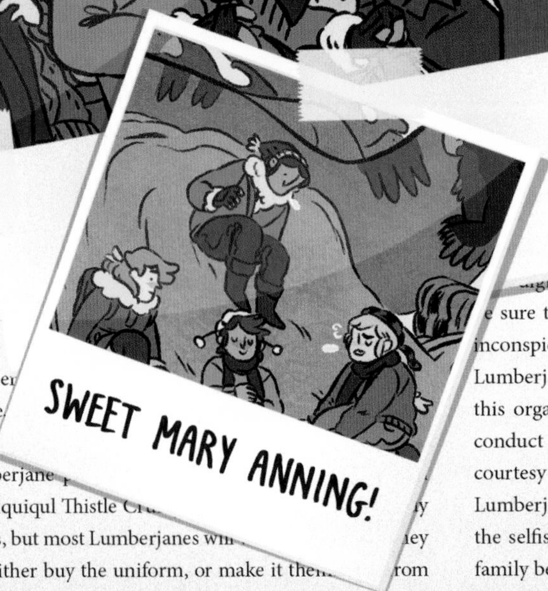
SWEET MARY ANNING!

The ...
helps ...
in a g...
active ...
another ...
future...
in or...
Lumberjane ...
Penniquiqul Thistle Cru... y
Types, but most Lumberjanes wi... hey
can either buy the uniform, or make it the... rom
materials available at the trading post.

COVER GALLERY

Lumberjanes "Out-of-Doors" Program Field

THE FRIGHT STUFF

"Fortune favors the bold."

Whether it's creepy crawlies or scary skeletons, there are more foibles and phobias in this world than there are letters in the word hippomonstrosesquippedaliophobia, a term which unfortunately means the fear of long words. Fear is a powerful and universal teacher. It protects us, reminds us of threats we've faced and ways we've kept ourselves safe. It keeps us alert for things we should beware of, situations to avoid, and people to distrust.

Many fears should be trusted. Being afraid of water may be irrational, but it also can keep us safe, whether from unknown creatures lurking in the depths, or simply from jellyfish. There are many possible ways to combat the way that your heartbeat increases and your adrenaline rises, from learning to swim better, or wearing inflatable water wings, to swimming with a little waterproof lamp for better visibility.

Some fears are more abstract—masks, or scary stories, or spider webs coating antique porcelain dollies up in the attic. These may give us the willies, but they are all the type of scary that can be fun, in the right circumstances. A thrill, rather than a chill, like a roller coaster. They become a gleeful way to give yourself a fright while knowing that you are safe all along. You feel alive, and grateful that the danger is over once the story has ended, the book has been shut tight, and the lights are all turned on again.

Plenty of fears, when pushed up against in a safe and planned way, are worth facing. Whether it's to learn to embrace new experiences and adventures, or to feel less fearful in your daily life, or even just to understand more about yourself, and why you were frightened in the first place.

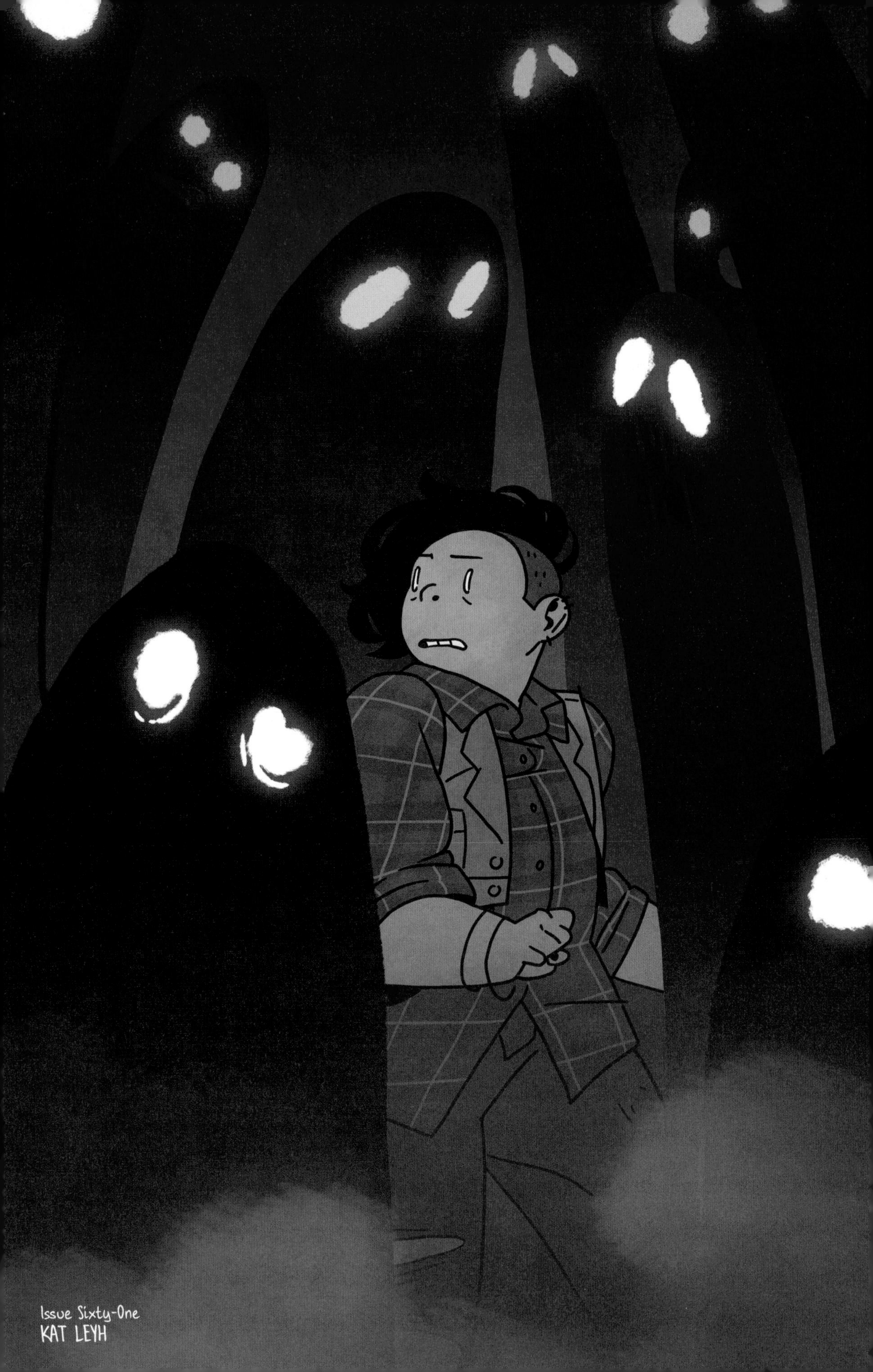
Issue Sixty-One
KAT LEYH

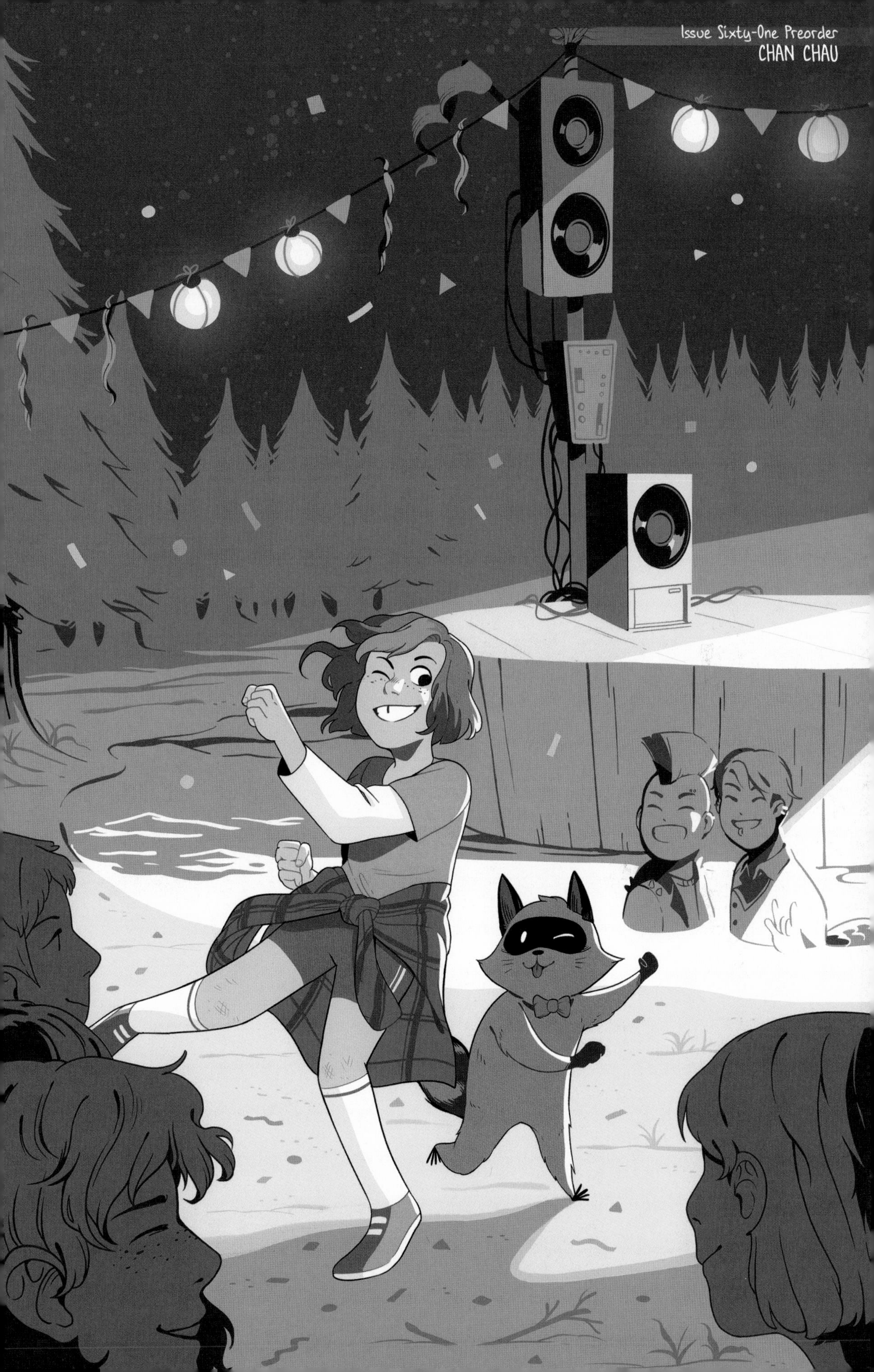
Issue Sixty-One Preorder
CHAN CHAU

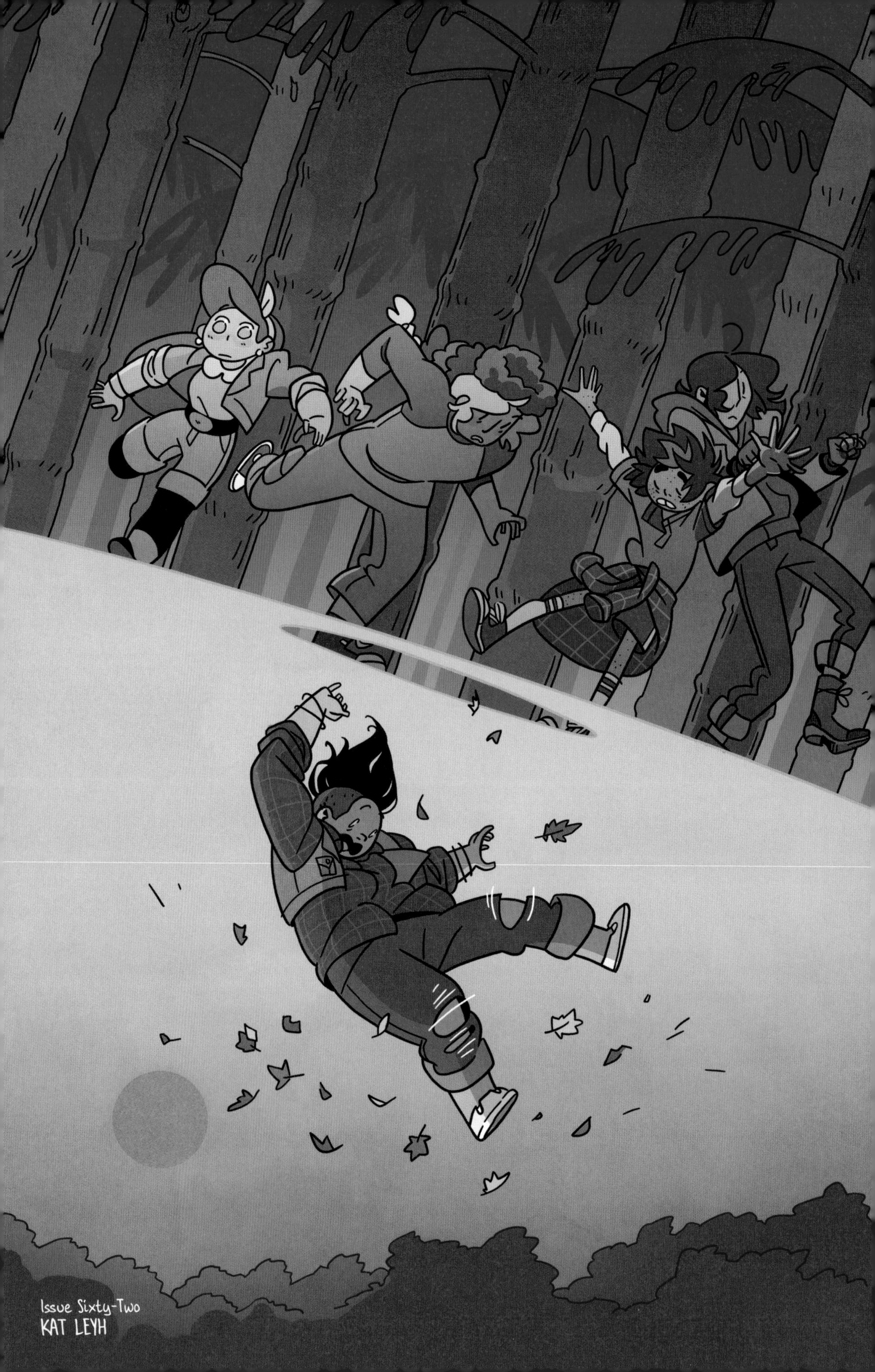
Issue Sixty-Two
KAT LEYH

Issue Sixty-Two Preorder
CHAN CHAU

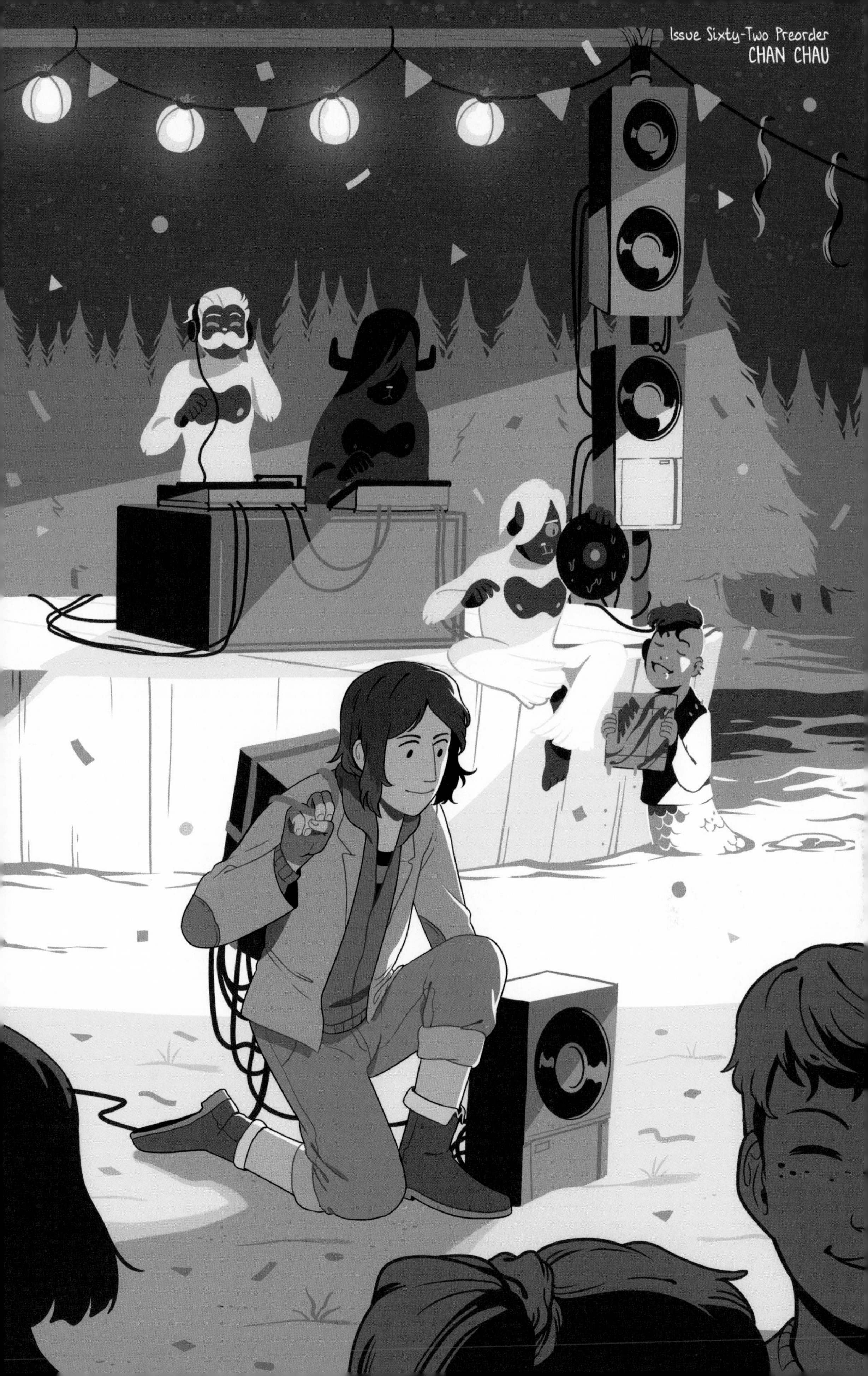

Issue Sixty-Three
KAT LEYH

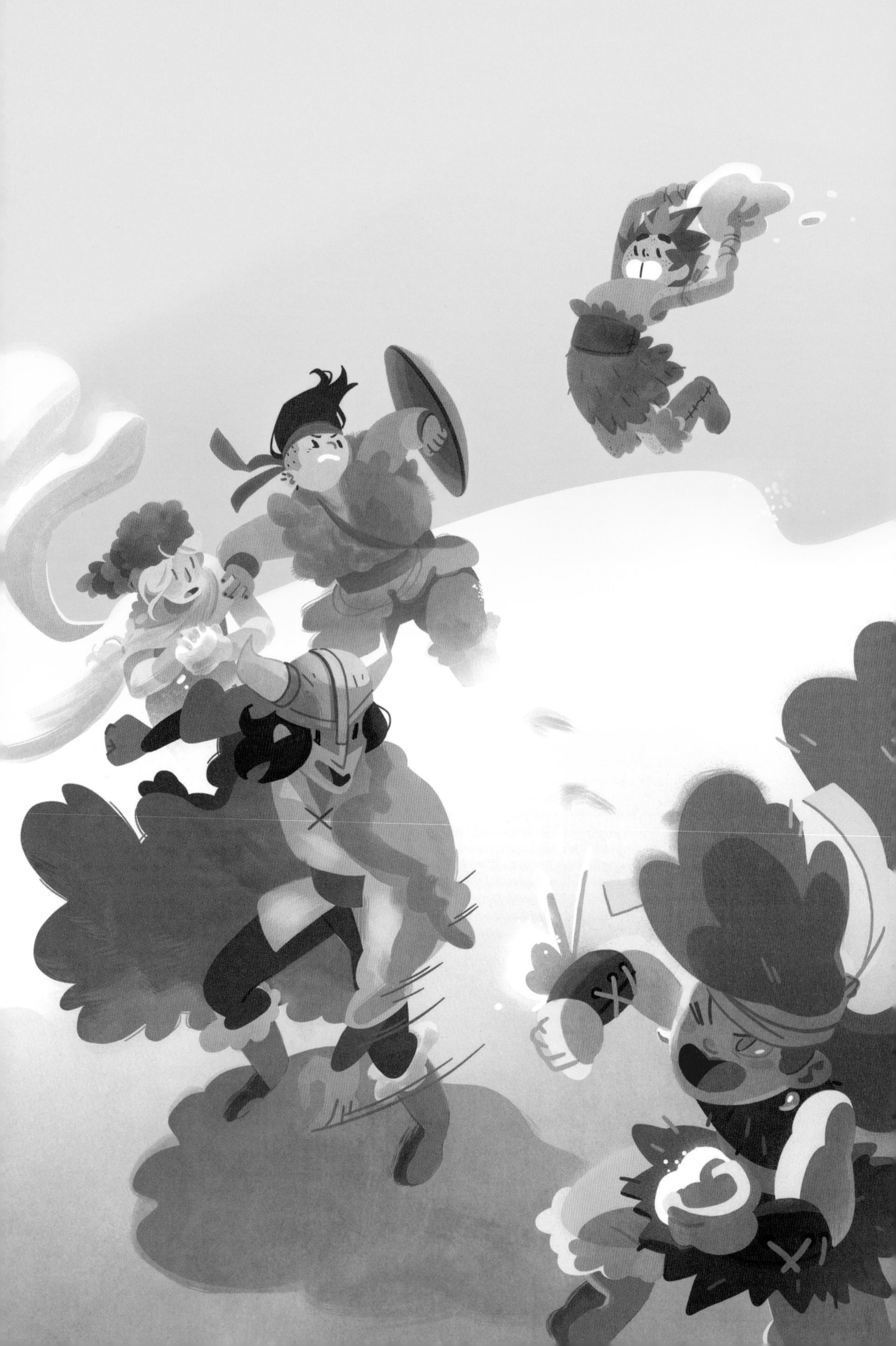

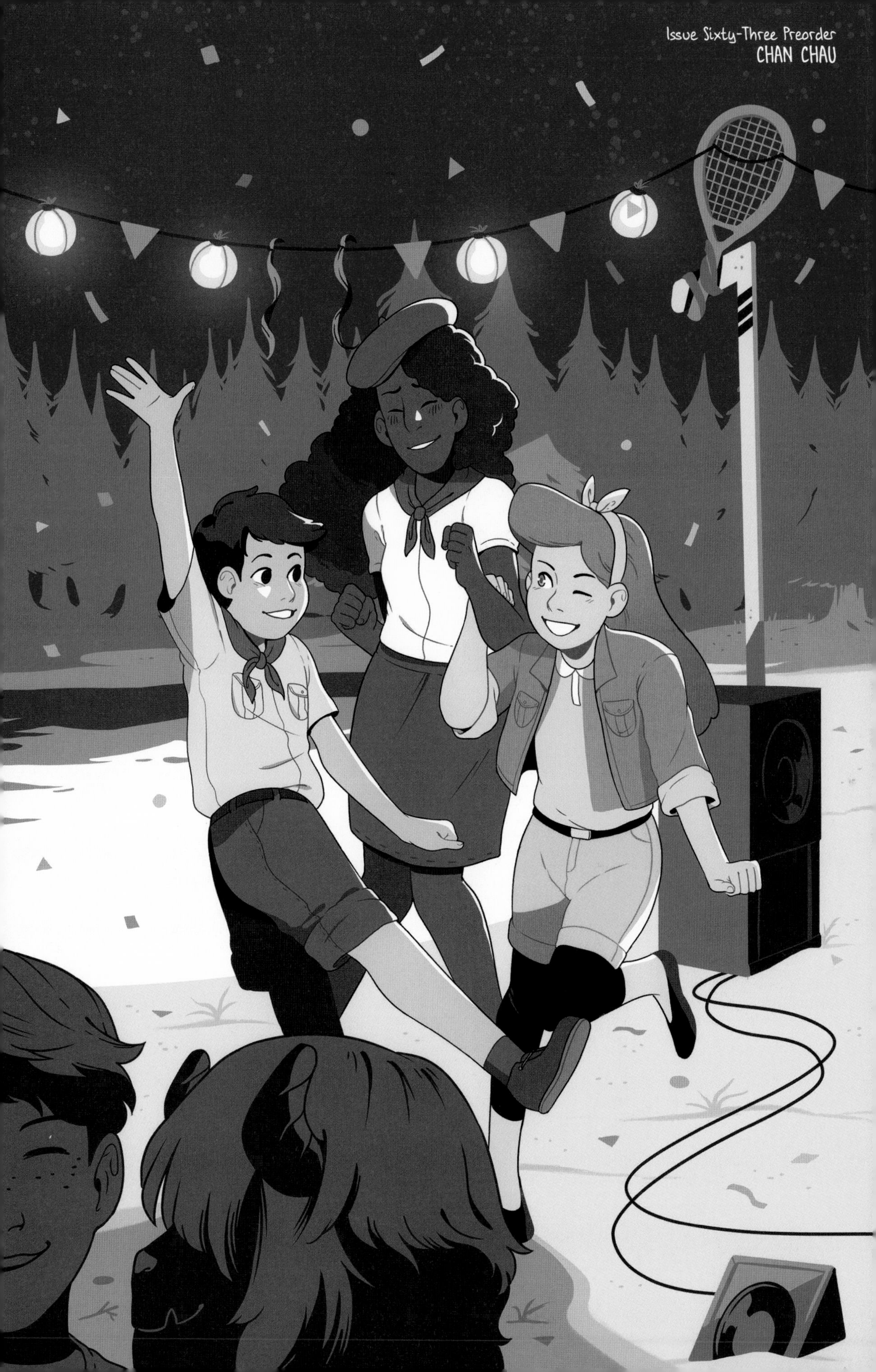

Issue Sixty-Three Preorder
CHAN CHAU

Issue Sixty-Four
KAT LEYH

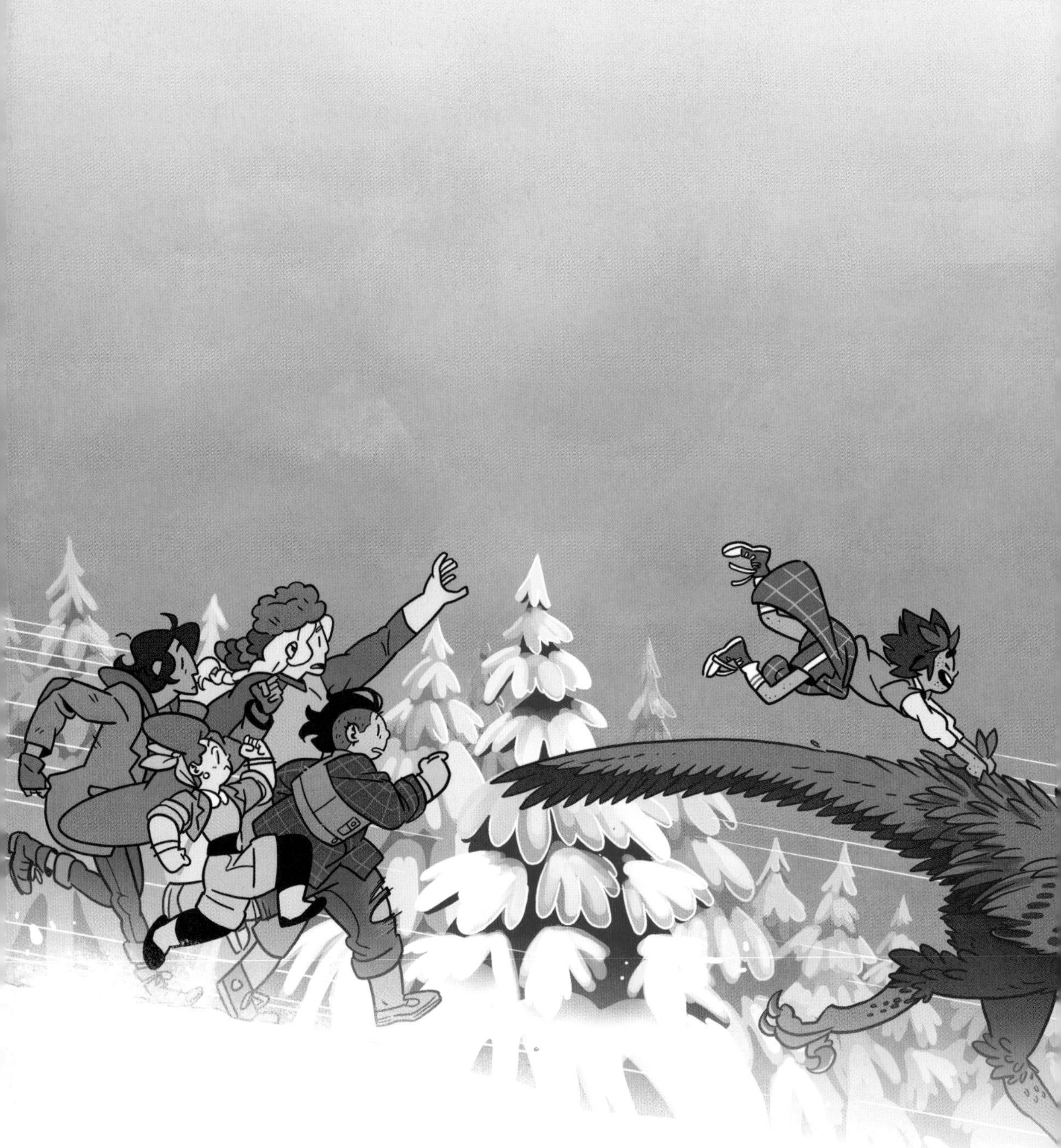

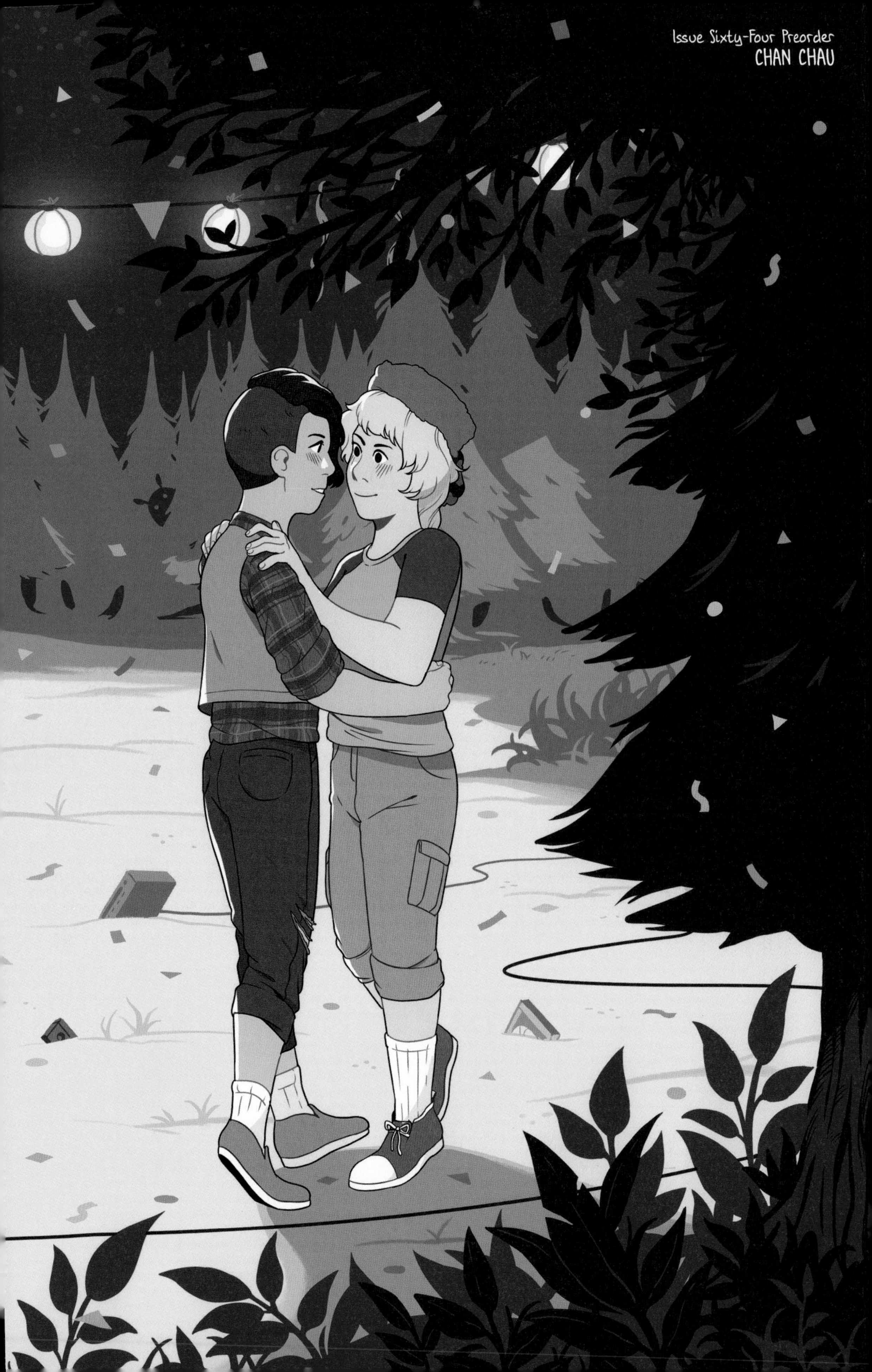
Issue Sixty-Four Preorder
CHAN CHAU

DISCOVER
ALL THE HITS

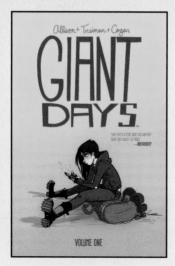

Lumberjanes
Noelle Stevenson, Shannon Watters, Grace Ellis, Brooklyn Allen, and Others
Volume 1: Beware the Kitten Holy
ISBN: 978-1-60886-687-8 | $14.99 US
Volume 2: Friendship to the Max
ISBN: 978-1-60886-737-0 | $14.99 US
Volume 3: A Terrible Plan
ISBN: 978-1-60886-803-2 | $14.99 US
Volume 4: Out of Time
ISBN: 978-1-60886-860-5 | $14.99 US
Volume 5: Band Together
ISBN: 978-1-60886-919-0 | $14.99 US

Giant Days
John Allison, Lissa Treiman, Max Sarin
Volume 1
ISBN: 978-1-60886-789-9 | $9.99 US
Volume 2
ISBN: 978-1-60886-804-9 | $14.99 US
Volume 3
ISBN: 978-1-60886-851-3 | $14.99 US

Jonesy
Sam Humphries, Caitlin Rose Boyle
Volume 1
ISBN: 978-1-60886-883-4 | $9.99 US
Volume 2
ISBN: 978-1-60886-999-2 | $14.99 US

Slam!
Pamela Ribon, Veronica Fish, Brittany Peer
Volume 1
ISBN: 978-1-68415-004-5 | $14.99 US

Goldie Vance
Hope Larson, Brittney Williams
Volume 1
ISBN: 978-1-60886-898-8 | $9.99 US
Volume 2
ISBN: 978-1-60886-974-9 | $14.99 US

The Backstagers
James Tynion IV, Rian Sygh
Volume 1
ISBN: 978-1-60886-993-0 | $14.99 US

Tyson Hesse's Diesel: Ignition
Tyson Hesse
ISBN: 978-1-60886-907-7 | $14.99 US

Coady & The Creepies
Liz Prince, Amanda Kirk, Hannah Fisher
ISBN: 978-1-68415-029-8 | $14.99 US